This is a novel about a murder, the kind of murder that has become horrifyingly commonplace in the Britain of the eighties.

Irene is the daughter of ordinary working-class parents, but she is abused by her mother, and after her father dies by the man who takes his place. She has no particular intellect or talent, but her strength of character carries her through childhood to a romantic marriage.

Her happiness seems secure, but the birth of their third child brings bitterness and isolation. It seems inevitable that her own childhood should be replayed through her son.

This is not a murder story of policemen assiduously collecting clues and making a final arrest, but one that features the helplessness of the social services, the realities of urban life and the downward spiral of human nature.

Sheila Johnson's previous novels have been praised for their authenticity and compulsion. Her writing here is even stronger and the story she tells will haunt her readers for some time to come.

VIOLENT HERITAGE

Sheila Johnson

MACMILLAN

First published in Great Britain 1986 by
MACMILLAN LONDON LIMITED
4 Little Essex Street London WC2R 3LF
and Basingstoke

Associated companies in Auckland, Delhi, Dublin, Gaborone,
Hamburg, Harare, Hong Kong, Johannesburg, Kuala Lumpur, Lagos,
Manzini, Melbourne, Mexico City, Nairobi, New York, Singapore and
Tokyo

British Library Cataloguing in Publication Data

Johnson, Sheila
  Violent heritage.
  I. Title
  823'.914[F]   PR6060.03/
  ISBN 0-333-40768-7

Typeset by Bookworm Typesetting Ltd. Salford.
Printed and bound in Great Britain by Anchor Brendon Ltd. Essex.

ONE

Only the sound of Irene's laboured breathing broke the silence of the room. The child was quiet, his dreadful keening had died to a low, plaintive moan before he had ceased to make any sound at all. Irene pressed her hands together, her glance leaping away from the corner and the small, huddled figure. Squeezing her eyes tightly shut she allowed her hands to separate, and they of their own volition crept about her slender figure to hug her as she rocked backwards and forwards in a paroxysm of remorse. Violent tremors shook her from head to toe, and she clamped her jaws tight, grinding her teeth together to still their chattering. Moisture, too hot for tears, coursed the agonised contours of her face to gather in a pool along her bitten lips. Tasting the bitter salt, Irene opened her eyes, making supreme effort to quell the spasm that racked her. Gaining some control she pushed cruel fingers through the strand of hair fallen across her damp face, dragging it back into place with a savage jerk that threatened to tear it from her scalp. The pain helped to restore her. Turning her back on the fallen child she moved as if in a trance, crossing the room to search among the bric-à-brac on the crowded side-unit for the cigarettes she had flung there earlier. A pot figurine teetered as her hand brushed against it, and she grabbed it up to hurl it across the room. It smashed with a small explosive sound against the wall, and the painted head with its vacantly smiling face rolled back to halt at her feet.

Irene stared at it, her eyes widening, and bit down on the scream of hysteria spilling from her throat. Her fingers snapped and tore the cigarette she had taken from the packet, and another fell from her grasp before she managed to place the last one she had between her lips. Using both hands she brought up the match to fire the end. Inhaling deeply, drawing the smoke down into her lungs, she fell to pacing the room in quick, nervous strides. Five paces one way, five paces back, until the cigarette was spent and she had nothing with which to occupy her hands. Cupping them under her elbows she scowled in sudden defensive anger. This was all Terry's fault. He should have known what would happen. And he had promised to be back this afternoon. So what was keeping him? Why didn't he come? He had promised, hadn't he? He should never have left her alone with the boy. He knew how she felt, knew what she was likely to do. Her foot knocked against the child's as her perambulations grew wider, and she jerked away as though stung. To hell with Terry! He should be here! The girls would be home from school very shortly, and she was in need of help.

A drink. Perhaps if she had a drink ... there was some whisky in the side-unit, but she would need to step over the child in order to reach it. She gave it only a second's thought before abandoning the idea.

Sliding a sideways glance from under her lids she permitted herself a fleeting glimpse of the small figure lying knees drawn up to his narrow chest, elbows pulled in to his stomach, in the foetal position, and felt the familiar tug at her heart. She took a half-step in his direction, her hand reaching towards him. She stopped, and drew back. Some small voice rose to torment her, whispered that it was not yet too late. If she acted now, she might help him, might be lucky enough to contact the people who would set all to rights.

A sly, guarded expression crept into her face, her lips tightened mutinously, and her eyes narrowed. No, she wasn't going to be fooled into doing anything stupid; let him lie there. Let him make as much of this situation as he chose, she was not prepared to answer the questions that would follow should she call people to his aid. Why should she? Why should she place herself in so tedious a position? She had experienced it all before, hadn't she? The innuendos, the false claims to understanding, the pose of being her friend. She wanted no more of it. It was all an act, she knew, put on to gain her confidence, and get her talking. And then ... then they would move against her.

6

She stole another, longer, glance at the child. He lay absolutely still. A low moan escaped Irene's lips, and she stuffed bitten fingers into her mouth to gag the sound. If only she knew what to do, how to help him . . . Why didn't Terry get here? What the hell could be keeping him?

Irene's fingers went automatically to the scar on her cheek as she resumed her nervous pacing. Even now, after more than twenty years, she could still feel the bite and tug of the doctor's needle as it passed through her skin. She grew still, her breath so shallow it seemed almost to have stopped. Suddenly, she gave a great, gasping sob, and turned abruptly, tearing her eyes from their mesmerised contemplation of the tiny figure, and strode resolutely towards the door leading from the room.

Face pressed against the bedroom window, Irene peered down the blank sameness fronting eight floors of council-owned flats to the car park far below, searching for the familiar shape of Terry's red Triumph. Most cars looked the same from this height, some longer, some shorter, but basically the same with their distinguishing rake and line wiped out by the angle, leaving them mere oblongs of repetitive colour.

She was always able to recognise Terry's car by the huge eye painted on its roof; done as a joke, he told her, to return the stares of the traffic cops ogling unsuspecting drivers from their vantage points on the motorway bridges. Oh, if only he'd come. Eyes clouded with anxiety, she strained to pick out that giveaway feature among the ranks of parked cars. 'Please, Terry, please,' she muttered to herself. 'Oh, please,' as her eyes searched diligently.

No wide, blue optic returned her gaze and she stood on tiptoe, flattening her nose against the pane in an effort to see into the corner close to the entrance hall. Sheets of waste paper, caught in the wind, swirled about the angle of the building, dancing like frivolous ballerinas to mock her desperate stare. Immediately to her left the narrow balcony fronting her living room jutted across the view; she could, had she dared, have opened the long glass door and gone out there, the better to scan the roads leading across the estate to the flats, but she had a terror of that dizzy perch and could not trust herself.

Withdrawing from her fruitless vigil she scrubbed at the

greasy splodge she had made on the glass with the side of her hand, spreading the misty film ever wider across the once sparkling window. Her daughters would have crowed to catch her at this; she was forever on at them for just this offence. Without thinking, she lifted the corner of the flower-sprigged curtain and used it to polish away the streaks. Before returning to the living room she unlocked the door on the communal landing, allowing it to swing back on the guard chain. Now she could hear the whine and rumble of the lift as it plied between floors, giving her time to prepare herself for the influx of her two lively daughters as they tumbled from the steel cage, bright eyed and eager, and agog to tell her their day's news.

Today she forestalled them. Meeting them at the door she asked brightly how they would like to take their tea at McDonald's.

Whoops of surprised glee answered her question, and the two girls bounced into the narrow hallway, satchels swinging.

'OK. Quick wash first, then get yourselves tidied up. And hang your school clothes in the wardrobe, don't forget.' Giving them no time to start asking questions, Irene swept their satchels from their shoulders and urged the girls towards their bedroom. 'Remember to wash before you put your clean clothes on and don't forget the bits behind your ears,' she directed.

'Aw, Mum.'

'Never mind the aw, Mum. Get along with you. Go on, get moving. Last one out is a donkey.'

Lauren and Debbie fought playfully to get ahead of one another, and hearing the gush of water from the bathroom tap Irene took an overcoat from the hall cupboard and carried it into the living room.

Her son lay as she had left him, and she caught her underlip in her teeth to still its trembling as she gently covered him with the coat. The lively sounds issuing from her daughters' room made the silence surrounding the child funereal. Irene brushed the back of her hand across her eyes, wiping away the threatening tears. 'Uncle Terry will be here soon, Lawrence,' she whispered. 'He will take care of you.'

She backed carefully away from the child, her hand groping

behind her for the obstacles made by the room's furniture, sliding around table and chairs alike, her eyes never leaving the hump made by the coat.

Shrieks of laughter warned that her daughters were almost ready. Irene shot a last look around the sitting room, snatched up her handbag, and was out of the door before the girls emerged, shiny-faced, from their bedroom.

'I won. I won.' Lauren pushed ahead of her sister as they came through the door. 'Debbie's a donkey.'

'Donkey yourself, parrot-face.' With a squeal of excitement Debbie dodged round her mother to shoot out of the flat and on to the landing where she turned to urge her sister to hurry. 'Now Mum's the donkey,' she cried, as they hopped up and down waiting for Irene to join them.

'Cheeky pair.' She pretended to cuff them. 'Just for that I think I'll let you buy your own tea.'

'Hard lines,' said Lauren with a grin. 'I haven't any money.'

'Nor me,' Debbie echoed.

'Hmm, fine pair. Looks like Mum's treat again.'

They entered the lift, mother and two giggling schoolgirls, without an apparent care in the world, happy to be together, enjoying each other's company.

'Did you bring Lolly home today, Mum?' Debbie asked as the lift descended. She had not particularly noticed her brother's absence, and asked after him only out of idle curiosity.

'I . . . he's out with Mr Garland,' Irene said sharply. 'And I wish you wouldn't call him that, his name is Lawrence.'

Lawrence . . . the name echoed round and round in her head, repeating itself in the staccato click of her heels. Lawrence, her own sweet, precious, long-awaited Lawrence. . . . Only he wasn't Lawrence, was he? He was a substitute, a sham. A stubborn, constant reminder of endless heartache.

Terry swore softly as the steady hum of the car engine stuttered, fading almost to silence before his foot, frantically pumping the pedal, managed to catch and restore the regular beat. He had been having trouble ever since he'd reached the motorway; a piece of grit, or some other small obstruction in the fuel supply, maybe lodged in one of the jets. Ordinarily he would have stopped at the service station to take a look, but he was going to be late enough as it was, and he was anxious to get back to Irene and the boy.

Pushing the accelerator to the floor he picked up speed, hoping to flush whatever was causing the trouble out of the system. Heading north he passed junctions thirteen, fourteen and fifteen in rapid succession, the car responding perfectly. With a grunt of satisfaction he allowed the revs to drop, and settled into an easier pace. Could be he was worrying unnecessarily, he told himself, glancing quickly at the clock on the dashboard. It was only just after six o'clock; the girls should have been home a couple of hours, their presence should help to defuse any potentially fraught situation. Irene would be busy fixing their evening meal, young Lawrence was unlikely to be in any danger. Subconsciously he allowed his speed to reduce even further. He'd be a fool to go breaking his neck rushing towards a situation that was well under control. Hadn't he already done all that he could? All that was humanly possible? Irene wanted things to work out even more than he did. Surely now was the time for him to display a little trust. Tomorrow the child was to start at the day nursery – tonight was for him and his mother to get to know each other again. Anyway, he was on familiar territory now, not more than ten miles from home. Another glance at the clock assured him he should be at Irene's place around seven, just in time to see Lawrence before he was tucked into bed.

The engine note petered out, and the car coasted for several yards with only the hiss of the tyres on the road, and the sigh of the wind for accompaniment. Terry steered towards the hard shoulder, glancing anxiously back through his mirror as he swung across the busy inside lane of traffic. A long insulting blast from a lorry driver, forced to take evasive action, expressed an opinion of all such fools. The car rocked in the slipstream of the lorry's boisterous passage before rolling gently to a halt.

Terry turned off the ignition. He sat drumming his fingers on the steering wheel while he debated his next move, then abandoned the action impatiently as it became clear to him that

10

fate had already robbed him of a choice. Releasing his seat belt, he swung himself out of the car, staring anxiously in each direction, wondering which would bring him soonest to the emergency telephones. This, he decided, was no place to attempt any amateur bodging. Christ, but he was going to be so late . . . He felt the sharp, disturbing thrust of anxiety rise like bile in his throat, and suffered a fresh spasm of discomfort over the role he was playing in this delicately phrased drama. Perhaps he had been wrong to take so much authority upon himself, maybe it would have been wiser to delegate some of the crippling responsibility. The thought nagged at him as he set off at a brisk pace along the sparse grass edging the motorway in search of the telephone.

'Mummy! Mummy, what's the matter?' Lauren's clear young voice pierced Irene's dark thoughts.

'Huh? What?' The endless babble and clatter of the busy eating place broke over her, and Irene became aware of her surroundings and the anxious expression on the face of her daughter.

'Mummy, why are you crying? What's the matter?'

Hastily brushing her wet cheeks with her fingers Irene managed a tremulous smile. 'Must have swallowed something the wrong way,' she said, affecting a choking cough.

'But you looked so sad.' Debbie edged closer to her sister, seeking reassurance.

'Wouldn't you, with half a beefburger stuck in your gullet?' she improvised, and succeeded in winning a relieved giggle from both girls. She glanced at her wrist-watch, frowned at the small oval face before flicking her wrist in sharp, impatient turns.

'It's still going, Mummy. I can see the clock over there, and it's five past five.' Lauren was staring over her mother's shoulder to the clock on the wall.

Irene turned with an exclamation of disbelief. 'God, is that all it is?' she asked of no one in particular.

'Well, what did you think? We've only just got here. I haven't finished my tea yet, and neither has our Debbie.'

Irene, glancing for confirmation at their half-eaten beefbur-

11

gers, and the cartons spilling chips, could scarcely credit the evidence of her own eyes. This was going to be a long, long, evening. Pushing aside her own untouched meal, she lit a cigarette. Would Terry have reached the flat yet? More importantly, would he have had time to do what was necessary? She drummed the fingers of her left hand on the formica table, her nails making sharp little clicking noises split seconds in advance of the drumming fingertips. Without noticing, she drew on the cigarette in quick, hasty puffs, the tobacco smoke scarcely hitting her lungs before she blew it out in tempo with her nervous tattoo.

'Mummy!' An exclamation of disgust broke from the girls as they flapped their hands against the choking smoke-screen.

'Oh, I'm sorry. I wasn't thinking.' She stubbed out the cigarette, wafted away the lingering cloud, then immediately lit another king-sized Rothmans from the packet she had purchased on their way across town.

Her daughters exchanged a glance that proclaimed mutual endurance of this adult stupidity before continuing their meal.

Irene spun out the time they spent in the restaurant for as long as she was able, plying the girls with ice-creams and bottles of coke until they began to regard her with uneasy suspicion. She checked her watch again, wondering if she dare take them home. Had she allowed enough time for Terry to deal with things back there?

'Shall we, er . . . How would you like to go to the pictures?' she asked, suddenly deciding she could not face returning to the flat. Her daughters' response made it easy for her to believe this was a normal family outing with no dark ulterior motive driving her to laugh and chatter too loudly and too long for it to be natural.

In the dark anonymity of the picture house she felt safe from prying eyes. Here she could relax and lower her guard, free of the need to talk or the pretence of listening; she could sit, eyes front, in faithful imitation of her neighbours, while her troubled mind made secret little forays of its own.

Terry was fortunate: the nearest telephone was a mere two hundred yards down the road, and the breakdown services had him located within twenty minutes. He rode into town in the truck towing his car, and asked to be put down close to the flats. By a quarter past eight he was knocking on Irene's door, feeling particularly self-righteous. He had done all he could to keep his promise to be here at no little inconvenience to himself. A lesser man might well have given up the struggle, and felt justified in returning home; the more so since this case was extraneous to his normal workload, he reminded himself somewhat smugly.

He knocked and waited, some small part of his attention given to an estimated cost of the repairs he would need to have carried out on his car. Having waited a considerable time and got no reply, Terry ran out of patience. Bunching his fist he assaulted the plain wooden door with no little force. His knuckles rang hollowly. He gained a distinct impression that the flat was empty. He tried the handle, and was surprised when the door swung inwards under his grasp.

'Irene?' There were no lights burning, no sounds of activity. Terry stepped into the hall, pushing the door closed behind him. 'Irene, are you there?' He felt foolish just voicing the words, knowing that had she been in the flat she would have answered him long before. He waited in the narrow hallway wondering what could have taken Irene from home today of all days. She hadn't said she would be going out, had in fact given every indication she would be spending the day at home with Lawrence. Had something gone wrong?

No premonition of disaster spurred Terry forwards, no inexplicable urge tugged at his feet. Instead, he frowned heavily as he arrived at his own conclusion that Irene had in all probability taken the children to visit that friend of hers in the flat some floors below. Terry's annoyance was twofold: he had now to go down and find her, and he was disappointed that Irene had shown by her action that she felt incapable of managing even so much as one evening alone with Lawrence.

It was not until Carol assured him that she'd seen neither Irene nor her children all day that Terry experienced his first twinge of anxiety. 'Are you sure . . . ? No, sorry, what I meant was, don't her daughters usually arrive home along with your children? Didn't they say anything?'

'What about?' Carol asked unhelpfully as she lounged in the open doorway obviously enjoying Terry's discomfiture. She had never liked this man, about whom Irene was so close-lipped. He needed bringing down a peg or two, in her opinion.

'Well, did they say whether Irene's girls had mentioned an outing, for instance? Or maybe an errand, or something like that?'

'No, and we don't live in Irene's pocket, you know. We don't keep tabs on each other to that extent.'

'I see . . . then you wouldn't have any idea where they might have gone?'

'No, like I told you, I'm not her keeper.' Carol drew herself upright, and made to close the door.

Terry stopped her with a quick gesture. 'Just one more thing. Is there a shop around here that might still be open? A grocer's, perhaps, or maybe a chippy?'

'There's an off-licence along the back road, Gregory's; they'll stay open while ever there's life on this planet.'

'Thanks. Thanks very much. You've been *most* helpful.' Terry felt unable to resist the touch of sarcasm, and he watched Carol's face darken as the shot went home.

He took the lift to the ground floor, walked through the passageway to the rear of the flats, and reached the off-licence after a brisk walk. The shop was busy, and, as Terry had guessed, catered mostly for the residents from the flats making last-minute purchases of those items that are always forgotten until the minute of need. Irene was not among the women selecting goods from the self-service display. Sight of their packages reminded Terry of his missed evening meal, and he considered them hungrily before turning away. He'd find Irene and the kids first, he decided, then think about feeding his face. A complete lack of ideas on where to try next convinced him he'd do as well to return to the flats and wait for their return, and since Irene had left her door unlocked, he considered he might just as well do so in comfort. Maybe he'd make himself a sandwich and a coffee, she shouldn't be too long now. Anyway, the children would be ready for bed, and she had shown herself to be conscientious in these matters where her girls were concerned.

14

A short, rotund man entered the lift along with Terry. He pushed the buttons for both the eighth floor and the ninth, a courtesy that passed completely unnoticed by his fellow passenger. Preoccupied with the mystery of Irene's whereabouts, Terry barely acknowledged the man's presence. His own, however, appeared to be causing the little man certain misgivings. He glanced at Terry's imposing breadth and fidgeted nervously as the lift began its ascent. At the third floor he moved as if to signal a stop, but his hand fell away from the bank of buttons as he apparently thought better of it. At the fifth level, he cleared his throat, and after taking several quick, anxious glances at Terry's set face, launched himself into speech.

'You the fella bin seein' that woman on the eighth?' he asked, staring fixedly at the rubber moulding edging the sliding doors as though planning a quick escape. 'Her as 'as the three kids?' he added doggedly.

'What? Sorry, were you speaking to me?' Terry looked at him in surprise. He had no recollection of having seen this man before.

''S'right. I asked if you were the bloke as is seein' that piece on this floor.'

The lift had now reached a halt. A slight bump indicated the stop before the doors reluctantly parted company to stand begrudgingly agape.

Neither Terry nor his companion made a move to alight, engrossed as they were in a thorough scrutiny of each other.

Deciding that the man was asking purely to satisfy his own curiosity, Terry fixed him with a sour glance. He was in no mood to deal with a nosey-parker seeking thrills at second-hand through the conjectured sex life of his neighbours. 'What business is it of yours who comes and goes in this place?' he snarled. 'Do the residents have no rights to privacy?'

'Here, keep your shirt on, mate.' The little man jumped forward as the doors threatened to close, thrusting his foot into the gap to hold them apart, and thereby holding the lift at its present station. 'I'm askin' 'cause there's something you can do fer me.'

'Oh?'

'Look, don't come sayin' "oh" ter me. I'm only tryin' ter do what's right. There's things bin goin' on in that there flat as needs lookin' into. An' I'm not above callin' the law ter do just that, let me tell yer.'

Terry listened to the man's broad Midlands accent and recognised he had made a mistake. Under his nervous belligerence this little man was so obviously concerned about something he'd seen or heard in Irene's flat as to risk tackling a stranger of almost twice his size and strength. Terry needed no second sight to appreciate the courage involved – nor was he in need of a clairvoyant to tell him some of the things he feared he was about to hear.

'I'm sorry. I was thinking about something else,' he said in apology. 'Look, why don't we let the lift go, and then maybe you'd like to tell me what's bothering you.'

Disarmed by this change of attitude the man stepped from the lift, to be closely followed by Terry.

'Well, it's like this, see. Me an' my missis, we're not nosey folk, only, well, there's bin' things as we've heard – we live in the flat above yon woman's.' His eyes flicked upwards indicating the next floor.

Terry made no attempt to hurry this preamble knowing from long experience that he would learn more if he allowed the speaker to find his own way of telling the tale.

'We've seen you comin' an' goin' in that car of yorn, so I thought, seein' yer in the lift like that, I thought I'd best have a word with you.' The little man was obviously finding it increasingly difficult to know where to begin and he cast about making several false starts, his nervousness becoming increasingly evident.

'The missis, she reckons as if you can find time ter paint eyes on the top of yer car, you can find a bit more ter see what's goin' on under yer nose.'

Terry swallowed his impatience, and assumed what he hoped was a look inviting confidence.

The man's courage swelled. 'She thrashes them kids, yer know. Well, at least, she thrashes that there baby. We've heard 'er. An' we reckon you must 'a' done too, seein' as how you've bin keepin' her company all this while.' He fixed Terry with an accusing eye, waiting for some denial before plunging on. ''T'aint right, yer know. All kids is buggers sometimes, we all know that, but ter knock 'em about . . . It ain't human.'

'What makes you believe she does that?' Terry deliberately kept his voice neutral.

'Why else would they scream an' yell like they do?'

'Maybe the sounds you hear are simply the noises all children make when they are forced to play in a confined space.' Terry glanced about him indicating the concrete structure of the flats.

'Nah, I know the difference, mate.'

Though Terry went through the motions of offering obligatory excuses, the sick, oily feeling deep in his gut warned he was wasting his breath. The little man bristled to think himself regarded as some kind of fool incapable of telling the happy sound of children at play from that of something far more sinister. He plunged into a heated recital of neatly catalogued incidents that served to support his theories; and confirmed Terry in his own opinion of gross, wilful, stupidity.

They had heard screams, the man said, winding up his tale. 'From that there baby. Screams as 'ud turn yer 'air white. An' then they'd stop, sudden, like. Too sudden to be natural. Me an' the missis 'ave bin on the verge of callin' the police many a time. Only, well, things quietened down a bit lately, an' yer don't like ter stick yer neb in where it's not wanted,' he ended apologetically.

'I see . . . and rather than interfere you allowed this thing to go on.' Terry was unable to hold back the accusation.

The little man looked uncomfortable. 'Like I said, things *did* quieten down. 'Sides, we 'ad no real proof. An', well, it's us as 'as ter live here.'

'But what does that matter? Supposing you were wrong? Who the hell cares if it helps to save a child from unnecessary suffering?'

'Oh, it's all right fer the likes o' you ter quibble. An' I ain't noticed *you* doin' so much, neither. So there's no cause ter come over so bloody righteous. But if we 'ad 'a' bin wrong, there'd 'ave bin no kid gettin' slapped around, would there? An' then where would we be? The whole damned block 'avin' us marked down fer nosey do-gooders. There'd 'ave bin no

17

livin' with it.'

Terry shook his head, his own sense of guilty neglect pointing up the man's ready defences.

'Any road, I'm tellin' yer now, an' I'll leave it to yer to see ter things as yer sees fit,' the man said, nodding at Terry as he shifted the burden of responsibility to the latter's broad shoulders.

Terry blinked at the sudden, sharp note of command, but immediately recovered himself. 'Right,' he said shortly. 'I'll make sure things get looked into right away. And . . . and thanks for taking the trouble to tell me. I understand that it can't have been easy.'

'Well, after today's little lot, I couldn't decide what to do. Then, as I said, seein' you in the lift, I thought I'd best take the chance. I knew as how you were seein' the woman, an' . . . Just so long as you don't hold no grudge, like?'

Terry heard nothing beyond the man's opening remark, and even that did not immediately make sense. He reached out to take hold of the man's arm. 'You said something about today? There's been no trouble today. I was *here*.' His whole manner pleaded to be told there had been some mistake.

'I . . . look, I don't want no bother.' The man broke free of Terry's grasp, moving quickly towards the sanctuary offered by the waiting lift.

'I'm sorry. I didn't mean to . . . you said today? There's been something today?'

''S'right. Better ask her yerself.' He paused outside the lift-cage, his finger covering the button that would bring the doors together. 'If yer ask me, things is gettin' from bad ter worse, an' the quicker yer gets her sorted out, the better!' The steel doors closed protectively in front of him, and the whine that followed signalled his ascent away from the terrible emotion he had seen building behind Terry's eyes.

TWO

Moving like an automatum, Terry approached the flat where he had meant to wait in such ease, all his senses telling him that he had made a most dreadful mistake. He had placed a child at risk through his own preposterous conceit, and his sin was about to be visited upon him.

Had it not been for his own blind refusal to accept that he was no more infallible than the next man he would not be entering this door now, not be groping for the light switch with the oily coils of dread clamped about his intestines. He pressed the switch, illuminating the narrow hall with the hard, direct light of an overhead bulb. Blinking against the sudden brilliance, he moved reluctantly to open the door of Irene's bedroom, releasing his breath in a long hiss of mingled concern and relief on discovering the room to be empty.

His glance into the room shared by the two girls was a mere formality; he had not expected to find anything there. He paused as he entered the sitting room, his senses groping across the dark shadows, fearfully probing the familiar shapes for some change, some unwelcome difference, before he dared to turn on the light. The window with its undrawn curtains sprang into dark relief, sending the glow from the electric bulb flashing back at him. He stared at the teapot, lying incongruously in the middle of the floor, before permitting his gaze to rove slowly about the room. He gaped at the obscenely headless figurine standing neglected against the far wall, then, as his senses grappled with this strange phenomenon his eye was caught and held by the small heap created by the spread overcoat, and all else was swept from his mind.

Fighting against the nausea clamouring for release, Terry advanced into the room, his gaze riveted to that dark shape. An overwhelming urge to scream a denial twisted his gut, stopping the breath in his lungs. He had no desire to learn of the horror he sensed had been perpetrated in this room, no wish to establish the root cause of the dread gripping him by the throat.

For several long minutes he held the truth from him, keeping it at arm's length by a conscious effort of will, refusing to accept the inevitable.

Then his feet betrayed him, carried him protesting across the endless acres of leaf-patterned carpet to a spot only inches from the tiny heap. Slowly, his knees cracking audibly in the heavy silence, Terry lowered himself to a crouch. His hand hovered above the spread coat unwillingly. He watched it fall to close on the woollen cloth, lift it gently aside, to lay bare the pathetic, cruelly misused body of the little boy he had held in his arms only a matter of hours ago.

As he gazed, daring to take only brief, fleeting glances at the child's appalling injuries, a sob ripped from his throat, and the pain that racked him as he stared into the face of his own inexcusable guilt doubled him over.

It was a long, long time before Terry could bring himself upright. Tears coursed down his face, losing themselves in the red tangle of his beard; it was for his damnably pathetic vanity that this child had paid such a terrible price, and the agony of that knowledge was so profound he was left in no doubt that he would carry it through the remainder of his life to the grave.

Moving hesitantly, groping his way by means of support from the furniture, Terry shuffled blindly across the room; without daring to hope for such a miracle his shaking fingers had detected the merest flicker of a pulse in the child's broken body. There was still a chance. . . . Terry felt as though he moved through treacle, his limbs refusing to respond to the urgency of his screaming brain. Only by the greatest effort of will was he able to shift his muscles into gear. There were people he needed to contact – a doctor . . . an ambulance – he was in the most desperate need of help. He wasted several minutes in a fruitless search for the telephone before cursing himself for his stupidity; Irene did not have one installed.

About to leave the flat he wavered, torn between his need to reach the pay-phone situated on the ground floor lobby, and his reluctance to leave the child unattended. Small use to tell himself there was nothing more he could do for the child while he was beset with the strange notion that for as long as he remained in the room all was not lost – that something was salvageable from this tragedy. Once he stepped outside the door, once the wheels of authority were put into motion, he knew the last vestige of hope would be gone.

Shrugging this strange fancy aside, and with a lingering glance for the tiny mound humping the spread overcoat, Terry forced himself into action. An encroaching rumble signalled the now familiar ascent of the lift, and he strode across the corridor to thumb the button that would bring it to a halt.

Irene entered her home with no show of reluctance, and having so far convinced herself that Terry would have restored all to rights, she made no move to check Lauren and Debbie as they hurried through the hall ahead of her to burst into the sitting room, tales of the things they had seen at the cinema bubbling from their lips.

Over the top of their heads Irene's gaze locked on Terry's. His eyes were coldly accusing, hers only slightly hesitant.

''Lo, Terry,' she said with every appearance of ease. 'I, I thought you would be here.' Her gaze slid away from his face to dwell for one brief astounded second on the child, covered now by the quilt from her bed, but lying still in the place where she had left him.

'Terry,' she faltered, one hand flying up to clutch at her throat. 'Terry.' She repeated his name, building into the one word a declaration of betrayal.

The girls ceased their chatter, turning as one to gaze from Terry's stern face to that of their mother.

'Take them out of the room,' Terry said in a colourless tone, jerking his chin at the door in a manner that brooked no argument.

Unable to tear her gaze from the eyes she felt to be boring into her soul, Irene spoke woodenly. 'I think you had better say goodnight to Mr Garland, you two. It's time you went to bed.'

Though neither adult made any move to enforce this suggestion, the weight of the silence stretching between them was so oppressive as to turn both children around, and send them suddenly subdued across the hall to their room.

Irene was only subconsciously aware of their going. Blanched as white as her face, her lips quivered as she struggled to make them offer some words of excuse for that which she knew to be inexcusable.

'Why, Irene? In the name of God, why? Can you answer me that?'

'I . . . he . . .' Shaking her head, she abandoned the effort.

'Irene.' He croaked her name in sudden appeal. 'It was all going to be so very different.' His voice flattened on a note of pleading. His face worked as he tried for understanding. 'He is your son. . . . Your son.' This in a hoarse, deep throated whisper.

Irene gazed at him wordlessly; her hands fluttered up from her sides as she made a desperate attempt to frame some sort of answer.

Before she could speak, the sound of the outer door being opened brought her head round in a quick, amazed glance. As the doctor hurried unceremoniously into the room she turned just as swiftly back to the man she had relied upon to spare her this confrontation.

'Terry?' Irene's quavering appeal was ignored as both men locked glances.

'I . . . he hasn't been moved . . . I thought it unwise.' Terry's shamed glance slid away from the granite expression which condemned him unheard, to flick briefly down over the child.

The doctor fixed on him a glowering censure of degrading contempt before bending to remove the enveloping quilt. His hands moved expertly and with great tenderness for several seconds; when he straightened his eyes were terrible. He made a half-turn to include Irene in their scathing, flesh-stripping gaze. 'Who is responsible for this atrocity?' he asked in a voice squeezed past the strangling constriction of his throat.

He neither expected nor received an answer.

He looked from one to the other of their stricken faces, treating them to a full-faced, silent castigation. 'There is an ambulance on the way,' he said, in carefully precise tones. 'I think I would prefer to wait outside.'

His footsteps were heavy as he crossed the room.

The ambulance attendants were quick about their business, their small burden scarcely warranting the lengthy stretcher that dwarfed his already shrunken frame. Irene and Terry watched in silence as they bore Lawrence away.

Once the men were gone and the door closed behind them, Terry lost his battle to appear professionally impartial. A sound that could only be described as a snarl broke from his throat and though he tried several times to speak his voice was too charged with emotion to express the words intelligibly. 'For Christ's sake! Why didn't you call somebody? . . . Anybody! You must have known what you were about.' Now his voice found its edge, sharpening to a stinging whiplash, and he spat the words at her. 'Even that so-called friend of yours from the flat downstairs – even her.' Afraid of what he might do or say he spun on his heel, wanting to shut her out of his sight, seeking escape. The uncurtained window beckoned and two long strides took him to the glass where he stared sightlessly out over the distant winking lights of the town, one hand bunched into a fist smashing again and again into the palm of the other.

The sound was ugly.

'Terry,' Irene ventured timidly. 'I . . . he wouldn't talk to me.' She stared at his broad back outlined against the dark sky, and stepped a little to the side the better to catch a glimpse of his face. 'I tried, Terry. Truly I did . . . I . . . I gave him the fire engine I'd bought specially for him, and the panda . . . he wouldn't look at them, Terry.'

He could hear her voice whining on the edge of his thundering self-condemnation; on and on it went, picking at him irritatingly, stinging and fretting like a hungry mosquito. He tried to brush it away, to block it out of his consciousness. Explanations were about to be demanded of him, his actions and motives would be called into question, and all that stupid, cringing bitch had to offer was some half-baked claptrap about a toy fire engine.

Since he did not turn, Irene sensed rather than saw the change that came over him. The sagging shoulders straightened, throwing off their crushing weight of guilt. The bowed head came erect by only a fraction, but she experienced a thrill of fear, and shrank away from him.

'Do you know . . . can you have any idea what you have done?' Terry whirled to face her, his face a mask of intense dislike.

Irene's eyes widened in shock. She had never seen such loathing on a human face. A whimper broke from her. 'Please,' she begged. 'Please, Terry, don't look at me like that.' Tears flooded her eyes and hung in glistening drops from her lashes before spilling down her cheeks, but failed to melt Terry's wrath.

'You make me sick, Irene. Sick and disgusted. And ashamed to be numbered among your acquaintances. If I had it in my power I would wipe you out of my life . . . and off the face of the earth. Creatures of your ilk should be exterminated – written out as if they had never been, then dumped somewhere far removed from human habitation like the worthless trash you have made of yourself.'

A deadly silence followed his words, holding them both aghast at the things he had said. It seemed that all the cruelty since time began had been concentrated in this place, scorching them both with its blistering presence, until they were changed out of all recognition.

Terry was first to recover from this baptism of hate. Shaking himself, he put a hand to his head, closing his eyes against the hideous, unforgivable accusations he had made.

Before he could guess what she was about, Irene gave a low moan, and launched herself at the door to the balcony.

'No!' Quicker than he would have believed himself capable, Terry grabbed her wrist and threw her away from that avenue of escape.

She dropped to the floor, howling like a baby.

'Stop that! Now stop it, Irene!' Terry squatted beside her. 'I shouldn't have said what I did, but jumping out of the window is no answer either. Come, dry your eyes.' He pushed his handkerchief into her hand, and tried to lift her to her feet.

Irene fought against him. 'Leave me! Leave me alone! Get out of here, you . . . you . . . Get out! Get out, and don't ever come back!'

Terry shook his head. 'Sorry, Irene. We're in this together all the way. You're stuck with me until the police and the rest of them get here.'

'Police?' Irene's tears dried as she stared up at him. 'Why? Who? What . . . what are they coming for?' She allowed Terry to help her to get up, then clutched at him, grabbed the front of his jacket with both hands, shaking it like a rag as she urged him to answer.

'I called them. I had no choice. And the Department.'

'Department? What are you talking about? Terry, what department?'

'The Children's Department. Social Services. Somebody will have to take charge of the kids.' His head wagged in the direction of the girls' bedroom.

'The kids? *My* kids? Lauren and Debbie? Why . . . why should they need anyone to take charge of them?' She was staring at him in dawning horror. 'You . . . you're sending them away? But Terry, why? Why? You promised. You promised, you know you did. You said you would never let anyone take my children away from me.' She threw herself at him, her fists beating at his head and face. 'I'll kill you! I'll kill you! You can't do this to me!'

Overcoming her wild struggles Terry pinioned her arms, holding her in a brutally restricting grasp until at last she was spent, and hung limply against him. 'Don't make a fuss, Irene. Don't let the girls hear you. You will only frighten them, cause them unnecessary distress.'

'I want them. I want to go to them. You have no right to try and stop me,' Irene said brokenly.

'Irene, don't you understand yet? It isn't only the girls they will be taking away,' Terry said softly.

Irene looked into his face and her frown deepened before giving way to incredulous disbelief as the truth burst over her. Her knees buckled as she began to babble and plead.

'So tell me, Mrs Rawding – Irene. What were your feelings when Lawrence was born?' Terry Garland's senior officer had arrived at the flat within ten minutes of the ambulance leaving. She was a small, bespectacled young woman of about half Terry's fifty-four years, and possessed of a mind geared exclusively to the work for which she held many academic and personal qualifications.

Janet Fouracres lived and breathed child care; the cause and effect of the parent-child relationship was a source of great fascination to this maiden lady, and her understanding of human nature surpassed only her ability to create an instant rapport with the distressed individuals on whom her interest was centred. She had entered Irene's flat in the guise of friend and helpmeet, and even her subordinate, lashed by his own feelings of guilt and inadequacy, had felt the subtle easing of the tensions running so dangerously near breaking point.

Irene gazed at her questioner. None of the quiet, seemingly casual conversation that had followed Janet's introduction had prepared her for a probe so close to the subject she had been at such pains to blot from her mind.

'I . . . I was . . . It was a very difficult time . . . so many things . . . so much trouble . . . My husband, my husband . . . ' Irene's white face was a stage for the emotions tearing at her. 'My little girls . . . ' She struggled to find the words to describe the hurt staring out of her eyes.

Janet Fouracre's innate compassion moved her to signal an end to this particular line of questions. 'Tell me about your own childhood, Irene,' she invited instead. 'Was that a happy time for you?'

Irene gave her a long, steady look in which both defeat and acceptance were mixed. The pain in her wide, grey eyes receded a little, became muted by the passage of time, and the long practice of dissembling. 'What would you like to know?' she asked in a dead voice.

'Everything.' Janet checked Terry Garland's move forward with a quick frown, and he retreated to his place behind the chair Irene occupied.

'Everything,' Irene said slowly. 'Well, I don't know where to begin.' Her fingers went automatically to the sickle-shaped scar on her cheek as her eyes stared back into the past.

Janet had not missed the action. She nodded her head imperceptibly, a little outward gesture in confirmation of her suspicions. She waited patiently for Irene to begin. 'Your mother,' she prompted after a while. 'What was she like? Was

26

yours a close relationship?'

'Close? Like did we get on, you mean?' Irene's voice became shrill.

'That's right.' The level, dulcet tones, which were Janet's habitual mode of speech, invited a more composed response, and Irene swallowed noisily before plunging into a reply.

'No, no, we didn't really get on,' she said, her fingers once again tracing the line of the scar on her cheek. 'She . . . she didn't like me very much, and . . . and she drank.'

After that hesitant beginning words flooded from Irene's lips, and her listeners were painfully appraised of a woman whose own personal afflictions had twisted and soured her relationship with her daughter.

THREE

No one ever mentioned the word alcoholic within Dorothy Cooper's hearing, and had any been rash enough to have done so that lady's renowned acid tongue would swiftly have thrust the words down their throats. She was not known to suffer any check on her behaviour. She glanced expectantly around the company in the smoke-filled, overcrowded public bar, and demanded to know who was buying.

'Here, I'll get these, Dot. You bought the last round.' Tommy Bastable pushed his empty whisky glass at the barmaid, waiting only for his wife to drain her own before ordering. 'Two more of the same, and a half of bitter for Dot.' He looked over his shoulder to the other couple making up their small group. 'You ready yet, Ida? – Stan?' An empty pint-pot and a half-full gin and tonic were hastily passed towards the bar.

'I'll just have a gin in there, Tommy. Got enough tonic, thanks.'

'Yours another pint, Stanley?'

'Please, Tom. Cheers.'

Glasses recharged, the five of them resumed their conversation, and what this lacked in erudition was more than compensated for by the variety of subject. From local politics to world affairs and the unwashed state of Maudie Brown's curtains, they gave them all benefit of their consideration. The quintet were, as usual, the last to leave the bar, and then parted company only after a further twenty-minute discussion held out on the street. Tommy Bastable and his wife went off to catch the last bus, leaving Ida and Stan to bear Dorothy company over the half-mile walk to their neighbouring houses.

Irene, lying wakeful in bed alongside her sleeping sister, heard them bid each other goodnight beneath her bedroom window. She pushed herself up from the pillows listening for the telltale sounds of her mother's entry into the house. If she stumbled over the threshold, knocking against the furniture on her way through the downstairs rooms, Irene had learned to expect trouble. Tonight, with her father being out at work on the night shift, she was especially wary.

The front door opened and closed behind her mother without audible mishap, and the girl breathed a sigh of relief before snuggling down under the warm bedclothes. Curling up against her sister's back she drifted towards sleep. When the bedroom light was switched on she was drowsy enough to imagine it part of her dreams, but the familiar and dreaded fumes of stale alcohol brought her swiftly awake.

'Wa's the matter?' she asked.

Her mother hung over the bed, one hand clutching the high wooden headboard to steady herself.

'Mam? What's the matter?' Irene asked again.

'Shh, shh, s'nothing. Jus' wanted to see you was all right.' Dorothy leaned closer, the beer on her breath surrounding Irene like a tangible cloud. 'Jus' wanted to be sure you were both covered up.' She made as if to kiss Irene on the lips, and the child drew back sickened by the smell and the fuddled approach.

'Why, you nasty little devil. Can't show me a bit of affection? Only wanted to kiss you.'

'I'm tired. You woke me up.' Irene pressed herself back on the pillow and closed her eyes.

The blow was even more severe for being so unexpected, and the sharp claw-setting of her mother's dress ring tore through the soft flesh of her cheek.

Irene's sister woke in a panic at her cry of pain, and started to scream as she became aware of the dark figure hanging over their bed.

'Be quiet! Stop your noise, you'll have the whole house awake.'

'It's all right, Sandra. It's all right. It's only our mam.' Irene fought down her own fear and distress in an effort to quieten her sister.

'How d'you mean, it's only our mam? Only in-bloody-deed.

29

Just what did you mean by that?' Dorothy took hold of Irene's shoulder, jerking her from the bed, shaking her back and forth until the teeth rattled in her head, and the blood from the gash in her cheek flew out to bespatter all three of them.

'Mam! Leave her alone! Leave her alone! She didn't mean nothing!' Sandra grabbed her mother's arm, hanging on like a small terrier.

'Stick together, you two, don't you? Stick together against me.' Dorothy began to cry. Maudlin tears of self-pity rained down her face, but she released her grip on Irene's shoulder allowing the child to fall back on her pillow. 'It's alu's been the same in this house. You two stand together against me,' she said through her sobs.

Sandra felt a rush of pity in spite of her fear, and reached out, longing to offer comfort.

Dorothy knocked her arms away with a vicious swipe. 'Don't come them tricks with me, madam. I know when I'm not wanted,' she said, before lurching from the room.

'Irene, are you all right?' Sandra whispered.

Irene buried her face in her pillow, muffling the sound of her weeping.

'Irene, there's blood everywhere. What shall I do?'

'Nothing. Don't do anything. Turn the light out and go back to sleep.'

'But there's blood,' the younger child protested, staring at the bright drops spattering the sheets and their pillows.

'I know there's blood. It's from the cut on my face, but don't let her hear you or she'll come back. Just put the light out, Sandra, and get back into bed.'

When she woke in the morning Irene's cheek was stuck to the pillow, and her frightened tears did little to ease the painful bonding between fabric and swollen flesh. 'Get me mam,' she begged of her sister. Go on, go and get her. Don't stand there.'

Sandra tore herself from terrified contemplation of the blood staining the bedding and ran shrieking for their mother.

'What is it? What's the matter?' Her face puffy with sleep and drink, her tongue thickly fumbling to frame the question, Dorothy peered bleary-eyed at her youngest daughter.

'It's our Irene. She's stuck to her pillow, an' her face an' everything is all bloody.'

With a groan of protest Dorothy pulled the bedclothes up over her head.

'Mam, you've got to come. She wants you.' Sandra tugged at the enveloping quilt, her small hands searching for a grip on her mother's arm. 'Come on, Mam. Don't go back to sleep.'

Dorothy pushed the quilt aside, but made no effort to rise. 'Aw, hell!' She drew several deep breaths before attempting to open her eyes. 'What time is it?'

'I don't know.' At three years old, Sandra had yet to learn to read a clock face.

'Isn't your dad home?'

'I don't know.'

'Don't you know anything?' Dorothy snapped, then lifted a hand to her aching head, instantly regretting the spurt of temper that sent the blood thumping inside her skull.

'Ma-am.' Sandra tugged at her arm. 'Get up, Mam.'

'I'm coming, I'm coming.' Gingerly swinging her feet to the floor, Dorothy came upright in a series of jerks and groans. Lifting the alarm clock from her bedside table she tilted it to catch the light from the window. 'Six o'clock? Christ Almighty, what a time to come pestering me.'

Afraid that her mother meant to climb back into bed, Sandra renewed her tugging; with her fingers now locked into the stuff of Dorothy's nightgown she tugged and pulled, her small frame rigid with the effort.

With slow, shuffling steps Dorothy crossed the dark room, hands groping for the familiar feel of the wardrobe and the end of the bed until she reached the clear space around the door. She found the light switch by instinct born of long usage and blinked against the harsh glare of the electric bulb as it sprang into life. Harassed and aggravated by Sandra, she plodded along the landing to her daughters' bedroom where Sandra released her maddening grip in favour of a place close to the side of the bed.

'She can't get up, Mam,' she said, with a worried glance at Irene. 'Her face is all stuck.'

'What do you mean, her face is all stuck? Here, move out of the way, let me see.' Pushing Sandra to one side Dorothy leaned over Irene who lay crying quietly, her face buried in the pillow.

'What's wrong, Irene? What's the matter?' Coming suddenly into full possession of her senses Dorothy gently stroked her daughter's hair back from her face and bent over the child to examine her cheek. When she attempted to flatten the pillow in order to see more clearly where the trouble lay, Irene shrieked in pain. 'Sh, sh, it's all right. I'm not going to hurt you, but you must let me look.'

'Don't pull it, Mam. Don't pull it, will you?'

'No, of course I won't.' Dorothy's voice was full of concern. 'Just lie quietly for a minute while I see what needs to be done.' Very gently Dorothy eased the pillow as far as it would go then took a closer look. 'I'll have to bathe it, my love. I have to wash some of the blood away. Can you be a brave girl while I try to take the pillow out of the cover?'

Irene's tears fell faster. 'It hurts, Mam.'

'Yes, I know, lovely. I know.' Dorothy pursed her lips as she studied the situation. Sandra watched with big, round eyes from the side of the bed, tears of sympathy starting down her cheeks. 'If I slide my hand inside the pillowcase and hold your head steady while I take out the pillow, we can get some nice warm water and soak away the cloth that is sticking to your face. Can you try, Irene?'

Irene made a small, frightened sound of agreement.

'Come on, then, let's give it a go.'

Roy Cooper, though one of the easiest men in the world to deal with, was certainly no fool, and when he entered his home at seven-thirty that morning to find his wife frying bacon and eggs for their two boisterous sons while their youngest daughter hovered protectively about her older sister, he was immediately concerned.

'You're up early for a Saturday, all of you,' he remarked mildly on entering the kitchen.

'Yes, it's a case of no rest for the wicked,' his wife answered lightly.

'And what has our Rene been doing to her face?' he asked, bending over the child and looking into her eyes.

Dorothy called the boys up to the table and began dishing out their breakfast, making unnecessary clatter with the plates.

'Rene?' Roy asked gently.

Irene lowered her eyes. 'I fell down,' she said softly.

Sandra glanced swiftly to her mother whose concentration appeared to be fixed on the breakfast plates.

'How did you manage that?' Roy persisted.

'Just did, that's all.' Irene fiddled with the fastenings of her cardigan, refusing to meet her father's eye.

'Let me look.' He reached out to lift the gauze pad she wore on her cheek and she jerked away with a cry.

'Leave her be, Roy. I'm taking her to get it seen to as soon as the surgery is open. Do you want any of this?' Dorothy indicated the frying pan she held.

'No, I'll have something a bit later.' A frown creasing his brow, Roy turned to consider his wife. 'I'll take Rene along to the doctor's if you like. Save you going out.'

'It's all right. I have the shopping to deal with, anyway.'

'Dorothy.' Roy moved across the kitchen and drew his wife to one side. 'Dot, I'm worried about her.' He indicated Irene with a jerk of his head. 'She has a lot of falls for a kid coming up five. The lads used to be more steady on their feet at that age.' His words carried no overtones of censure, but his keen grey eyes, searching his wife's face, spoke volumes.

'She's clumsy, that's all.' Dorothy met his gaze squarely.

'And that's all it is?'

'That's all,' she said positively, and Roy was obliged to accept her word.

Doctor Court had known Dorothy all her life; he had delivered her into the world in the small back bedroom of the terraced house long since swept away in a road-widening scheme. He had monitored her childhood and watched her grow into a healthy young woman, and was constantly surprised at the rapid passage of the years that had brought her to marriage and a family of her own. He'd attended her diligently through her four pregnancies, and kept a professional eye on the usual childish ailments contracted by her infants. In Dorothy Cooper *née* Townsend, he saw a neat, tidy mother of clean, tidy children who suffered nothing out of the ordinary by way of either injury or disease. When Dorothy was ushered into his surgery leading her elder daughter by the hand he gazed at the pad covering the child's cheek, and pursed his lips expectantly.

'Well, well, and what have we here?' he asked of Irene in the jovial avuncular manner he habitually used when addressing his junior patients.

'She's cut her face, Doctor.' Dorothy drew Irene forward to stand at the doctor's knee. 'Fell down, she said. It's pretty bad. I thought maybe you should take a look at it.'

'Well, then, let me see.' The doctor gently removed the dressing, a frown gathering between his eyes as he examined Irene's bruised and swollen cheek. 'You know, this should have been dealt with as soon as possible after it happened,' he said in mild reproach.

'It was late. The surgery was closed,' Dorothy said quickly.

'Hmm, even so . . . Turn your head this way, lassie.' Irene winced as his fingers pressed against raw flesh. 'And how did you come to do this?' The doctor was talking merely to put the child at her ease, he anticipated no contradiction of Dorothy's explanation.

'Fell over,' Irene whispered. And her mother expelled her breath in a ragged gust that sounded loudly in the quiet atmosphere of the small room.

'Worry you to death, don't they, Mother?' Mistaking the reason for her anxiety, Doctor Court smiled sympathetically at Dorothy over Irene's head. 'Never mind, we'll soon put this young lady to rights. A couple of little stitches and she'll be as good as new.'

A cry of fear escaped the child, and her eyes filled with tears. Dorothy dropped to her knees hugging her daughter protectively. 'It's all right, my pet. Don't you cry. Doctor's not going to hurt you.'

Irene bit on her lip, her tears spilling down her cheeks.

'There now, this won't do. See, you are making your face wet.' The doctor swabbed the flowing tears with a tissue. 'I think I might have a sweetie for a big girl,' he said by way of encouragement. 'So you just stand perfectly still for one little minute, and we'll see what we can find, eh?'

34

With one cheek distended to accommodate the striped humbug, and the other hidden behind a thick gauze pad, Irene's solemn little face bore slight resemblance to its customary beauty. Her father, studying her as she followed her mother into the house, thought the child looked positively ill.

'What did he say?' He addressed his question to Dorothy, but his gaze remained fixed on his daughter's face.

'She's all right,' Dorothy said briefly. 'I thought you would have gone to bed by now.' She took Irene's coat to hang it next to her own, pausing to straighten the sleeves and twitch the skirt smooth. This whole operation apparently demanding her full attention, prevented her turning to meet her husband's eyes.

'So what did the doctor say?' Roy persisted.

'I've got stitches,' Irene told him, childishly proud of her suffering now that the worst of the pain was over.

'Stitches!' Roy forgot himself so far as to allow the shock he felt to sound in his voice. He recovered himself quickly, and bending down to look into his small daughter's face asked on a note of admiration, 'Have you, sweetheart? How many?'

'Er . . . ' Irene thought hard, then turned enquiringly to her mother. 'How many, Mam?'

'Five, I believe.'

'Five! My God, how badly is she hurt?' Roy pulled Irene into his arms, his hand moving automatically to the pad held to her cheek by two strips of pink sticking-plaster.

Irene flinched away with a cry of alarm.

'Leave her be, Roy. The doctor said we've not to take the dressing off.'

'But I want to see. She'll be marked for life.' His face worked as he considered this possibility.

''Course she won't. It's not anywhere near as bad as you imagine.'

'But five stitches . . . *five*. They don't put those in for nothing.'

'They're pretty close together. And young flesh heals quicker than you'd expect.' Dorothy made to pass along the hall and through the door into the living room, but Roy caught her by the arm, holding her in a grip that was none too gentle. She made no effort to pull away.

'Go and see what Sandra is doing, Rene.' Roy indicated the back room with a jerk of his head, and Irene, sure of her sister's warm sympathy, went eagerly to tell her of her ordeal.

Roy waited for the door to close behind her before turning a look on his wife that made her blood run cold. 'I think it's time you and I had a little chat, Dorothy. Let's use the front room.'

The front room of their pre-war semi was kept sacrosanct by Dorothy, as the front room of her childhood home had been so kept by her own mother. It was used on only one day a year, Christmas Day. For the remainder of the year it stood unheated and rigidly tidy, the chilly inhospitable testament of a house-proud woman.

There was always the faint odour of soot on the damp air of the room, emanating from the unused firegrate, despite the quantities of crumpled newspaper Dorothy used to blank off the chimney. She was conscious of it now as Roy propelled her across the well-preserved carpet. In the act of closing the door firmly behind them he seemed to Dorothy to be distancing them both from the warmth generated by their children, at play in the next room. She steeled herself to face him. This was not the easy-going man she had lived with for close on sixteen years, nor yet the credulous idiot she hinted at to her drinking cronies. This was a man with a purpose, with a strangely direct way of looking at her that gave her to feel he might read every thought that passed, or had ever passed, through her head.

'What's this all about?' She tried to bluster, but under his gaze the aggression deliberately injected into her tone faltered and ebbed. She found herself unable to meet his gaze, and thought to conceal this fact by ducking her head in an act of pretending hurt. 'You are so besotted with that girl, you can't even see straight, that's your trouble.' She mouthed the words in wounded accents. 'None of the others get so much as a look in. And as for me . . . ' She allowed her voice to die on a pitiful note.

'Now come on, Dorothy. That's not true, and you know it. I treat them all equally.'

Hoping to divert him from the grim purpose she believed had caused him to bring her into this room, Dorothy pressed on with her counter-charges. 'Well, I've never seen you nursing the lads the way you do her,' she said with a snort.

'And they'd love that, wouldn't they?' Roy was equally derisive. 'Them an' me in football kit having a fatherly kiss and cuddle. I can just imagine their faces.'

'Ah, now you've said something there, haven't you?' Resentment, long simmering, came to the boil causing Dorothy to completely lose her head. 'It's all getting a bit past fatherly, to my way of thinking, the way you kiss and cuddle Irene. And her nearly five years old at that.'

An awful silence met her words, during which she had time to wish she could bite her own tongue out.

Roy looked at her as though he was witnessing something vile.

'My God! I can't believe I heard you say that,' he said at last, his voice a hoarse croaking, rising scarcely above a whisper as the full horror of his wife's implication was borne on him.

Dorothy looked down at her fingers, twisting her wedding ring round and round as she was wont to do when she was distressed. 'Well, I don't care,' she muttered, her chin pressed into her chest, muffling her words. 'You've never had time for me since that kid was born.'

'Time for you? Time for you? Who else do I have time for, then? Answer me that. I work all hours God sends to give you the things you need – I've never begrudged you anything . . . no, not anything. You come and go as you please, you never go short . . . what more do you want?'

There tumbled unbidden into Dorothy's mind words she knew she would never find the courage to speak. I want you, she longed to tell him. To love me and cherish me, and to treat me like a desirable woman – not like some half-forgotten companion who is comfortable to have in the background. I want romance and love and desire; all of these things and more. I want to fill you with an ache for my body, to have you court me, woo me, want me, before we are both too old, and too busy being father and mother to care any more.

Instead of speaking she sighed and turned away from the hard light in her husband's eyes that branded her as cold, ungrateful, and worse.

'I want you to tell me, Dorothy. Did you cause the injury to

37

that child? And if you did, what are we to do about it?' There was a gentleness 'in Roy's manner of asking that startled Dorothy. Threats and recriminations she had been prepared to outface, but not this, this kindly indication of understanding that completely overthrew her. She turned to meet his gaze, words trembling at her lips; if only she might tell him . . . Her eyes dropped abruptly as she struggled to find the right words. How could she explain her feelings to him when it was only with the greatest reluctance that she ever acknowledged them to herself?

'Come on, Dot. Make the effort. Tell you what, I won't look at you if it'll help. See, I'll sit over here, and you can stand behind my chair.' Roy took the easy-chair with its back to the door leaving Dorothy to choose her own direction. He had long suspected the cause of Irene's many bumps and scrapes, had tried to bring it out in the open on several previous occasions only to find himself cleverly thwarted by some reasonable explanation that put him to shame for his suspicions. He gave Dorothy time to collect her thoughts, before prompting her quietly.

At this point Irene, too, paused to consider her situation. She looked at Janet Fouracres as if seeing her for the first time, and must have found reassurance in the mild blue eyes staring back at her from behind the heavy spectacles, for her nervously twisting hands became still, and she took time to arrive at the question she asked next.

'I don't suppose this is helping at all, is it? I mean, you want to know about Lawrence, and I've just been going on and on about me.'

'Which is exactly what I wanted to hear,' Janet assured her. 'The things you have been telling me help me to understand the whole picture.'

'Understand? How can you understand? How can anyone?' Irene half turned, seeking support from Terry Garland. He found himself incapable of meeting her gaze, choosing instead to look at his colleague, silently urging a return to the question of Irene's behaviour.

Janet, correctly interpreting his gaze, felt a surge of exasperation. Had he followed prescribed methods, this scene might well have been avoided. 'Why don't you take a seat, Terry?' Pity for his predicament overcame her momentary impatience, and she waved him towards a straight-backed chair just to the left of Irene's lounger.

Terry seated himself but continued to look uneasy.

Janet leaned forward in her chair, her whole manner conveying her willingness to listen. 'Go on, Irene. You were telling us about your parents, and about your childhood. What happened after you'd had the stitches put in your cheek?'

'But what about Lawrence? Will he be all right?' cried Irene in sudden sharp anxiety. 'You let them take him away, Terry. You let them take him!'

Janet's expression urged her colleague to answer this accusation.

'They have taken him to the hospital. They're going to make him better.'

'Like they did before?' Irene pleaded.

'We must hope so. We must all hope so.' His words had about them the nature of a prayer. 'Please, Irene. There is nothing we can do now but wait, so why not go on with what you were saying?' He met Janet's speaking glance. 'Your parents – they had a good marriage, would you say?'

'What have they to do with anything? Why do you ask so many questions?'

Janet spoke quickly, hoping to avoid the hysterical outburst she sensed was about to overtake Irene. 'We are just trying to help pass the time. It's better, don't you think, to keep our minds occupied?'

'Occupied with my business,' Irene said darkly. She took several deep breaths, and glowered at the social worker from beneath lowered lashes before allowing herself to be led back to the point where she had departed from her story.

Though she tried her utmost to be frank, Dorothy was unable to admit that sexual frustration played a major role in the troubled relationship between herself and her eldest daughter. Sex had not been considered a proper subject for discussion when she and Roy were growing up, and by the time the 'swinging sixties' with their permissive society and greater awareness caught up with them, their inhibitions were already too deep-seated to be lightly discarded. Their courtship had been virtuously proper, with Dorothy's mother warning at every turn of the trouble that came to young girls who were silly enough to go too far. What exactly she had meant by that she had never elaborated on, and it had been left for Dorothy to glean what misinformation she could from her contemporaries. The explanations, based often on knowledge as sketchy as her own, were as varied as they were misleading, and she had gone down the aisle to meet Roy entirely deserving of her white wedding gown.

Married as soon as they reached twenty, and both of them virgins, they had fumbled their way into parenthood without ever fully understanding the demands of their flesh.

Two sons were born to them, coming as though planned, Roger a blameless two years after their wedding, and Martin a further two years after his brother. Dorothy then declared her family complete, and herself blissfully happy. She idolised her two little boys, enjoyed being paramount female to three lusty males, and might have continued feeding her ego on their affections had not Irene put in her appearance after an interval of seven barren years. Finding herself ousted from supreme position as both boys and their father came under the spell of this endearing new arrival, Dorothy failed completely to understand her own resentment of the child. She considered it no favour when Roy got up in the night to give the baby her bottle, and was deeply hurt when he refused her inexpert, but longing advances with the plea of being too tired when he eventually returned to their bed. Aching to be reassured of her place in his affections she took his refusals on a personal level to which she retaliated by withdrawing altogether from any outward demonstration of love. Towards the baby she was always showily attentive, ensuring the child was clothed in only the most expensive outfits. To such an extent did she carry this fetish that all her spare cash went into buying little dresses, coats and shoes until Irene was possessed of a wardrobe far in excess of any child's needs.

'Blimey, Dot. Not another new outfit,' Roy lamented when Dorothy showed him her latest purchases. 'Hasn't she got enough clothes? Buy something for yourself for a change.'

But Dorothy went on buying the frilled and ruffled little-girl dresses, determinedly changing Irene out of one and into another before ever they became the least little bit grubby. Always she looked for some sign of gratitude from the child, waiting for a smile of pleasure or some gesture of thanks, but Irene was forever solemn-faced in her mother's presence and it took her father or the boys to persuade her to smile.

As Irene approached her first birthday Dorothy made plans for a birthday treat. 'I'll invite the little girl from over the road, and her cousin Julie, and of course there'll be Roger and Martin,' she told Roy in some excitement.

Roy shook his head in contradiction of his indulgent smile. 'You spoil that kid, Dorothy. You really do. What does she want with birthday parties at twelve months old? She's far too young to understand.'

'Well, I just thought it would be nice.' Dorothy moved to pass him, and he caught her round the waist, pulling her down to sit on his knees. 'So what about being nice to the old man for a change, eh?' he hinted broadly.

Dorothy struggled to free herself. 'Let me up. Don't be so daft,' she said angrily.

Roy laughed and held on to her until her struggles became more determined. Suddenly losing patience he thrust her to her feet. 'Well go, then,' he said harshly.

Heart beating furiously, her throat full of tears, Dorothy took a chair on the far side of the hearth and hid her face behind a newspaper. Loving Roy as she did, wanting him, needing him to want her in return, she could not have explained her action. Somehow, it was all mixed up with the way he was forever kissing and hugging the baby. Irene won his affections without lifting a finger; no matter how much she cried or played him up, he was never short or impatient with her.

That evening when she was bathing the child, the zinc baby-bath she had used for the boys drawn up to the fire, she watched the way her daughter's face creased into smiles at the sight of her daddy, and her fingers clenched on the soft little body brutally pinching the tender skin.

Irene shrieked, her gurgles turning to howls of outrage and

pain. Dorothy snatched her from the water, enfolding her in the towel she held ready across her lap. She rocked Irene in her arms, soothing, comforting, staunching her tears.

'What's the matter with her? Was the water too hot?' Instantly concerned, Roy plunged his hand into the bath water, testing the temperature. 'What made her scream like that, Dot? Is she all right?'

''Course she is. Just a touch of colic, I expect. Honestly, the way you fuss.' In spite of her assurances a cold hand clutched Dorothy's heart. What had she done? What in heaven's name had made her do such a cruel, spiteful thing to her own child? She felt she would be sick, and struggled against the nausea, clutching the baby to her breast. She continued to nurse Irene long after her tears had stopped, holding her tenderly in her arms, gently caressing the dimpled limbs. Irene yawned and stretched, her eyelids drooping. 'Who's a tired little girl, then? Come on, sleepy-fleas, time you were in bed.' Dorothy carried her up the stairs still wrapped in the downy towel.

In the room she and Roy had decorated as a nursery she placed Irene in the crib while she assembled the child's nightclothes. Then, unable to postpone the moment any longer, she unwound the towel, forcing herself to examine the purple bruises staining her baby's silky skin. With a swift intake of breath Dorothy stared at the angry weals rising under her fingers and knew a fresh burst of self-loathing.

'I'm sorry, darling. Mummy is so very sorry,' she whispered.

Irene stared up into her troubled face, wide-eyed and uncomprehending.

From that first act of deliberate cruelty, Dorothy made a conscious effort to be more loving of her baby. It should not have been difficult: Irene was a pretty child, the beauty of whose white-blonde curls and big blue eyes could only be enhanced by the expensive, ultra-sweet dresses and coats that were her mother's delight. Dorothy received as her due all the extravagant compliments paid to the child, but found it very hard to show enthusiasm for her baby's achievements. When the boys had been small she had never stopped marvelling at their first step, their first word, their ability to understand;

every little advance they had made was a source of constant wonder to her, and she had bored glassy-eyed anyone unwise enough to ask after her sons. She merely went through the motions in respect of her daughter, forcing every word through reluctant lips, hoping each time she did so that they would strike some sort of warmth from the cold, empty space in her heart.

Roy watched them together, his wife and his little girl, and knew a pride he did nothing to hide. 'My very own sweethearts,' he would say, placing an arm about each, with always a kiss for his daughter's fair curls. 'And my big, handsome lads,' he would add should the boys come within earshot. 'My two special pals.' The boys would grin bashfully while Irene would return her daddy's kiss with enthusiasm leaving Dorothy to wriggle free of this shared embrace.

'You get dafter in your old age,' was her usual rejoinder before she turned away to busy herself with whatever came to hand.

So clever did she become at concealing her feelings that it was not until Irene's second birthday that Roy caught his first glimpse of the unhappy relationship existing between his wife and their only daughter.

Following the pattern of the previous year, a birthday party had been arranged; a cake, entertainment for Irene's little guests, everything Dorothy imagined would delight and please the child. In this atmosphere of nervous anticipation Irene grew over-excited long before the tea-table was spread and was unable to swallow more than a mouthful of the tempting jellies and creams her mother had taken such trouble to prepare. Dorothy cleared away with a fixed smile on her face, contriving as she did so to catch the side of Irene's head a sharp knock with the base of the heavy cake-stand.

She was instantly contrite, bending to smooth the bump already swelling under the child's curls, making crooning sounds of apology.

Roy started from his place at the head of the table prepared to help curb the expected tears, only to be halted by his daughter's stoic silence and the empty expression on the child's face as she suffered her mother's fussy ministrations. Roy

43

returned to his place, brows drawn together in a frown of reluctant understanding.

After the party guests left, each little girl coaxed into politely expressing her thanks by her attendant parent, Roy drew his wife into the kitchen out of the way of their two sharp-eyed, keen-hearing sons. 'You clonked that child deliberately, Dot. Didn't you?'

Dorothy hotly defended herself. 'When? This afternoon, you mean? Don't talk so daft.'

'That seems to be your favourite expression just lately. Well, let me tell you, I'm not so daft as you might believe. I know what I saw, and I saw you fetch that baby a crack with the cake-stand as sure as eggs are eggs.'

'You are being ridiculous. Why would I do such a thing?'

'Why would anyone? You tell me.'

'Well, they wouldn't, would they? Isn't that what I'm saying?' Dorothy turned away, making as if to start on the dishes piled in the sink, but Roy deliberately placed himself in her way, dropping his hips against the sink edge and reaching for Dorothy's hands. She snatched them away. 'Oh, don't start that, Roy. Can't you see that I'm busy.'

'You are always busy when I try to touch you these days,' Roy said bitterly. 'And anyway, you needn't flatter yourself. I wanted to speak to you about this business with the baby, that's all.'

'She's not a baby. She was two years old today, in case it slipped your notice.'

'I noticed all right, just as I noticed the other thing, but she is still a baby to my way of thinking. Too young to have you vent your spite on her the way that you did, even if she was twice her age. So come on, Dot. What is it? Why did you do it?'

'It was an accident, I tell you. If I'd wanted to hurt her I'd have given her a smack, ungrateful little madam that she is.'

'Ungrateful? What the devil are you talking about?' Roy was patently amazed.

'All the trouble she's put me to. All the work I've had. And she never so much as touched a bite of her tea.'

'My God! Is that what it was all about?' He studied Dorothy for several long minutes, his gaze neither kind nor flattering.

44

'You have got to be sick, woman,' he said finally. 'I suggest you see a doctor. And in the meantime' – he wagged a finger under her nose – 'if I should catch you as much as laying a finger on that kid – on any of the kids – so help me, Dot, I'll clout you myself.'

After Roy had stormed from the kitchen Dorothy drew hot water into the sink and went calmly about the task of washing the piles of dirty, sticky-fingered glass and crockery. As she lifted the last plate from the suds she paused to study her own image, reflected again and again in the fast-disappearing bubbles. It was not an evil face, she thought. Plain, maybe, but not unattractive. Her eyes clear and well spaced, her nose short and tip-tilted above the wide, generous lips. Her honey-blonde hair curled as naturally as did Irene's, and was her one vanity. Endless bubbles like miniature mirrors showed her the rippling waves that she wore long to her shoulders. The boys called her Goldilocks when they wished to tease, and she would pretend to be annoyed while inwardly basking in their flattery. With a quick swish she scattered the reflections and pulled the plug allowing the water to drain. Tonight she was in no mood for such silliness.

She returned to the living room and began getting Irene ready for bed. Roy watched her remove the child's frilled party dress and slip the sprigged cotton nightie over her head with a strange, unfathomable expression on his normally open face.

'I'll take her up,' he said when Irene had been divested of her socks and shoes. 'And you two had better start clearing all this away.' He indicated the Meccano pieces littering the floor, bringing quick howls of protest from Roger and Martin. 'By the time I get down,' he warned them. 'You've done very well today between you, now it's time to give it a rest. Me and your mam want a bit of peace and quiet this evening,' he added, bringing Dorothy's head round in surprise.

She waited nervously for him to return. Was he going to start on again about that business with the cake-stand? Roy was gone quite a time, she could hear him in their daughter's bedroom speaking too softly for her to distinguish the words. What was he asking her up there?

'She wanted a story,' Roy said as he returned to the room.

'Now, come on, you lads. Your turn next.'

Hoots of laughter from their young sons greeted this as they deliberately chose to misunderstand. At nine and eleven years old respectively, they considered themselves far too grown up for bedtime stories.

It was quiet after the boys went to bed. Dorothy fidgeted with some knitting, unable to relax. 'Why don't you put the telly on?' she asked, desperate for something to break the silence born of her unease.

'Because I want to talk to you. Put that knitting down and come to sit over here.' Roy patted a place beside him on the settee.

Dorothy hesitated before sticking the needles through the ball of wool. It had been a long time since she and Roy had shared the intimacy of the sofa.

'Now, then.' Roy placed an arm about her shoulders, drawing her head to his chest. 'Now tell me all about it, love.'

'All about what?' She fiddled with the buttons of his shirt, dreading any further attempt on his part to draw more details from her.

'This afternoon, Dot. It wasn't like you. Now I've cooled down I can see that. So what's wrong?'

'I . . . nothing. There's nothing wrong.' She struggled to sit up, to draw away from him, but he held her fast.

'Aren't you well? Is that it?'

'I'm all right.'

'But there has to be something. Aren't you sleeping? Do you get enough rest? Now I come to think of it, you do look a bit drained.' He held her away from him, the better to study her face.

'I'm all right, I tell you.'

'Well, was it the kids, then?' Roy was losing patience. 'I did try to persuade you not to invite so many. Six two-year-olds plus our lads can make for a lot of aggravation.' Dorothy made no answer but tears glistened on her cheeks, leading Roy to believe he had arrived at the root of the problem. Holding her close once more, stroking back her hair as he might have done Irene's, he chided her softly for being over-ambitious. 'You do too much, love. You always have. I know you're thrilled at

46

having a girl to dress up and show off after our two rough-and-tumble lads, but you try too hard. No one is going to notice if she wears the same dress two days running, or even if she gets a bit grubby every once in a while. She's not a chocolate-box doll, you know. And she'll survive without you knocking yourself out trying to give her the very best of everything.'

'Roy . . . I . . . It's not that . . . I . . . '

'Shh, shh. Let it go. Don't try to explain. Just do a little bit less running about after her in the future, eh?'

Dorothy struggled to hold on to the truth. A few minutes ago she had been on the point of letting it all out; of telling Roy about the many times she had been . . . a bit rough, was how she thought of it, to their little girl. Suddenly she was afraid he would draw away once he knew. Afraid she would lose him entirely. There had been little display of affection between them since Irene's birth, and while she was aware of her own fault in this, she couldn't bear that he should stop loving her altogether.

She allowed the moment to pass, and Roy to go on believing that afternoon's semi-accidental blow with the cake-stand an isolated incident.

That night she and Roy made love with all the stored up longing of two long years of misunderstanding and frustration, their hungry need of each other sweeping away all inhibitions, carrying them both helplessly along on an overwhelming tide of passion.

Recalling the flagrant abandonment of Sandra's conception, Dorothy felt the hot blood rush to stain her cheeks; there would be no repeat of that shameful lack of restraint at the conclusion of today's catechism, she promised herself. No matter what interpretation Roy chose to place on the excuses she made for her continued abuse of their eldest girl, she would never allow herself to descend to that animal level again.

Keeping out of Roy's line of vision she stumbled through a series of explanations so weak and so lacking in conviction he begged her impatiently to stop.

'I can't understand your insistence that young Irene is always

47

to blame. She's no angel, I'll grant you that, but then neither are the other three, yet you seem to find no difficulty controlling them without resorting to bully-boy tactics. It seems to me that it's time we looked for some advice about all this. I always said your obsession for overdressing the kid wasn't natural, and now it's come to this.' Roy turned fully to face her, his expression at once regretful and accusing.

'You're not trying to make out that I'm crackers, I hope.' Stung by her husband's championship of the child, Dorothy sought to retaliate with a show of temper.

Roy refused to be drawn. 'Whatever you like, Dorothy,' he said wearily. 'Just so long as you understand that we've reached the end of the line in as far as young Irene is concerned.'

FOUR

Tasting the salt of tears on her lips, Irene blinked. She had been unaware of any emotion attendant upon her recital of this grim episode from her childhood, but now, suddenly, all these years later, she was weeping bitterly for the death of that brave new beginning her father had promised after his insistence on taking both her and her mother to see Doctor Court. . . .

Irene had not been party to the whole interview. After the stitches were removed from the healing cut in her cheek she had been puzzled but not alarmed to be left in the care of the receptionist while the grown-ups continued their lengthy discussion. Whatever might have been said during that interview she had never been told, but there stemmed from that time an abrupt change in her mother's attitude. Her frantic, never-ending obsession with dressing her daughter in one beribboned dress after another gave way to a marked disinclination to clothe her at all, and Irene was allowed the freedom of getting herself gloriously and childishly dirty for the first time in her young life. Now she could join her younger sister happily sloshing poster-paint all over herself, or drape her neck with the bright ropes of sticky plasticine jewellery they both loved to fashion. A whole new world was opened up for her, one in which she found her mother's outward indifference amply compensated by an equal lack of her more painful attentions.

On the day she started school, Irene's brave new independence led her into mischief of the worst kind. She had been taken to the classroom where the other first-day pupils were assembled, neatly dressed, as were they, in the prescribed navy blue gymslip and pleated white blouse of the infant school uniform. Watching her mother depart with never a pang of regret she had thrown herself wholeheartedly into the dizzy experience of being with girls of her own age, and no apparent restrictions placed on their behaviour. Their teacher, occupied with the task of reassuring the more reticent pupils, failed to note that Irene had drawn a little clique about herself, and was currently fostering their awe-inspired admiration by cutting patterns across the front of her gymslip with a pair of blunt-nosed scissors she'd discovered on a windowsill.

By the time Mrs Bannister was free to turn her consideration to the remainder of her class, Irene had joyfully mutilated her beautiful new outfit beyond all repair.

'Oh, good heavens, child. What on earth are you doing?' Snatching the scissors from Irene's grasp her teacher gaped at the ruined gymslip. The quality navy blue serge sported a rash of holes across the front which parted with every breath Irene drew to flash the startling whiteness of the pleated blouse beneath. 'Whatever made you do such a thing?' she demanded weakly.

Irene smiled at her serenely. 'It doesn't matter,' she said reassuringly. 'My mam won't mind.'

'Not much she won't!' Appalled at the damage, and her own slipshod grammar, Mrs Bannister drew a trembling hand across her brow, and made a fresh attempt. 'Why?' she pleaded. 'Why had you to do such a thing?'

'I thought . . . I thought it would look pretty,' Irene faltered, some of the teacher's shocked dismay finally registering.

'You are a naughty, silly, destructive girl,' Mrs Bannister said harshly, visions of irate parents demanding that she make compensation out of her own pocket causing her to speak even more severely than she had intended.

The dimpled smile was sponged away. The red, sickle-shaped scar, with the stitch punctures still clearly visible, took on new prominence as Irene's expression flattened into blank acceptance of impending punishment.

'Go and sit at that desk over there.' Sudden pity softened the teacher's manner and she found herself inexplicably determined to defend this child against retribution.

Irene crept behind the desk indicated, there to remain, solemn-faced and subdued throughout the day.

Greatly perturbed, Mrs Bannister directed her to stay behind when class was dismissed in the mid-afternoon, and waited with fast-beating heart for the senior girl she'd appointed as look-out to return with the news that Mrs Cooper had arrived to take Irene home.

'Will you bring her in here to me, please, Sadie.' Keeping an eye on her young pupil she waited uneasily for Dorothy to be admitted.

'Mrs Cooper, I . . . You mustn't blame Irene. This is entirely my fault. If I hadn't been so taken up with my other children I would have noticed.'

Dorothy paused on entering the classroom, her puzzled gaze flicking swiftly from Mrs Bannister to her daughter seated, apparently unharmed, at her small desk in front of the teacher's large oak table.

'I'm sure Irene didn't mean to be naughty. And I never should have left the scissors within reach,' Mrs Bannister babbled.

'What is it? What has she done?'

Gazing into the sharply anxious face, Mrs Bannister motioned for Irene to stand.

Dorothy's gaze travelled slowly to scan her daughter, her swift intake of breath the only expression of her anger as she surveyed the ruined clothes. Without a word she reached forward to haul Irene clear of the desk, and into the open space beneath the tall blackboards where she examined the damage with deliberate thoroughness.

Alarmed at the expression on the woman's face, Mrs Bannister placed a supportive hand under Irene's thin arm. 'Please, Mrs Cooper. I know these things are expensive, but . . .'

The child was whipped from her grasp as Dorothy spun her about before propelling her rapidly from the classroom.

Half running, half stumbling, Irene dangled like a puppet from her mother's grasp, fighting to keep her feet as Dorothy charged at a frantic pace along the school corridors and out across the enclosed playground. Without pause she was dragged through the streets towards home with never a sound leaving Dorothy's lips, and only her own whimpers of pain and fright to mark their passage.

Each gasping breath tore at her throat, each flying step brought hot, knifing stabs from the stitch in her side; her head swam, and she was barely conscious by the time they reached home.

Without slackening her speed Dorothy marched her across the worn grass fronting the house, and along the side entrance to the rear garden, and the small wooden shed where Roy stored his gardening tools. Dragging the door open Dorothy thrust her daughter inside, shooting the stout bolts after her the minute she was clear of the door.

So swiftly was this accomplished Irene found herself sprawled at full length across the musty-smelling sacking heaped in the far corner of the windowless shed, while her legs still windmilled to keep up that punishing pace. Gasping for breath, and unable to swallow against the burning dryness of her throat, she had no time to recover herself before her mother's voice, icy with loathing, penetrated the thin wooden walls to warn that should she make so much as a sound, she would be made to regret it.

'I'll set fire to this place, an' you in it! D'you hear me?'

Heart racing, her legs still twitching and jerking in nervous reaction of that enforced march, Irene sucked in the earth-permeated air of the garden shed, filling her starved lungs before managing to croak, 'I'm sorry. I'm sorry. I didn't know . . . Please, Mam, let me out. Let me out,' she whimpered over and over again in a mindless, terrified chant which served to fill her ears and help block out the horror of her mother's threat.

Having once caught his sons surreptitiously using the place to puff on a forbidden cigarette, Irene's father had lectured both them and her on the dangers of bringing matches into his shed. He had gone so far as to give them a demonstration, using paraffin-soaked waste, of the rapid and uncontrollable spread of fire. Both Roger and Martin had been suitably chastened, but Irene, for whom the demonstration was intended to be purely incidental, had suffered nightmares in which she found herself trapped and surrounded by flames.

Caught up in this horror, she crouched on the damp sacks, afraid to move, afraid to cry out as one dread-filled hour moved leadenly into another. She was not aware of the failing daylight, nor conscious of either hunger or thirst as evening turned into night. She felt only a fevered paralysis, anticipating those scorching flames licking her flesh, burning her to death before anyone came to save her.

Dorothy was in no hurry to tell Roy the news of the day. On his return from working the late afternoon shift, she served him his supper and waited for him to ask after Irene, and how she had coped with her first day at school before casually mentioning that their daughter was even now locked in the garden shed.

Roy dropped his knife and fork with a clatter, sending his chair rocking back from the table as he sprang to his feet.

'Have you taken leave of your senses?' he demanded in strangled tones. Waiting no answer he was already on his way to the door.

Dorothy blinked, her mouth pursed in a self-righteous little pucker that swallowed her lips. 'Oh, sit down, do! She's right enough.'

Roy halted his headlong rush just long enough to subject his wife to a stare of amazed condemnation.

'Right enough? Right enough, you say? Dorothy, it's coming up midnight, would you be right enough locked out there?'

'But you don't know, Roy. You don't know the half.' Dorothy made a desperate appeal for understanding, running to place herself in the doorway, effectively gaining Roy's full attention. 'You don't know what she did. You should have seen her. It was like she'd flung everything I've ever done for her right back in my face. She . . .' Her voice trailed away as Roy put her firmly to one side.

'So tell me the rest – *after*,' he said in chilling accents. Now he moved like a man possessed, clearing the room in two strides, letting himself out of the back door with scant regard for the catch which he hardly bothered to release or the hinges which snapped back under the slamming weight of the door.

It was black as pitch in the garden shed. Roy hadn't waited to collect a torch and there was no mains electricity out here. As he hung in the open doorway waiting for his eyes to adjust to the unrelieved darkness he called Irene's name, sharply at first, then more softly when she failed to answer. It occurred to him that she might be waiting in fear of further punishment for whatever crime she was supposed to have committed.

'Rene, it's me, your dad. Don't be frightened, sweetheart.' No sound reached his straining ears. 'Rene? Irene, are you there?' He held his breath, listening for the slightest indication of her whereabouts. His eyes could pick out no shapes within the inky darkness. His heart gave a leap at the continued silence. She's having me on, he told himself in a wash of exasperated relief. He had been worse than a fool to imagine that Dorothy could leave the kid out here all this time, even allowing for the difficulties of their relationship.

As he was about to turn back indoors some sixth sense picked up the vibrations of another presence, and he cursed as he fumbled through his pockets feeling for a match.

'Rene, are you there, love? Ah!' He found the matches and struck one, holding the wavering flame aloft, peering into the misleading shadows that loomed and danced and retreated in the uncertain light.

Gripped in a vice of dread Irene saw only the leaping flame. Her slender hold on sanity fled as her tortured brain accepted the inevitable, and she fell into a merciful void.

'Irene.' The name was torn from his lips in a hoarse exclamation and the reflected whiteness of her school blouse confirmed her presence as the match burnt down to his fingers. Swiftly striking another he bent quickly, his precipitate action causing the flame to blow out. Too concerned to bother with lighting another, he groped along the dusty floor until his finger encountered the cold flesh of his daughter's bare legs.

'Irene. Irene, love. Answer me.' He had her in his arms now, stretched rigid as a corpse, stiff and unyielding in his grasp. Clutching her ever tighter he stumbled from the shed towards the welcome light showing from the house.

Kicking the doors wide, he carried her through the kitchen, and along the hall to the stairs, taking them three at a time. Shouldering his way into the bedroom he shared with Dorothy he placed his daughter gently on the wide double bed.

Irene lay without moving, her eyes wide and staring, distended pupils reflecting nothing but unspeakable fear.

Chafing her small hands between his own calloused palms

Roy bawled for Dorothy, and was startled to find her already at his elbow.

'What's the matter with her? Why's she looking like that?'

'She's scared bloody stiff, that's what's the matter. Can't you understand, woman, you've frightened the poor little beggar to death.' Roy continued to chafe his daughter's icy limbs, the sound of flesh on flesh filling the accusing silence stretching between man and wife.

'I didn't touch her, Roy. I put her in the shed so's I wouldn't go for her. I swear to you, I never laid a finger on her.'

'Don't go on, for Christ's sake. Don't go on or I'll . . . I'll . . . Go and get the doctor. Quick! Go on. Don't just stand there.' He switched abruptly from the half-hysterical cry to a softer, more menacing tone. 'Go and get the doctor, Dorothy. Get him here. Let him see what his half-baked attempts at psychology have done for this child.'

'Irene! Irene!'

She became aware of a hand on her shoulder, and looked up into the glint of light reflected by Janet Fouracre's spectacles.

'Don't distress yourself. I think we can guess how terrible an ordeal this was for you.' The social worker was warmly sympathetic.

Irene shuddered convulsively. 'I . . . I'm sorry. I . . .'

'It's all right, you don't have to say any more.'

'But . . . but it was a dreadful thing to do,' Irene said, unable to rid herself of the memory.

'Yes, I agree, it was . . . and you would never do anything like that to your children, Irene?'

She looked horrified. 'No . . . never,' she said vehemently.

'So how do you punish them?'

'I . . . I don't know what you mean.'

Terry Garland stifled an impatient exclamation as he listened to this naïve evasion, and earned himself a swift frown of reproof from his superior officer.

'How do you correct your children?' Janet substituted the milder phrase. 'Do you send them to bed, for instance? Or maybe withhold their pocket money? How, Irene?'

Irene glanced nervously towards the door leading into the

hall. Lauren and Debbie were unusually quiet; was this what the woman was hinting at? 'N-no, I . . . I usually . . . well, sometimes, only sometimes, I have to smack their bottoms. But I never really hurt them,' she added swiftly. 'And anyway, I'd much rather they had a sore bum than lock them in some garden shed. I hated my mam for that . . . Hated her.'

'And what was your mother's attitude towards you following that episode?' Janet asked gently. 'Can you tell us that?'

'It . . . changed, for a time. She sort of . . . sort of . . . well, my father and I were very close. That helped.'

'Can you think of anything anyone might have done, other than your father that is, that might have helped?'

Irene shook her head. 'I can't remember much about that bit at all. It's all sort of hazy, and very mixed up.' She paused, then in a voice scarcely above a whisper once more took up her tale.

Though mercifully unable to recall any detail, Irene had been a long, long time recovering from her nightmare ordeal in the locked garden shed. It was a painfully timid, insecure little girl who emerged from the trauma of deep shock which held her silent and cowed despite all Doctor Court's best efforts to rouse her.

Mindful of the serious implications of Dorothy's action, Roy was careful not to reveal all the facts relating to his daughter's breakdown. He had no wish to see his family broken up or his child placed in care, and was therefore obliged to protect his wife along with his daughter. Dorothy accepted this consideration with a certain sour satisfaction.

When it was judged she was sufficiently recovered, Irene made a fresh start at the primary school, her demeanour totally lacking the brave confidence which had led her into such mischief on her previous debut. Mrs Bannister could not help but note the marked change and be shocked by it. Dim stirrings of concern kept her eyes fixed to the child, and she remembered uncomfortably the manner in which she had seen her pitched from this very classroom. Wondering at the possible connection between Dorothy's obvious rage on that occasion, Irene's subsequent absence from school, and her current nervousness, she drew a long, troubled breath; was there something here that she, as a teacher, should concern herself with?

The morning bell signalled the start of lessons; Mrs Bannister had perforce to put Irene and her problems to the back of her mind while she struggled to impart the rudiments of the alphabet to the remainder of her class.

As the days passed, and Irene outwardly appeared to make slow recovery, Mrs Bannister came to regard her initial concern as unfounded, and thankfully dismissed the need to become involved.

For all her improved confidence there remained with Irene a blank and terrified refusal to pass anywhere close to her father's garden shed. And when Roy saw the look on her face as she scurried along the back yard, hugging the side of the house, scraping along the brickwork to keep as much of a distance as possible between herself and that dreaded place, he knocked it to pieces, waiting only until she was out of the way before putting a match to the broken timbers.

A sort of uneasy truce developed between Irene and her mother, with Dorothy studiously avoiding all contact with the child, and Irene turning more and more to her own devices. She and her sister Sandra shared a close bond, and their brothers, big enough at twelve and fourteen to seem like young men to the two little girls, treated them with a careless affection which more than compensated for any neglect on the part of their mother. Not that Dorothy was ever cold to the rest of her brood. Roger and Martin still held first and equal claim to her heart, but little Sandra suffered no lack of maternal affection. It was as if Irene alone shouldered the blame for all the misdeeds of her siblings, leaving Dorothy free to love three out of four without let or hindrance.

With this sort of balance a semblance of normal family life was maintained in the Cooper household, and was not overset by the long evenings Dorothy continued to put in with her drinking cronies while Roy was at work on the late shift. The warm, fuddled haze engendered by alcohol helped to take the edge off her loneliness, and under its benign influence she could forget the cold, empty space in her bed that Roy never troubled to fill.

Often, on those nights while their father worked and their mother pursued alcoholic oblivion, Roger and Martin would entertain their friends over a game of Monopoly, and on such an occasion they were hilariously engaged with the sale of Park Lane, complete with two hotels, when the police officer knocked at their door.

Thinking perhaps this was one of their mother's bad nights when she had returned too well oiled to fit her door-key into the lock, Roger rose from his place at the board, and with a grimace for his brother went to let her in.

The dark blue uniform with its officiously gleaming buttons stopped in his throat the greeting he'd prepared. Swallowing the words of teasing reproach Roger gazed blankly at the police sergeant.

'Is your mother in, son?' The policeman's face was filled with compassion as he gazed at Roger.

'Er, no. No, she's not. There's only me and our Martin, and . . . and some of our mates,' Roger heard himself gabbling. It was almost as if he hoped to prevent the bad news he could sense had brought the man here by denying the presence of an adult.

From the shadows behind the policeman came a young woman, also wearing uniform. 'Do you know where we can find her?' she asked as she joined her colleague on the door-step.

'Me mam?'

'Yes, your mam. Where is she likely to be?'

'I . . .' Roger hesitated. Did he ought to tell them his mother was in the pub? 'I . . . she . . . went out,' he said finally.

'Out where, lad? Come on, you must know where she's gone.' The policeman fixed Roger with a stern eye.

'The Stars, I think.'

'The Seven Stars, down on the Blid'orth road?'

Roger nodded.

'Who else did you say was in the house?' the policewoman asked, peering past Roger. In the back room the three lads had fallen silent, no doubt trying to guess what, and who, was keeping their companion, and the house seemed to wait for Roger's reply.

'Me brother, and two of our mates. Oh, and me sisters, but they're in bed.'

'Who is your mother with, do you know?'

Roger shook his head.

'Look, I think I had better come in and wait while the sergeant here goes to find her. Is that all right?' She looked from the policeman to Roger, a winning smile deliberately called to her face.

'Er, yeah. Yeah, I suppose so.' Roger took a pace to the side to allow her to enter the house.

On the door-step she paused, and turned to her colleague. 'This is where I'll be then, Sergeant Mosely. Until you get back.' Without waiting for a reply she turned her smile back to Roger and motioned for him to lead the way indoors.

Dorothy took the news of Roy's death very badly. The sight of the sergeant's uniform had wiped out the rosy euphoria she'd purchased over the bar of the Seven Stars leaving her with nothing to cushion the shock. As she reeled under the blow her first passionate feeling had been a deep and abiding regret. Often deliberately hidden, always badly expressed, the love she felt for her husband had grown none the less ardent for all the misunderstandings they had known over the years of their marriage.

Too late now to tell him how much she adored him, how his very touch could cause her knees to turn to jelly, or how she used the panacea of drink only to blunt the pain of hopeless yearning. As she stared with dry, burning eyes at the man who had broken the news of Roy's massive and fatal heart attack, she experienced an agony so fierce, and so all consuming, she prayed she too might soon be dead.

'Here, you'd better drink this.'

She was handed a glass of water which she took with trembling hands. As she raised the glass to her lips she began to laugh. A harsh, mirthless cackle that grated on the ear. To think she should be given water at a time like this! Her, of all people. Quelling the hysterical snigger she choked down a mouthful of the cold fluid.

'Thank you.' She released the glass into the policeman's broad hand.

'Better now?' he asked.

Dorothy nodded automatically, all the bitter replies she

might have made to that fatuous question screaming like demons in her brain. 'The kids,' she said suddenly. 'Do they know?'

'I . . . I believe the lad who answered the door half guessed something of this nature. I left a female colleague at your home so I imagine they will have been told. Feel up to joining them? We'll need you to identify the remains, of course. But that can wait.'

'Remains.' Dorothy baulked at the use of the word in connection with Roy. She chewed savagely on her lower lip as she tried to consider the man who had left their home that afternoon, his pocket bulging with the packet of sandwiches she'd prepared for his mid-shift break, reduced to something casually labelled remains.

'Take me home,' she said dully.

They left the private back room of the Seven Stars with only a nod from the policeman by way of thanks to the landlord's wife for her silent chaperonage.

FIVE

If Dorothy had looked to alcohol for comfort and consolation while her husband was alive, she now pursued this palliative with the utmost zeal. Numb with shock and grief, she had coped with the harrowing necessity of the post-mortem and borne her sorrow dry-eyed and bravely throughout the funeral; it was during the late afternoon, when the mourners had gone and she was alone with her children, that her iron reserve finally broke.

Wandering aimlessly into the little-used front room where the scent of funeral lilies hung on the still air, she retrieved a flower petal from the place where Roy's coffin had rested, and cradled it to her breast as the storm of weeping swept away her control.

Hearing the racking sobs, the four children in the next room deliberately avoided each other's gaze. They had cried themselves empty through the night and the length of this slow, plodding day and they had nothing left to wet their cheeks; their reservoirs were burned dry.

Unable to bear the sound of their mother's harsh weeping, Irene slipped from the room and went to offer the only comfort she had. Her arm fell like a feather across Dorothy's bowed shoulders, but hardly had her words of sympathy left her lips before she felt herself hurled bodily across the room.

'Get away from me, you sly little bitch! Creeping in here, making up to me now he's gone.' Crouched like an animal, teeth bared in her tear-drenched face, Dorothy turned her pent-up emotion into a glorious rage against her daughter.

Stunned by this display of raw, seething hatred, knocked breathless by her fall, Irene could only stare.

'Just you keep out of my way, d'you hear me? I don't want you around, all the trouble you've caused.' Slamming out of the room, Dorothy made directly for the remains of the bottle of sherry she had served after the funeral tea, and finding less than she had expected took up her outdoor coat.

'I'm going down the road,' she told Roger and Martin. 'See that the kids get to bed.'

Her return, in a state of brutal drunkenness, marked the beginning of many savage nocturnal beatings for Irene.

Missing the strong, dependable championship of their father the boys were at a loss to prevent what they knew was happening. Conscious of their approaching maturity they formed a unit denying the weakness they felt in their mother's presence, and tried between themselves to find ways of baulking her wrath. Her growing dependency on drink was never spoken of outside the privacy of their bedroom, and it was there they repaired to consider their plans.

'We have to find some way to keep her away from Irene.' Roger chewed his fingernails, making them bleed before hitting on a possible solution. 'We'll have to take turns waiting up for her, maybe if we keep her talking while the drink wears off. . . . You know she never gets too mad at us.'

Martin groaned. 'God, I'll be shattered. She doesn't get home much before midnight.'

'I know, I know. But think what it's like for Irene. How would you like to be dragged out of bed and clouted for no good reason night after night?'

'Well, can't we see somebody about it? I mean, there has to be somebody who can stop her. It's only the drink.'

Roger shook his head. 'No, better not. If we get it around that she's an alky . . . No, better not, Mart.'

'You know, it's dead funny. She never bothers our Sandra. What is it with her an' Irene?'

'No idea. Perhaps Irene's different, somehow.'

'Yeah, perhaps she is, poor little kid.'

Having reached this mystifying conclusion the boys were agreed that Sandra might safely be left in their mother's care during the day, but Irene, then as always, would be better off out of her way. Since Roger was due to start work in the spring and was already making applications for jobs, Martin made it his duty to escort his sister to and from school every day. And if she was the first child in the playground each morning and the last to leave when the afternoon came to a close, that was no reflection of her brother's timekeeping.

Lacking the warm, safe haven of her father's embrace, Irene found her infant world a very cold place. There was no one now whom she wished to please, no one to care how well or how badly she did with her studies, and no eagerly awaited presence to bring joy to her days. Despite the concern shown by her brothers for her well-being she became a very withdrawn, silent child, going quietly about home and school alike, afraid of drawing attention.

Her self-effacement earned her nothing but spiteful little prods and pokes from her mother, who seemed to find the child's presence a constant irritation. Nor was her cause helped by the many well-meaning friends who remarked on her altered state, attributing her subdued manner to lingering grief for her father. In death, as in life, Dorothy wished to share the man she had loved with no other, least of all this daughter she resented so strongly.

'Why can't you at least try to look cheerful,' she would snap at Irene. 'Things are bad enough without your miserable face.'

On these occasions the boys quickly learned not to jump to their sister's defence. Better she suffered a constant nagging while in their presence, than yet another beating once they were out of the way.

Resenting the affection her sons held for their sister, yet finding herself powerless to curtail it, Dorothy fastened on the close harmony which existed between her daughters, seeking to use this as another implement with which to inflict injury.

Sandra became a child who could do no wrong, the recipient of many expensive treats and toys. Irene was never an acquisitive child but as the gifts and privileges grew ever more preposterous, childlike jealousies became inevitable. She and Sandra began to bicker.

To help the widening gap Dorothy made Irene responsible for cleaning up after her sister, encouraging Sandra towards selfish ingratitude and petty spite.

Increasing insecurity affected Irene's nerves with disastrous results, and for the first time since she was a baby she wet the bed.

In the morning when her disgrace was discovered she was mortified.

'You are disgusting.' Dorothy's lip curled as she surveyed her daughter. 'Dirty. Filthy. Disgusting.'

The two boys eyed each other across the breakfast table, their expressions mirroring concern at the relish in Dorothy's tone.

Irene hung her head, her face washed with shame, while Sandra looked on with keen interest.

'A great girl like you. Near on seven years old and still pittling the bed. Well, let me tell you, madam, the sheets and bedlinen will be here for you to wash when you get home from school.' Dorothy made her daughter subject of a withering glance before turning away to clatter loudly through the process of making breakfast.

Martin and Richard sighed in relief. They had anticipated a far more vigorous punishment. Washing a few sheets wouldn't hurt the kid – even if it did seem a bit hard on a child of her age.

At seven-thirty that evening, exhausted by her struggles with the weight of wet sheets, Irene was preparing to follow Sandra up the stairs to bed when Dorothy's sharp demand that she explained where she was going halted her feet.

'I'm going to bed,' she said, the apprehension to which she'd been subject all that day making her tongue feel thick and clumsy.

'Oh no you're not. Not in this house, anyway.' Dorothy's face was narrow with spite.

Irene's blank stare invited her punishment.

'If you behave like an animal, you must expect to be treated like one,' Dorothy informed her coldly. 'Cats that aren't house trained are put out at night.'

Her face flattening into disbelief, Irene gazed at her mother. Sandra sniggered from her place by the stairs, and the two boys lost all interest in the television screen.

Pretending to believe this was their mother's attempt at a joke, Roger affected a strained giggle. 'Are you expecting her to dig a little hole in the garden?' he asked, keeping his face schooled in an appreciative grin.

'No, I'm waiting for her to get out.'

Mesmerised by her mother's unwavering stare Irene backed slowly towards the outer door.

'Don't be so daft, Irene. She don't mean you to go out there. Blimey, it's as black as pitch.' Martin grabbed wildly for a return to sanity.

His mother's icy stare flicked him like a lash, causing the words of protest to die in his throat.

Irene stumbled backwards through the door, and at the sound of it closing behind her a dreadful silence settled over the house.

Now Irene became solitary indeed; openly shunned by her mother and sister, painstakingly avoided by the two boys, she had no one to whom she might turn. Her brothers in attempting to come to her aid had only made matters worse.

'I'll have her put away if you interfere,' Dorothy warned when they protested at seeing her turned out of the house.

Martin paused on his way to open the door, his outstretched hand falling short of its mark. 'Put away?' he asked incredulously. 'Put away where?'

'In an asylum, where she belongs,' said Dorothy.

Martin looked to his brother.

'You can't.' Roger joined him in his stand against their mother.

'Oh, can't I? We'll see about that.'

'But she's not crazy,' Roger protested hotly.

'Isn't she? What about all the daft carryings on when she locked herself in the garden shed? Or had you forgotten that?'

The truth of that episode had been concealed from the boys by their father who had believed knowledge of his wife's conduct on that occasion altogether too heinous to be supported by her sons. They had been left to believe their sister's breakdown had come about as a result of her own actions.

There was a pause while they both considered what they knew of Irene's strange illness following that incident.

Roger was first to cast doubt aside. 'No,' he said firmly. 'Our Irene's not daft. She was poorly, that's all.'

'And if being locked in the garden shed for a couple of hours makes her so poorly, how do you think being walled up in an asylum will suit her?' Dorothy asked maliciously.

'But you can't leave the kid outside all night. She'll be frightened to death.'

'She goes out of the door until she learns to behave herself in a civilised manner.'

'Aw, come on, Mam. She only wet the bed,' Martin pleaded.

'I'm warning you. One more word and to the asylum she goes,' Dorothy threatened. And there was that about her expression that persuaded her sons she would make good her intent.

Irene's night-time banishment continued for the better part of a week, her brothers' furtively agreed plans to smuggle her indoors defeated by Dorothy's vigilance. She bore her punishment stoically and made no complaint, but she grew alarmingly thin and hollow eyed, a fact remarked upon by her school teachers.

'Have you seen the Cooper girl lately? Looks like a wraith.' Miss Hanbury asked of her colleagues.

'Grief, I should think, over her father.' Mrs Bannister offered the explanation in self defence. Her conscience refused to be quietened where Irene was concerned yet she was reluctant to better acquaint herself with the child's circumstances. If she was to have her worst suspicions confirmed, she would be required in all humanity to act upon them, and that might become tiresome.

'You don't think perhaps we should have a word with the Head?' Miss Hanbury taught needlework to the senior girls, and having devoted her life to the school saw herself in loco parentis to each group of infants as they came along.

Mrs Archer, the second-form teacher, made allowances for this trait. 'No, I don't think we need bother the Head, Rosemary. There's nothing to be done, after all.'

'I suppose not, but it does seem such a shame, that child looks positively haunted.'

Mrs Bannister said nothing. To mention her earlier fears at this stage might point to her own lack of appropriate action.

'I'm sure that the girl is grossly underweight.' Miss Hanbury continued to fret.

The school doctor echoed Miss Hanbury's concern. He examined Irene as a matter of course during a routine visit, and was not only concerned with the child's emaciated condition, but was far from satisfied with the explanations she offered for the numerous small bruises and contusions covering her body. As a newly qualified practitioner he kept assiduously abreast of medical news, and the newly coined phrase of one Dr Kempe concerning non-accidental injury to children came unbidden to his mind. Battered babies, Kempe had called them, or rather battered children, and that, in his opinion, might have been a phrase conceived expressly to fit young Irene Cooper.

He made a note to pursue the matter with her family doctor.

Doctor Court read his young colleague's hastily scrawled letter with a grimace of wry indulgence. He could remember the fervour he'd applied to this work himself when he was fresh out of training. No doubt young Brewster would settle, given time. He balled the young doctor's well-intentioned missive in the palm of his hand, tossing it in the general direction of the waste-paper basket before touching the bell that would summon his next patient. Wait until Brewster had worked through two surgeries a day, six days a week, with house-calls all the hours in between, he told himself, as an elderly man wheezed his way into the consulting room. Then let us see what he makes of the knocks and bruises kids inflict on themselves at play.

'Did you try to tell anyone of the things your mother was doing to you at the time?' Janet Fouracres asked gently, temporarily putting an end to Irene's haunting disclosures.

'I . . . no, who would I tell?' Irene asked in some surprise.

'Well, your teachers, or your doctor, or . . . or a close relative, an aunt, maybe?'

Irene shook her head. 'I couldn't . . . that would have been snitching.'

'But you were being ill-treated, for heaven's sake!' Terry Garland so far forgot himself as to break in on his colleague's steady questioning.

Irene stared at him, her fingers caressing her scarred cheek. 'Yes, but . . . but she was – is, my mam,' she said plaintively.

Terry and Janet exchanged a speaking glance.

'So you put up with it,' Janet said matter-of-factly.

'Well,' Irene shrugged. 'What else was there?'

67

Another long exchange of glances between the two child-care officers spoke volumes. 'Go on, Irene, what happened next?'

'I . . . this has nothing to do with Lawrence, you know. He hurt himself. It was an accident. A terrible accident.' She gazed wildly from one to the other of their carefully schooled faces. 'It was, I tell you! It was, it was!' She sprang to her feet in great agitation.

'I know, I know. Now sit down. Sit down, take a deep breath, and try to calm yourself. Terry, a cup of tea, do you think?'

Terry nodded, and moved towards the kitchen.

'Now then, Irene. You were telling me what happened after the death of your father,' Janet prompted. 'You must have felt very distressed . . . lonely? In need of someone to turn to?'

'Yes,' Irene whispered. 'I didn't know . . . there was no one . . . nothing.'

So Irene continued to keep her silence, doing whatever she might to avoid the worst of her mother's dislike, and resigning herself to the loss of Sandra's sisterly affections. Time passed bringing inevitable changes, blunting the edges of grief. Roger left school and took a job, Martin followed in his turn, and Sandra was enrolled in kindergarten. Dorothy grew increasingly lonely. She was in need of an adult companion, someone with whom to share her life.

It was John Forster's good fortune to make her acquaintance while she was in just such a mood, and before the mellowing clouds of the alcohol she'd consumed were dispersed she had fallen easy victim to the charms of this divorced man some five years her junior, and about whom none could find a good word.

'He's a sponger, Dot,' her old friend Tommy Bastable warned. 'You want to watch what you're doing where that one's concerned.'

Dorothy pursed her lips. 'Well, he's not the first man I ever met to hand me his empty glass,' she said tartly with a significant glance at the foaming pint in Tommy's fist.

'Now come on, there's no need for that. We all pay our corner,' Tommy was stung to reply.

'Just don't kid yourself that gives you the right to criticise my friends.'

'Friend, is he? Then you'll not need many enemies, girl. Let me tell you that.'

Before the furious retort trembling on Dorothy's lips could be delivered they were joined at the bar by a man wearing the confident air of a professional voyeur. He immediately endorsed Tommy's opinion of his character by the nonchalant manner in which he accepted the whisky and soda from Dorothy's hand.

John Forster, though possessing a certain attraction, was not especially handsome. Tall, rather slightly built, with crisply curling hair, and girlishly long eyelashes, there was about his face a hint of weak self-indulgence that his full lips and dimpled chin did nothing to contradict.

He downed the whisky in a swallow before turning the studied charm of his smile on Dorothy. 'By golly, I needed that,' he said feelingly. 'It's been one bitch of a day.'

'Another?'

'Why not? Then we'll find ourselves a seat, eh?'

'Suits me. It's getting too crowded for comfort around here.' Dorothy sent a withering glance in Tommy's direction as she handed John's empty glass to the hovering barmaid.

In defiance of her friend's dislike of the man, Dorothy continued to meet John on a regular basis, devoting herself exclusively to his company until she had estranged all her former drinking companions. She knew John had been divorced by his wife on grounds of adultery, and gathered from the hints well-meaning acquaintances let fall that she was not the only woman he was currently seeing, but she didn't care. It had been four long and lonely years since any man had looked on her as anything other than a drinking companion, and she was hungry for attention.

Forster was a sales rep for a company manufacturing perfume and cosmetics; a job, he was quick to explain, that entailed a certain amount of socialising with prospective customers, be they buyers for retail outlets, women in business for themselves, or merely salesgirls who might be persuaded to put in a word for him in the right quarters.

Dorothy accepted this blanket excuse for the predilection he displayed for her sex, and made allowances in this respect she would not have entertained for her late husband.

Since Forster confessed to finding money a bit tight Dorothy made no quibble about financing their outings. Roy had been responsible in the matter of insurances, and as a consequence she was now quite comfortably endowed. She found John's open gratitude of her generosity rather pleasant, and preferred to ignore the comments made by the likes of Tommy Bastable.

For several months Forster paid assiduous, but platonic court to Dorothy, guessing from her lack of response to his initial attempts at deeper intimacy that she would not welcome an approach for casual sex. Better play your cards right, he cautioned himself, wouldn't want to frighten the golden goose.

Dorothy found his restraint admirable, and was encouraged in her belief that his intentions were serious. So much so that she was persuaded to introduce him to her family.

Roger and Martin accepted Forster at face value. Busy now with their respective jobs and girlfriends of their own they saw no objection to this friend of their mother's. Sandra loved him instantly, and he made capital of her partiality, sitting her on his knee, adopting a role that was not quite that of a father, nor yet that of a sweetheart. Only Irene viewed him with mistrust, backing away from his advances, and earning herself a quick slap from her mother for being so stand-offish.

Taking quick inventory of the comfortable home, comparing it with the cheerless bedsit in which he'd been living since his divorce, John Forster formed the opinion that he'd be worse than a fool to pass up the opportunity of making it his own. He was finding little pleasure lately travelling the roads under threat of a hernia lugging those blasted sample cases. He allowed himself a more leisurely glance of appraisal. Two lads, well grown and earning their own living, one little girl eager to show her affection, and one budding young lady whose very antagonism presented the sort of challenge he was least able to resist. Add to these one well-endowed widow whom he was certain could be persuaded to match her generosity in the matter of ready cash with those of her not inconsiderable favours, and he was in clover.

Untutored in the delights of sexual gratification, Dorothy was ill prepared for the clamouring that John's expert lovemaking aroused in her. With the one shameful exception she had allowed herself to take no more than a passive role in her relationship with Roy, and John found her as shy and as reticent as any young virgin. His own jaded palate titillated by this, he employed all the artistry at his command to bring her to the peak of desire. When he was certain she was his for the taking, he affected a slight cooling of interest, and Dorothy, afraid of losing him, allowed him into the bed she had preserved so chastely.

Without waiting for formal invitation John Forster took up permanent residence in the Cooper household, gambling on Dorothy's newly awakened sexuality to bind her unquestioningly to his side without benefit of clergy. He could see no point in reducing their income by the amount of pension she would lose if they made their union legal, though he made no mention of this to his besotted partner.

The cup and saucer Irene was nursing shook so violently that Janet reached to take it from her grasp. She handed it to Terry to dispose of, her keen gaze never leaving Irene's face.

'You didn't like this man Forster?' she asked.

Irene shook her head, her teeth clenched, tears jetting from the corner of her eyes.

'Were you – jealous, perhaps?'

Irene's eyes flew open. '*Jealous*! Oh, God! God, if only you knew.'

'So tell me, Irene.'

'I . . . I can't.' She dropped her head, hiding her face as she gazed fixedly at her fingers twisting and writhing now they were empty of the cup and saucer.

'Your brothers – and your sister. Did they like him?'

Irene nodded.

'You felt he was taking your father's place?'

'No-oo!' Irene screamed the word at her. 'Never that! Not him. Not that . . . that bastard!'

Janet Fouracres narrowed her eyes, her face, despite her best efforts to keep it neutral, betraying a certain reluctant understanding. 'But you all lived together as a family, with Forster as the head?' she said flatly, her apparent lack of

71

emotion defusing Irene's outburst.

Irene fell back in her chair, only the tremors shaking her body betraying the weight of her feelings. 'We . . . we didn't stay together very long,' she said, gulping back her tears. 'He soon managed to get rid of our Roger and Martin. Persuaded them to take a bachelor flat. Didn't want them around.'

'I see. But are you sure you didn't misjudge him? After all, your brothers were young men by this time, maybe they felt the need for a place of their own.'

'No, they would never have left but for him. I know they wouldn't.'

'And you were upset about that?'

'Yes. Yes, I was . . . it . . . they . . . I didn't want them to go.'

Irene missed her brothers most keenly. She felt alone now in a household that held no place for her, and vowed that as soon as she grew up and left school she would follow their example and leave home. In the meantime she continued to keep out of the way as much as possible, ticking the days off her calendar as she left her childhood behind. As she approached her teens and began to show promise of womanhood, her gaunt hollow-eyed sharpness gave way to the sweet roundness of youth, made even more lovely by the lingering shadows in the smooth planes of her face.

Forster watched her guardedly as she moved about the house, his overtly jocular attempts to draw her into the rough and tumbles he staged with her sister gaining him nothing but scowling rejection.

Dorothy, remaining besotted with her sexual Svengali, read nothing more in those advances than a desire on Forster's part to make friends with the girl.

'Spiteful little bitch,' she accused Irene on one such occasion. 'Always were. Even when you were a baby.'

Irene shrank from the malice in her mother's expression and sidled towards the door, hoping to escape from the room with no greater hurt than that inflicted by the words.

'Where d'you think you are going?' Dorothy checked the move.

'Up to the bedroom. I . . . I've got homework,' Irene lied.

'Liar! Your homework's finished. I saw your books.'

Irene stared into her mother's face, now almost on a level with her own, trying to conquer the fear churning in her stomach. A pinch or a slap was the worst she had come to expect since Forster had moved in to engage her mother's attention, but it was waiting for the punishment to be delivered that kept her nerves at full stretch.

'Why can't you be sociable for once in a while? Or is that too much to ask of my lady?'

'I . . . I didn't mean . . . I only . . . I really do have homework. Some extra. Mrs Corner gave it to me.' Irene glanced desperately about the room, afraid to meet her mother's searching gaze.

Help came from the quarter she'd least expected or desired when John, fending off Sandra's laughing attempts to plait his hair, came to place an arm about her shoulders. 'Leave the kid alone, Dot. If she's got schoolwork, she's got schoolwork, it's as simple as that.'

'Like hell she has. Bloody stand-offish, that's her trouble.'

Irene held herself rigid in Forster's encircling arms, disliking the man's closeness, but hesitating to move away for fear of provoking fresh assault from her mother.

'Go on, Irene. Go and get your bookwork done. Maybe we'll have a hand of cards later, after I've sorted this young lady out.' Before turning to resume his playful fight with Sandra, Forster allowed his arm to slide down Irene's body, trailing his fingers down her spine to finish with a quick squeeze of her buttocks.

Irene turned and fled from the room.

After that unmistakable demonstration of Forster's impudence Irene was doubly careful to give him no opportunity of catching her alone in the house. Though very hazy and uncertain about the taboo subject of sex, all her basic instincts warned her against the man. She watched from a distance the games he played with her sister, noted the familiar patting and touching of the younger girl's body and wanted to scream at Sandra to tell him to stop. Sandra, unlike Irene, appeared to enjoy this contact.

Dorothy, it seemed, found nothing objectionable in her lover's partiality for her youngest daughter, taking their romps together as nothing more than outward proof of filial compatibility. The straying hand, the intimate, questing fingers, Irene noticed, were usually kept to Dorothy's blind side.

Frightened and confused by the revulsion Forster's behaviour aroused in her, Irene determined to speak to her brothers, and succeeded in catching Martin alone as he left the house following his weekly courtesy visit to their mother.

Red faced and acutely embarrassed, Irene kept her gaze fixed on the silver tack pinning Martin's tie as she blurted out her misgivings. 'The really horrid thing, Marty, is the way Sandra giggles and makes up to him . . . and all the time he is putting his hand up her clothes.'

Martin stared at his little sister. He felt sick. It was as if an angel had opened its mouth and spewed forth filth. His brain refused to accept the enormity of what this child was saying.

'Martin, you have to do something.' Irene tugged at his sleeve, embarrassment forgotten as she tried to convince him of the need to act.

Martin withdrew his sleeve from those clutching fingers and took a backward pace. 'Irene, I'm going to tell our mam what you've just said,' he told her, fixing her with a stern expression. 'I know you don't really understand all you're saying, but you can't go around spreading those sort of tales.'

'No! Martin, please. You can't tell our mam. She'll . . . Oh, Martin, please.' Tears starting in her eyes, Irene stared at him beseechingly.

Martin appeared to remain unmoved.

'Martin, I'm sorry. I won't ever say it again. Please, Marty, please don't tell on me.'

Martin frowned, pondering what best to do. 'Look, Irene. I don't know what to say. I don't know where you learned that sort of filth, or what sort of girls you are mixing with at school, but you want to watch it. Saying things like that can get you into serious trouble.'

'I know. I know, and I'm sorry,' Irene gabbled, terrified that Martin might carry out his threat to tell their mother. She hadn't considered that possibility when she'd approached him for help. Her dislike of Forster paled in the face of the punishment Dorothy would exact, and she renewed her pleas for his silence.

'Well, all right, then. But mind, if I hear one more word. . . .' Martin allowed the unspoken threat to hang between them.

As the months passed Irene grew adept at avoiding contact with Forster. So skilfully did she manage to efface herself in his presence, and so quietly did she contrive to vacate any room he entered, few beside herself and him were aware of their cat and mouse activities.

Certainly Dorothy had no suspicion of the deceptions practised beneath her roof. Secure in her belief of Forster's devotion she formed no connection when he made business an excuse to absent himself from the bar of their local on the evening that Irene, by custom, stayed home to wash her hair.

He promised to be gone no more than an hour. The lusting desire burning naked in his blue eyes as he gave his word left her awash with scalding floods of anticipation.

Never dreaming his passion could be for any but herself, she begged him not to delay.

Stripped to her plain cotton petticoat, busy with the spray-fitting on the handbasin taps, Irene was not aware of Forster's presence until she felt his hands, hot through the fine cotton, sliding around her body to cup her tenderly thrusting young breasts. Her shriek of alarm drowned by the hissing spray, she struggled ineffectually against her captor.

'Don't fight me, sweetheart. Don't pretend you don't want this as much as I do.' Forster clutched her fiercely, holding her tight against his throbbing male hardness. 'Relax, my darling. Just relax. You are going to enjoy this.'

For Irene, that night marked the beginning of a new age of unspeakable terror and nightmare. When it seemed that her pain had reached its zenith, and she could endure no more, Forster suddenly released her. For a time she lay motionless on the cold floor of the bathroom, afraid to move as he gasped and panted above her. When she whimpered and tried to push herself into a sitting position his fist shot out, his fingers taking a bruising grip on her jaw. Forcing her head back he caused her to look into his reddened, sweat streaked face.

'Not a word. Not a word to anyone, do you hear?'

When she found herself incapable of making a reply his fingers tightened cruelly on her face crushing her features into a distorted mask.

'Want some more, do you? Maybe this time we could try some variations.'

Paralysed with fright she allowed him to draw her head into his groin before outrage and revulsion gave her the strength to jerk clear of his grasp. 'No! No! Leave me alone!' She collapsed into sobs, her fingers opening and closing uselessly, her fingernails rasping and scraping against the smooth black and white tiles covering the floor.

'So do as you are told, you hear? One word, just one squeak out of you, and I'll have you put away in a home for the rest of your life.'

His threat stemmed her tears, and she lifted herself on one elbow to stare at him in stunned disbelief.

'Shouldn't be hard to convince your mother that you'd thrown yourself at me, do you think? Hates you already, she does. One hint of the old hanky-panky on your part, and she'll be only too willing to see you carted off.'

Irene's eyes widened above the livid weals left by his fingers, and she caught her breath.

'Wait while I tell your old girl how you taunted me, flashing your tits and giving me the old come-on. She won't give you a chance to deny it.' Satisfied his warning had gone home Forster began to right his clothing. Standing over her he adjusted his dress, finally zipping his trousers with showy vigour. 'Remember, keep your mouth shut, girl. Unless you want it filled with more than you've bargained for.'

After Forster had gone, Irene filled the bath and rolled her bruised, aching body into the steaming water, allowing it to grow cold, topping it up time and time again, before reaching for a towel.

SIX

Throughout this difficult and heart-rending narration Terry Garland was kept in check only by Janet Fouracre's quelling glance. The whole gamut of emotions swept across his face, leaving it in turn dull puce or ashen white above his fiery, bristling red whiskers. This particular revelation came as a complete shock to him. Most of Irene's previous disclosures had been commonplace, and fairly predictable, but this – this was a fresh laceration to a man who had believed himself equal to any situation. Gross sexual abuse, either by a member of the child-victim's own family, or a close associate, was no surprise in itself, but the fact that he had never made that connection in Irene's case – given all the information at his disposal – shook him to the core.

Unaware of the questions, accusations, and self-recrimination flooding his brain, Irene continued her story. Looking to neither of the child-care officers as she spoke, the hesitant, almost inaudible, phrases issued from her mouth.

Knowing her mother would readily accept Forster's word over her own, and terrified of prodding her undisputed hatred into violent reaction, Irene allowed herself to be trapped.

Sickened now by the mere thought of Forster's presence, she found every excuse to absent herself from home. At school she threw herself into all extra-curricular activities taking place outside of school hours; here was the one place she could be safe from that man's demands.

Since that first night, Forster had waited his time, giving her increasing hope that she might further avoid his attentions. Then, when her guard was relaxed, he seized fresh opportunity to molest her, coming into the bedroom she had inherited from her brothers, choking her cries with her pillow, confident that the sound of her thrashing limbs would not disturb Sandra asleep in the room across the passage, nor awaken Dorothy from her drunken stupor. His visits became more and more frequent, and when Irene was finally brought to submit without further protest or fight, his lewd and prurient brain devised fresh ways to torment her. Now she could never allow herself to relax, never be sure that any innocent occupation would not draw from him some deviation to enhance the sex act.

Driven to utter despair Irene clutched at any excuse to avoid her persecutor, even going so far as to attach herself to Dorothy, following her around like a second shadow, a circumstance which earned her little credit.

'I wish you would get from under my feet,' Dorothy complained. 'It's getting so's I can go nowhere without you tagging after me.'

She thought desperately of seeking help from her teachers, then dismissed the idea, accepting she could never bear to tell them of the dreadful things Forster had made her take part in.

Her brothers she dismissed out of hand. Martin, without doubt, would go straight to their mother, and Roger would probably follow suit, then she would have lost their affection for nothing. Only by keeping within Dorothy's sight could she be sure Forster would not approach her. She was willing to endure her mother's irritation in exchange for that much relief.

In spite of all Irene did to avoid him, Forster found ways to outwit her; for him this was all part of the game. With Dorothy so besotted as to find no fault, and Sandra in likewise condition, it was not difficult for him to manipulate them both. Accordingly, they were persuaded to run some errand on his behalf, leaving him the run of the house, and Irene, all unsuspecting.

Thinking to find her mother and sister at home, Irene returned from a contrived outing to be confronted by Forster, grinning in most unpleasant fashion.

'Thought you were being clever, didn't you?' he asked, stepping behind her and leaning his shoulders against the door by which she had entered. 'Thought you'd get away with hiding behind your ma's petticoats.'

Irene shot a swift glance about her, wondering which way to run.

Forster read her expression. 'No use you taking off, darling. I've locked the other door, and the windows are all fastened. . . . But you can make a try for it, if you like,' he added softly, the familiar light of anticipation kindling in his eyes.

Irene resigned herself to the inevitable. She had learned long since that resistance merely served to increase his appetite. She collapsed inwardly, allowing her shoulders to sag as she faced him with dull acceptance across the narrow hall.

'Come on, darling. Don't spoil the fun. Here, I've brought you a present. I want to see you put them on.' Forster held a rustling paper bag, shaking it under her nose. 'Take it, damn you,' he snapped as Irene made no move.

Reluctantly, she took the bag from his hand.

'Well open it, then.'

Slowly, her eyes never leaving his face, she opened the neck of the bag.

Forster snatched it impatiently, grabbing the contents with one hand, and discarding the wrappings with the other. 'Here, put these on.' His fist, clenched about the scraps of red and black lingerie, was thrust into her face.

Irene flinched but took the scanty bra and panties from his hands, her face registering nothing but blank acceptance.

It had been some time since either Roger or Martin came to call on their mother. Their initial weekly visits had grown less and less frequent until now each needed the support of the other before showing his face. So it was that both were witness to their sister's shameful and degrading attempt to excite desire in their mother's friend by parading herself before him wearing nothing but tawdry scraps of scarlet and black lace, designed to do little more than invite ravishment.

Strutting the hearth in precariously high-heeled sandals, twitching her buttocks in time to Forster's enthusiastic hand-claps and calls for more effort, Irene turned to discover her audience.

With a strangled, whimpering sound, like that of a tethered dog cruelly beaten, she clasped her arms about her near-naked body, and stared transfixed at her brothers.

'Looks like the game's up, darling, no use to be coy.' Forster stifled a suave yawn, quick to recover from his surprise at this unexpected intrusion, and even more quick to assume the bored air of a practising roué caught up to his tricks with a more than willing partner. 'Seems they've caught us good and proper so you can spare us the maidenly blushes,' he said on a note of resignation.

With a low moan of mortal hurt, Irene stumbled from the room, brushing past her brothers standing open-mouthed in the doorway.

Once she had gone Forster sent a sheepish glance at the two young men. 'Sorry you walked in on us like that, must have come as a bit of a shock, what with me being part of the family, so to speak.'

'Part of the family! Why you . . . bastard.' Roger was first to recover his power of speech, and with it a sense of outrage. He advanced on Forster, his fists clenched.

'Now, Roger, there's no need for that.' Forster hastily put the settee between himself and Irene's brothers. 'We'll get married just as soon as we're able. Only, well, you know how it is . . . Warm little beggar, your sister. She wouldn't wait.'

'And you think that excuses your dirty goings on, do you? My God, if our mam ever finds out she'll bloody kill her – an' you, too.'

'Steady on, there's been nothing between your mother and me to make her think she has any claim.'

'Why, you dirty, lying toad. Get a hold of him, Mart, and we'll see about claims.' Roger urged his brother forward, making to trap Forster in a pincer movement as they skirted the settee.

Had Irene not picked that most inopportune moment to appear in the doorway, her brothers might have thrashed the truth out of her tormentor. Her presence, wrapped in a dressing gown, and weeping floods of tears merely endorsed Forster's declaration that theirs was a mutually satisfactory relationship. Nor did she help matters with her choking, bungled attempts at a truthful explanation. Too overwrought to plead her case coherently her cries for understanding fell on their ears as hasty excuses for her wanton behaviour, and called from them increasing disgust.

'Please, oh, please. Please don't be mad at me,' she begged, groping tentatively for Roger's arm. 'I tried to tell you, I tried to tell Martin . . . It . . . It wasn't . . . I didn't . . . he, oh, Roger, please.'

Knocking aside her trembling fingers Roger turned on her in fury. 'You dirty little whore! Parading up and down like a cheap prostitute – a kid of your age – and in your own home at that. Get away from me, girl! He's welcome to the likes of you!'

Sinking to the floor, mindlessly allowing the dressing gown to fall open to display once more the provocative strips of lace, Irene clasped her brother's knees. 'Don't Roger. Don't, I beg of you. Please don't say things like that. I'm not a bad girl. I'm not, I'm not!'

Roger, goaded beyond rational thought by his sister's overtly sexual attire, flung her from him. Face drained of colour, eyes blazing contempt, he surveyed her sprawled figure for only a second before turning to his brother. 'C'mon, Martin. Let's get out of here. No wonder she acted so shifty last time we came.'

'No! Oh, no. It wasn't like that. Listen to me. Listen, please.' Irene tried one last desperate appeal.

'Give over, Rene. They caught us at it, didn't they? No need for all this carry on.' With a show of irritation, Forster effectively quelled her hopes of gaining further hearing.

That night, without stopping to make any preparation, Irene let herself out of the house. With no clear idea of where she might be heading she tramped through the hours of darkness, seeking only to put as much distance between herself and the home that had become her prison, as her strength would allow. Mile after mile she trudged, her fear of being caught and forced to return causing her to spurn the major roads, and with them all possible hopes of getting a lift. Keeping to the quiet back lanes and the open fields she stumbled blindly along until she dropped from sheer exhaustion. Her childhood phobia of becoming trapped in a burning shed prevented her seeking shelter from the winter rain in some outbuilding or barn, and she slept where she fell. She was soaked to the skin, and her clothes, of necessity, dried on her body. She had not thought to bring as much as a change of underwear away with her.

Hunger made her light-headed, but she had nothing with which to ease her cramping stomach pains, no money to buy bread, and no hope of succour from the barren ground. She grew delirious, drifting in and out of coherent thought, waking from dreams of hot, steaming puddings to find her sore feet plodding round and round the same patch of scrubland she had believed to be miles behind her. A tearing cough racked her chest, doubling her over with pain, and as she tore a path through bramble and thicket the lights of a distant town drew her invitingly. Seeking warmth and ease she forced her protesting limbs to carry her towards the tantalising spectacle of busy roads and teeming crowds that shimmered like a mirage on the edge of her vision.

She was discovered slumped on a public bench, babbling incoherently of warm beds and hot dinners, dirty beyond recognition, and suffering from exposure.

She awoke forty-eight hours later in the blissfully clean, starched and polished atmosphere of a hospital ward, and was allowed three days free of constraint or question to recover from her ordeal. When the time came for her to attempt an explanation of her flight from home, she maintained a stubborn silence.

'I told you, didn't I? Told you what it would be like.' Dorothy turned in justification to the woman sent by the Children's Department in direct response to her request. 'Three days, nearly four, I've been half out of my head with worry. And what do I get? Well, you can see for yourself that she's quite beyond me.'

Primed by Forster on the line she should take, encouraged by him to seize this opportunity of ridding herself once and for all of the wearisome responsibility of this wayward child, Dorothy had summoned the woman here with the demand that her daughter should be taken into care.

The Child Care Officer, an elderly woman who, in spite of her iron-grey hair and military bearing, seemed to exude an all-embracing sympathy, listened to this tirade and kept her face impassive. 'Won't you try, Irene, to explain what you intended by running away from home?' Her voice was evenly pitched and non-committal.

Irene stared at her, shrinking back into the safe, firm support of the pillows piled at her back. She was wearing a borrowed hospital nightgown, too big for her slender frame, and the falling shoulders and over-wide sleeves added to her waif-like appearance. She plucked nervously at the starched cotton sheets, her eyes fixed on the Child Care Officer, deliberately blotting out sight of her mother's angry face.

'It must have been miserably cold out there. All that rain and sleet. Weren't you afraid?'

Irene refused to be trapped into speech.

'Well, I know I would have been. I'd much rather be safe and warm in my own home than alone out there on the streets.'

Something moved behind Irene's grey eyes, some flicker of expression that was instantly quelled by the snort of disgust that seemed to burst from Dorothy's throat.

'Her? Rather be safe at home? Don't I keep telling you she cares nothing for her home. Nothing! Nor for me or her dad.'

'He's not my dad!' The instant denial came on a high, wailing shriek of protest. The first words to leave Irene's lips since the interview began.

'There! You see? John's done all he can to be a father to her, and you can imagine the thanks he gets.'

'He's not my dad! He's not my dad! He's not, he's not, he's not!' Irene's small face was suffused with angry colour and she beat her fists on the bed in rising hysteria.

'I think perhaps we'd better leave matters there for the present, Mrs Cooper. I'd like to visit you at home, if I may. And maybe later, when Irene is feeling a little better . . .' Olive Ridgard stood face to face with Irene's mother, but her eyes were turned in a sideways, speculative glance to the girl now sobbing denial from the hospital bed.

Whatever Olive's private opinion of Irene's home background, she had no hesitation in recommending that Dorothy's application to have her daughter taken into care should be speedily endorsed.

Frightened and apprehensive, intimidated by the legal jargon used to acquaint her of this decision, Irene viewed her future with considerable misgivings.

'What will it be like?' she asked Olive Ridgard when she

came to escort her from the hospital to the reception centre where she was to spend some time under close observation before she would be assigned a permanent place.

'Well, it will be a little strange to begin with, I suppose. But nothing for you to worry about.'

'Yes, but will it be like prison?' Irene asked anxiously, thereby betraying the fears which haunted her.

'Good heavens, no. Not at all. You'll be well looked after, Irene. And there's a strong possibility that you will be sent to a private foster home. I'm sure you'd like that. So don't worry, we're all on your side, you know, and I'm certain you will soon make friends.'

In this, at least, the Child Care Officer was wrong.

It had been discovered during the medical examination on Irene's admission to hospital that she was no longer a virgin, and this fact, noted on her case-papers, was enough to condemn her from the start. Questioned by the Care Officers grimly determined to discover the identity of her seducer, Irene remained unco-operative, feelings of guilt and shame cleaving her tongue to the roof of her mouth, holding her silent.

'Was he some boy from school?' The question was put to her with professional impartiality.

She shook her head, her gaze fixed to her hands lying clasped in her lap.

'Then someone from the youth club?'

Her head moved in another negative gesture.

'Were you forced?' This question, snapped at her in direct departure from their previously gentle enquiries, brought her head up in panic.

'No! No, I . . . No.' She subsided, but not before the Officers had seen the fear in her eyes.

'Someone raped you, didn't they? When? . . . Where? . . . Who? . . .'

Slow tears spilled down Irene's cheeks.

'Was it someone you know? Some man or other you'd had previous contact with?'

'No! No, I tell you.' Suddenly her head snapped back, and she answered them brazenly. 'It was more than one man. I have boyfriends. I'm not a kid, I enjoy sex!'

Her words slammed into them like a hammer, dealing a blow that stunned them all.

They shifted uneasily in their chairs, small creakings and rustlings of hastily shuffled paperwork sounding loud in the void Irene's words had created.

'Hrrmph.' Throats were cleared preparatory to the conciliatory noises designed to win her from this shocking and unexpected stand.

Irene outfaced them, maintaining her defiant pose, her terror at being discovered lending inventiveness.

Distressed, deserted, and regarded by everyone as a potential trouble-maker, Irene accepted her incarceration in local authority care as a punishment for the sins committed against her. She made no friends at the reception centre to which she was first assigned, neither among the staff nor her fellow inmates. She was wretchedly unhappy, and grew daily more so. Olive Ridgard had promised a place of refuge, a second home; Irene found neither. The centre had the cold feel of an institution hanging in its disinfected air, echoing along the bare corridors, and creeping onto the dinner table with the warmed-over mutton and soggy cabbage. Night after night Irene curled into a ball of abject misery oozing slow tears of lonely grief until sleep came to offer a few hours of forgetfulness. Now that she'd had time to consider her position she bitterly regretted the audacity of her replies to the questions she had been asked on admission. If only she'd been wise enough to keep her mouth shut, instinct told her she'd be in receipt of far greater charity from the people she had come to regard as her gaolers.

The professional staff studied Irene like a bug under a microscope. They observed her demeanour, her facial expressions, her manner of speech, and her solitary habit. They discussed her upbringing, her orphaned state, and her boasted promiscuity; weighing all these things against the alternatives they might apply for her future control and guidance. A place in a foster home with a surrogate family was discarded as being too much of a risk – for the foster father in particular – and it was finally agreed that only a closely supervised family-group home might offer Irene adequately monitored care.

Irene accepted this decision with the same apathy she'd come to display in respect of all matters concerning her future. She no longer cared what they did to her, or for her. She felt forgotten, unwanted, a second-rate person of no potential. Her mother sent in her clothes without so much as a note to wish her well, and Irene watched the social worker go through them with critical appraisal, checking their suitability for everyday wear.

On the day she left the reception centre to take up accommodation in the local authority family-group home, she experienced a suffocating sensation of panic. She turned swiftly as if about to run. What if they shut her away and forgot about her? What if she was left to mould forever in that place while her former schoolfriends grew up free to do as they chose?

A firm grip on her elbow steered her from the door of the centre to the car where the social worker waited to drive her to the children's home, and the brief moment of rebellion was over. She allowed herself to be led away.

Irene had been resident at the children's home almost three months before her condition became manifest. She had not been well since the day of her admission, but had stubbornly tried to hide her swelling stomach, and almost constant nausea. An innocent still, despite the use Forster had made of her body, she identified her symptoms with the dropsy graphically described in her history books, and as a consequence now believed herself to be in danger of dying. For a time she childishly welcomed the idea of death. It would serve everyone right, she told herself fiercely. If she was to die, then they'd all be sorry.

When common sense reasserted itself, and the nausea that had plagued her finally stopped, she was brought to recognise that she had no wish to exchange her lodging, however miserable, for that of the graveyard. Mortally afraid she sought counsel from Mrs Garland, the woman appointed as her house-mother.

'I . . . Your wife was very cross with me . . . I didn't understand why that should be . . . I really thought that I was dying.' Incredibly, Irene's lips curved into a smile as she directed this remark at Terry Garland.

He shifted uncomfortably in his chair, unhappy with this disclosure. 'She probably thought you were making it up,' he said defensively. 'Playing for sympathy.'

'Oh, no. It wasn't that,' Irene said without heat. 'She was frightened that I'd try to accuse you, or some other male member of staff. She guessed straight away that I was pregnant.'

Terry kept his gaze averted, not choosing to face either Irene or his colleague as this mild accusation was made. He remembered all too well his wife's defensive anger, and the way she had railed against the child newly brought into their care. Could she have had her way, Irene would have found herself brought under the strict discipline and close supervision found in a home for wayward girls. At the time he had preached tolerance, taking the news of Irene's pregnancy philosophically; though he would have been the last to say so, Terry Garland was a man totally attuned to his job, and nothing he ever discovered about the children in his care ever shocked, worried, or dismayed him.

A big man, standing well over six feet tall, broad and rumpled, he had about him the air of a friendly, much patted dog. His sweaters were never without holes, his habitual corduroy trousers hung like floppy, creased concertinas, but his shoes, like his smile, always gleamed. His hair was sparse, even in those days, clinging about his balding pate in a gingery tonsure that paled against the flaming luxurious beard springing flamboyantly from his chin.

In respect of his job Terry Garland was somewhat unique, since very few men were appointed as Child Care Officers, it having been decided somewhere in the development of the social services that this was primarily a woman's province, but Terry filled the role admirably. He had an innate understanding of children, a warm avuncular personality which earned him their trust. When he and his wife had learned that their marriage must be forever childless his present post of house-father had offered consolation, and might have been designed especially for him. Terry applied for a transfer from the Probation and After-care service and, with his wife, had moved into the custom-built house to take up the complex role of acting father to an instant family of children with problems.

The fact of Irene's pregnancy did not alarm him as it had his spouse. In his judgement Irene was a child more sinned against than sinning, and he saw nothing in her manner to suggest promiscuity.

'She is going to need help, Erica,' he said in response to his wife's angry and over-dramatic presentation of the news. 'She is far too immature to cope with this alone.'

'Now don't you get taken in, Terry. Next thing you know she'll back you into a corner and start screaming rape.'

Terry smiled at his wife's bristling indignation, but took care that she did not see. 'Oh, I think I could manage to beat her off,' he said mildly.

His wife gave a snort of disgust. 'It's all right you thinking it funny,' she said sharply. 'But she could cause us no end of trouble, what with that sweet, innocent face, and that air of being misused.'

'There you are then, Erica. You've seen it for yourself. How did a baby like her ever get mistaken for a *femme fatale*?'

'If she's as innocent as all that, you great buffoon, ask yourself how she got pregnant in the first place.' Erica quelled him with a glance. 'It's men like you her sort get into bother.'

'How, er, did she react to the idea of becoming a mother?' Terry asked, hoping by this slight diversion to escape the lecture he sensed was coming.

His ploy succeeded better than he might have hoped. 'Oh, Good Lord! I haven't told her.' Erica clapped a hand to her mouth. 'I left her upstairs in her bedroom and came down here with the doctor. Then I came straight to tell you. I'd better go up to her now.'

'I was terrified,' said Irene, breaking in on Terry's recollections.

Terry shot a quick glance at Janet, seeking approval before venturing to reply. At her nod he turned back to Irene. 'But she soon put you right, didn't she? Erica – my wife, I mean. She looked after you?'

'Oh, yes. She . . . she was very kind once she got used to the idea. She arranged for me to help out in the nursery, if you remember. That was one of the best times in my life.' Irene's face softened at the memory. 'I loved the babies. And Matron was really nice.'

'Do you still love babies, Irene?' asked Janet in a conversational manner.

'Of course I do,' Irene said without hesitation.

'And your own? Baby Lawrence included?'

'Yes! Yes, I do. And I wish you wouldn't try to trick me like that. Of course I love him. And Lauren, and Debbie. I love them all.'

'Even when they are naughty?'

'Yes. Even then.' Irene faced her defiantly, her hands gripping the arms of her chair, her chest heaving as her eyes flashed fire.

'So tell me some more about the nursery. Did they teach you how to care for your baby?'

'Yes,' said Irene sullenly.

'And did you enjoy that?'

'Yes.'

'What about the babies in the nursery? What sort of nursery was it?'

'You know all about that.' Irene refused to allow herself to be won over.

'Not really. I'm fairly new to this area. The nursery and the children's home both closed down before I came.'

'It was a sort of temporary shelter for babies who were taken into care,' Irene said slowly, measuring Janet Fouracre's reaction to her every word. 'They usually got adopted, or taken into foster homes. They didn't stay in the nursery for very long.'

'And you helped to look after them,' Janet prompted, gently returning Irene to her story.

'Why do so many babies come here?' Irene had asked.

Matron, a trim, efficient woman whose angular figure belied her warm, comforting nature, sent a 'you should know' glance toward Irene's swelling stomach.

'Oh, you mean . . . But they aren't all . . . all . . .'

'No,' Matron relented. 'They aren't all illegitimate, some come to us from broken homes, and some simply because their mothers cannot cope.'

'And what about little Michelle here? She's neither of those.' Irene kissed the petal-soft hands of the child she held in her arms.

Matron's face darkened. 'Michelle was maltreated. When she was brought to us she looked like a victim of famine.'

'Oh, but that doesn't mean they'd hurt her, surely. I mean, I've seen her mum and dad, they look ever so nice. Perhaps they just don't understand how to look after her properly.'

'Take off her socks and shoes,' said Matron in a thin voice, and as Irene gazed at her, perplexed, said again, 'Take off her socks and shoes, Irene. Go on, take them off.'

Wondering what this was about Irene removed the button-through shoes and began peeling the lacy tights from the child's legs. The baby grew instantly still, her dimpled knees and wriggling limbs held rigid, her smile fading as her face puckered.

As Irene pulled the tights from her legs the baby began to scream.

With a gasp of shocked disbelief Irene stared at the scars covering every inch of the child's buttocks and legs. Nausea threatened to overwhelm her as she grasped the significance of her own deeply pitted cicatrice.

'Look at her feet, Irene. Take your time, examine them properly. Never mind her screams, it will take years for her to grow out of doing that.'

As Irene took the small feet into the palm of her hand, her face drained of colour. 'She . . . she's got no toes,' she said at last. 'She . . . they . . . oh.'

Matron scooped the child from her faltering grasp, pushing her into a chair. 'I'm sorry. I shouldn't have made you do that, but every time I hear someone say what nice people Michelle's parents are, I could do murder.'

'Oh, Matron. How could they?' Irene wrapped her arms protectively about her stomach, closing her eyes with a shudder.

'Oh, quite easily, so I'm told. She cried, you see. And kicked out when her mother stuck the nappy-pin in her. So of course she had to be punished.'

'But how? All those scars. And her poor little feet.'

'Scalding water. In her bath. Gangrene. They pleaded ignorance, of course. But those sort of monsters always do.'

'What will happen to her?' Eyes staring, she waited for Matron to reply.

'She'll be sent home in due course.'

There was a poignant silence during which even the baby seemed to be holding her breath.

'And in due course, when they discover she is unable to walk as other children, their twisted, evil minds will dream up some new atrocity.'

'But, I . . . But, Matron, why don't you *do* something?' Irene's horrified gaze was riveted on the woman's face.

'What would you suggest?'

The question was asked so matter-of-factly that Irene gasped. 'Well, *do* something! Like . . . like call the police. Or . . . or keep Michelle here, where she can be safe.'

'And what reason would I give for such action?'

In the face of such stupidity Irene began to lose her temper. 'I'd have thought that would be obvious,' she said hotly.

'Yes, of course you would. And so would anyone of a right mind. But look at it this way – the way the average parent is made to see it. On the one hand you have this nice, loving couple – you did say Michelle's parents looked nice, didn't you? – And on the other, you have the ugly, unfeeling face of bureaucracy. Our loving couple produce a child that to all outward appearances they love and cherish. They live a pretty normal sort of life, one or two rows, but then who doesn't? The baby they have produced cries a lot, perhaps. The neighbours start asking questions. The child looks thin and peaky, maybe has a few bruises. The social services are told. Not openly, you understand, because that would be sneaky. So they learn in some roundabout manner that may take several months.' Matron paused to confirm that Irene was following this, and the expression in the wide grey eyes urged her to continue. 'Well, here we are, then. Armed with the suspicion that all is not as it seems, our social workers find some acceptable excuse to call at the child's home. But here they tread on delicate ground. What if the stories they have heard are merely evil gossip? What if neighbourhood spite has exaggerated some unfortunate, but perfectly innocent incident? Let's suppose for instance, they discover Michelle has a black eye. How did it happen? She fell, says her mother. Or one of the other children hit her with some toy. She walked into a swing on the park. She just happened to stand in the way of the door. Remember, Irene, these are *nice* people. What would you believe?'

Irene dropped her gaze. 'I don't know. I suppose I'd have to be sure. Maybe I'd talk to the father separately. Perhaps he knows how these things happen, and, and he'd like someone to help.' Her fingers strayed to the scar on her cheek, and Matron's eyes widened in sudden comprehension.

'But supposing these injuries are inflicted by him?' she asked gently. 'Or if both parents are equally guilty of maltreating their child?'

'I don't know.' Irene admitted defeat.

'You understand, then? Some of the difficulties?'

'Yes, but I still think something should be done. I mean, we know Michelle has been scalded,' she said stubbornly.

'Of course we do, but her parents said that it was an accident. Are we then to go out on the streets kidnapping every child who shows signs of injury?'

'Don't be silly.'

'If you think that's silly you should hear the hue and cry that goes up whenever we remove a child from its parents.'

'But you know! You *know* Michelle's parents are hurting her. Why can't you keep her here?'

'Because public opinion is against us. Because most parents are guilty at some time or other of giving their children a slap. Even some of the best of them come close on occasion to doing their child some permanent damage. Their feelings of guilt work against us when we fight to bring a child into care.'

'I don't believe you! Not everyone is as wicked as you say.'

Matron smiled, a slow, sad smile for the dreams that were dying behind Irene's eyes. 'I didn't mean to imply that there are no happy families,' she said gently. 'Only that they are all vulnerable to some degree.'

'Well, I don't know that I understand all that exactly,' Irene said stubbornly. 'But I can tell you one thing, no one will ever ill-treat my baby. Least of all me.'

SEVEN

Having surrendered the care of her daughter to the local authority, Irene's mother was advised of her pregnant state only as a matter of courtesy. On receiving the letter officially stating the fact, she paid her one and only visit to the children's home where Irene was lodged.

'You'll have it adopted, of course,' she said emphatically. 'You're not but a kid yourself, so you don't really have much to say in the matter.'

Irene stared at her in shock and dismay. 'I . . . I don't know . . . I thought . . . I wanted . . . Perhaps . . .'

'Don't be so stupid. How could you ever hope to take care of a child?' Dorothy demanded, guessing where her daughter's inclinations were leading. 'And don't imagine I'd be daft enough to help you, 'cause I'm not. I've had enough with my own, more than enough, without taking on any more. Besides,' she said coyly, 'it's odds on I might be getting married. And I'm sure John wouldn't like me tied down by no illegitimate brat.'

At this unconscious reminder of her child's parentage, Irene reeled. She had been accustomed to thinking of the baby as no one's but her own. Her mother's disparagement carried a warning; what if Forster should guess the child was his, and use the fact to make her return to their former relationship? She blanched at the thought.

'Does he know?' she asked quickly. 'About the baby, I mean.'

'Well, I've not been in any hurry to tell him I'm about to become a grandmother,' Dorothy said with unaccustomed candour. 'He's a bit younger than me.' She fluffed her hair, and primped in a sickening fashion. 'Wouldn't do to remind him of it too obviously.'

'I see . . . Well, well maybe I will think about adoption.'

'Think about it? Don't be so bloody ridiculous, girl. What option do you have? Haven't we just been over all that? You'd better get it adopted, and quick, if you want any sort of a life for yourself once they let you out of this place.'

'It was you that put me in,' Irene muttered darkly.

'Don't give me that, you ungrateful little sod. It was for your own good. And it'll be to your own good to get rid of that brat!'

This was a sentiment, though far more charitably expressed, that was shared by Terry and Erica Garland.

'Give it some time and thought, Irene. You are so very young. What sort of a life can a girl of fourteen hope to offer a tiny baby?' Mrs Garland asked kindly.

Terry gazed at his wife from beneath raised brows. He had been surprised by the sure and certain way in which she had gone straight to the only argument which would influence Irene. He decided to leave her to handle the situation. Too much pressure, too many opinions would only stiffen the girl's declared resolve to keep the child. Had Irene been just a couple of years older he would have supported her stand, but he knew only too well the hostilities she would encounter once she left the protected environment of the home. He had seen too many unmarried mothers forced into a life of drudgery and petty crime to want that for Irene.

And so it was on the strength of Erica Garland's prudent counselling that Irene was brought to sign away her right to the tiny boy whom she laboured so long and so painfully to bring into the world.

When she had first learned of her pregnancy she had been frightened, but once she had grown used to the idea, and had been disabused of the old wives' tales she'd gleaned regarding the mystery of birth, she had begun to look forward to nursing her child. When her pains started she was filled with the joy of that impatient life, and newly determined to put up a fight to keep her son. They endured so much together, she and him, his lusty birth-struggle forging a bond through the agony that would bring them to separate existence. And when, with that last, white-hot, severing pain, the child had burst from her, Irene, already forgetting her travail, had reached between her blood-spattered thighs to scoop the squalling infant to her aching breast.

Waking from fulfilled, happy sleep, turning in blissful anticipation of finding her son by her side, she had been shocked and confused to find herself alone in the small, private side ward.

'Nurse! Nurse!' Struggling to climb from the high hospital bed, she cast frantic eyes about the room, searching for the cot she had expected to find close by.

'*Nurse!*'

Her screams brought a harassed young nurse running into the room.

'What is it? Whatever is the matter? Are you bleeding?' Without waiting for a reply the nurse stripped back the coverlet, quick professional hands lifting Irene's starched hospital gown.

'My baby! My baby! Where is he?' Irene clawed at the cool hands, pulling the nurse down to the bed, screaming at her to return her child.

'Don't get so worked up. You'll make yourself ill. Lie down, I'll get Sister.'

'No, no. Don't leave me. Tell me what you have done with my baby.'

Unable to tear herself free of Irene's fevered grasp, the nurse stabbed the emergency call button hanging close to the bed, and prayed for swift assistance.

Sister answered her prayer with a speed that drew groans of indignation from the wide-flung door. Air swirling in her wake, she reached the bed.

'What is it? Is she haemorrhaging?' she demanded of the nurse.

'It's the baby. She's just discovered he's gone.'

No words, however carefully chosen, could deliver the truth in any manner that would make it acceptable. No amount of cold common sense could make her believe she had done the only wise thing when she had put her signature to the documents which deprived her of the right to her child. And it was very small comfort indeed to hear it suggested that the infant might be better accommodated with the strangers to whom he now belonged.

Irene sank into a deep depression, her young breasts aching for the feel of her baby's searching lips, her arms and stomach empty of that warm, tender life. For days and weeks she sat alone in the midst of the clamouring, busy turmoil of the children's home. Surrounded by people, she existed in total isolation.

Her house-parents tried everything in their power to breach the barriers of misery she had built about herself, but to no avail.

It was left to a chance remark by a young woman working as a domestic in the home to bring about Irene's slow and hesitant return to health.

'What's up wi' 'er?' the domestic asked of her elderly colleague as they cleaned around Irene in the communal sitting room. 'What's she sittin' around like that for – right in everybody's way?'

'She's like you, she's just lost a nipper. Well, a few months ago now.' The buxom figure heaved, threatening to burst the narrow seams of the woman's flowered wrapover apron, as she drew a deep breath of commiseration.

'What, 'er? Blimey, she don't look old enough.'

'You're not so long in the tooth yourself, my girl.'

'I'm nearly eighteen.'

'She's nearly fifteen, so I hear tell, so there's not much between you,' the senior woman pointed out with a defensive sniff.

'Well, at least I'm married, so I'm entitled . . . Still, poor little sod, 'spect the kid was all she 'ad. Never gets any visitors, does she?'

'Not all the while I've been here.'

'Has she al'us been like she is now? Y'know . . .' The girl tapped her forehead significantly.

'Oh, she's not daft. Least, not so's you'd notice. Right as anybody she was 'til she had that baby. Reckon they should have let her keep it, myself.'

'Oh, so it did get born?' Her duster poised in mid-air, the girl took another look at Irene.

'Got born all right. Little lad, it was. They made her have it adopted.'

'Yeah, they would. 'Er bein' in 'ere, an all. Cruel sods.'

Having completed their work the two women collected their materials and were about to leave the room when the younger, struck by Irene's unhappy solitude, crossed to her chair to give her a warm hug. 'Don't you worry, ducks. You'll 'ave other kids. That's what they told me when I miscarried, an' 'ere I am, already startin' another. So don't you let 'em get you down, eh?'

Irene made no immediate response, but as the girl crossed the room she turned her head to follow her progress; her first spontaneous action since she had been released from the hospital.

Quietly, and with infinite patience, Terry Garland had been watching for just such a sign. Now he knew how to reach beyond the veil his young charge hid behind, now he could help her make a start rebuilding her shattered life. Ignoring his wife's pleas, and her well-intentioned refusal to allow Irene near the children in the nursery, he took her there himself, and signalled for the Matron to leave the shambling, trembling girl alone with the babies.

After one strangled sob Irene gathered up the nearest child, raining kisses on its hands and face as the pain of loss poured from her heart.

For all her continued air of melancholy and grief, strength returned to Irene's ravaged frame. She was young, and she was learning resilience; one day, when she was free of this place, she would make them tell her who had taken her child.

Meanwhile she found ease from her heartache in caring for the babies other women did not love.

'You took a real gamble there, Terry,' Erica said as they compared their notes on Irene's progress. 'Her sanity was precarious, to say the least. You might have driven her right over the edge, you know.'

Terry smiled, a self-satisfied, knowing quirk of his lips behind his bushy red whiskers. 'Not really, old girl. I had the situation well in hand. And now I'm going to try a real experiment. The Irish girl, Dolores, she finds it difficult to make friends. Maybe Irene . . .'

'Oh, no. No, Terry. I wouldn't,' Erica spoke forcefully across her husband's half-whimsical musings. 'She'd steal the eyes from your head, that one. She should be in a remand home rather than here. It's far more likely she'd corrupt Irene than acquire any morals from her.'

'I'm not looking to have Irene act as her mentor, although I should hope, of course, that some good might come for the girl from such a relationship. No, what I'm looking for is an anchor, someone to whom Dolores can attach herself. Irene has an excess of motherly love, and the other girl starves for it. It's my belief their individual problems might cancel the other's out.'

'You'll get too big for your boots one of these days, you old fool.' Though her words were harsh Erica regarded him fondly. She knew how much the welfare of these children meant to him, and how hard he worked to send them on their way free of the problems that had brought them into his care.

'So could you arrange for them to share a bedroom, maybe?' Terry asked, smiling as he scented her co-operation.

'Maybe . . . Terry, will you tell Irene? About Dolores's habit of stealing, and the rest?'

'The rest, I think,' Terry said after some consideration. 'There's very little she could steal from Irene, so I have few worries on that score. And why spoil my chances by painting too black a picture?'

Irene listened with quiet acceptance, displaying only a token interest while Terry explained how Dolores had been brought to England as a baby in arms, and then abandoned by her mother.

'She has six other children, you see. Her husband had no work, it was too much of a struggle to keep her.' There were occasions when Terry found it hard to be charitable in respect of the actions of certain parents. If he felt this now he deliberately kept it hidden. Irene needed to know she was not alone in her failure to provide for her child. 'After a spell of two years, during which Dolores was passed from one member of her mother's family to another, she was placed in a foster home, but things didn't work out.' Terry shrugged in negation of the trouble the undisciplined youngster had caused, and continued.

98

'She was sent to another couple, and might have been happy there, but her mother – her real mother – suddenly decided she wanted her daughter home, and took her back to Ireland. A few months later she brought her back and returned her to the second set of foster parents without explanation. After refusing to allow them to adopt Dolores, she went back once more to Ireland. The foster parents were too upset to try again.'

Terry scanned Irene's face hoping she understood the mental cruelty inflicted by this callous disregard of the child's feelings. His gaze was met with a deep-eyed defensive stare that registered a guarded empathy. Encouraged to believe he might break through one to reach the other Terry resumed his lengthy narrative.

'Well, after that, Dolores was placed in a community home for a while – an orphanage operated by the nuns. Dolores is a Roman Catholic, you see.'

Irene nodded, concerned to discover where all this was leading. She understood, and in some respects shared, the other girl's misery, but so far failed to see what she was expected to do about it.

'They, er, they tried to place her with first one family then another, but there was always some problem, some difficulty. Dolores doesn't always stick to the truth, she . . . romances, a little.' And so do you, Terry Garland, he thought to himself, because Dolores had shown herself to be as accomplished a liar as she was thief. 'I expect she does it as a protection from the hurt of thinking nobody wants her.'

'How old is she?' Irene asked.

'Coming up twelve. And already she has had eight different foster homes.'

'Who sent her here? Was that her mother?'

'Not exactly. You see she got herself into a spot of bother, and, well, this seemed like the best place to put her.'

Suddenly abandoning his mentor-pupil role, Terry took Irene by the shoulders and appealed to her as an equal. 'She needs help, Irene. She needs to know somebody cares. If she is ever going to make anything of her life she needs lots and lots of love and affection. Do you think there is anything you might do for her?'

'I don't know.' Irene shrugged. 'And anyway, why should I?'

'Well, I was rather hoping . . .' Terry suddenly realised that he could hardly explain his theories of a mutually beneficial therapy to one of the unsuspecting participants, and hastily swallowed his words. 'I thought,' he began again, more firmly, 'that it might be a kindness on your part to help the child out. She has no real friends here, no one she feels she can trust. But obviously, if you don't want to be bothered . . .' His eyebrows shot upwards, twin question marks on his bald forehead, silently posing the invitation he deliberately left unspoken.

'It's not that,' Irene said, faintly ashamed of herself. 'It's just . . . well, I have no one either. Not really, and nobody helped me, so why should I do anything for her?'

Terry sighed, a gusty exclamation of sorrowing acceptance. 'No, no, of course not. I shouldn't have been so thoughtless. Forget it, Irene. You are quite right.' He turned to walk away, but allowed himself to be detained by a small sound from Irene.

'I . . . Look, I don't know if I'll be able to do anything. I might not even like what's-her-name. But if you want me to have a go, I don't mind.'

'Oh, Irene. That's very generous of you.'

Irene hung her head, the colour mounting in her cheeks. 'I'm not making any promises, mind,' she mumbled into her chest.

Terry's mouth was drawn in a grimace of mocking self-congratulation which he was careful not to allow her to see. 'OK,' he said lightly. 'I'll leave it to you, then. If there's anything, I'll be grateful. If not, no need to worry. At least I'll know you made a stab at it.' Anxious not to overplay his hand he left her then to mull over all he had said, confident that he had contrived yet another solution beneficial to both protagonists.

Irene was not immediately enamoured of the brash, cocky young girl who moved in to share her bedroom. She found Dolores somewhat alarming with her very abundant, very black hair, her dark flashing eyes, and her tendency to lie about almost everything. Nor did she find the girl's habit of loudly and wetly snuffling when she ought to have been using a handkerchief particularly endearing. Terry's scheme to bring them together might have foundered from the first had not Irene noticed the snuffles become even louder and wetter after the lights were put out, and her new room-mate supposedly asleep. She was reminded of her own first few weeks in this place – the feeling of utter loneliness and despair, and the many tears she had shed into her pillow.

Sliding out of bed she crossed the narrow strip of varnished flooring to reach the other bed. Without waiting for invitation she lifted the bedclothes, and made a space for herself alongside Dolores. The beds were narrow and it was a natural move for her to place her arm about the other girl's waist and snuggle up to her. The snuffles stopped immediately as Dolores held her breath, lying rigid in Irene's embrace, feigning sleep.

'I'm frozen,' Irene said with a realistic shiver. 'These bedclothes aren't very thick. I thought we could keep each other warm, if you like.'

Dolores expelled her breath on a ragged sob, and while she said nothing in answer to Irene's proposal she did not pull away.

'I used to sleep like this with my sister,' Irene told her. 'We were always lovely and cosy.' An unexpected wave of nostalgia made her voice wobble, and she bit her lip remembering the way things had been between her and Sandra before their mother had thought to drive them apart. Suddenly she found it a comfort to have someone to cuddle, and for the first time since the birth of her baby, the cold, empty spot in her middle began to feel a little less icy. She fell asleep holding Dolores in her arms unaware that the other girl was feeling equally comforted.

The following morning both girls rose and dressed, neither giving outward indication of the small breach in the wall of defence they each habitually hid themselves behind.

Their friendship was a hesitant thing, progressing only by very slow degrees, but Terry Garland observed and was satisfied.

Though Irene occasionally spoke of her life before she was admitted into care, Dolores remained tightlipped on the subject. She listened to Irene's deliberately tailored descriptions of a rosy childhood as she might have listened to any bedtime story, and made no attempt to question or elicit greater detail. But always after such episodes she would go off by herself for a time, and the warmth would die from their relationship.

They had been sharing a bedroom and this strange on-off fraternity for some months before Irene so far lost her temper with Dolores's constant snuffling as to upbraid her about the use of a handkerchief.

Dolores stared at her, those dark, flashing eyes smouldering, before she burst into a tirade that set Irene gasping.

'It was all right for you,' Dolores shouted at the conclusion of her outburst. 'To hear you go on, you were so damned precious to your fancy-pants mother she'd have gone so far as to lick your snotty nose dry.'

Irene stared at her, too dumbstruck to make any reply.

'What I'd like to know,' Dolores said, her cheeks bright with the red flags of anger, 'is how the hell you came to be here at all.' And with that, she fled to the bedroom they shared, and there proceeded to tear into shreds every handkerchief Irene possessed.

Irene made no attempt to go after her, feeling both justified in her complaint of the girl's snuffling, and more than a little hurt by her subsequent outburst. But her conscience smote her when Dolores failed to put in an appearance for the evening meal, and nagged her uncomfortably as bedtime approached without a sign of the girl. Deciding she would go up to bed early and make her peace before lights-out, she entered the bedroom to find Dolores sitting fully dressed on the side of her bed. She kept her back turned towards Irene and refused to look up when the older girl took a seat on the bed opposite.

'I'm sorry, Dolores. I shouldn't have shouted at you . . . but it is a bit off-putting, you know, when somebody keeps snuffling and snorting.' She tried to take Dolores's hand, but Dolores snatched it away, twisting about on the bed, keeping her face turned away from Irene.

'Well, I'm a bit fed up, too,' she said at last. 'With always hearing about your marvellous family, and all the rest . . . and how do you expect me to use a hanky when I haven't got one?' she demanded.

'Oh, Dolores, don't be so silly. There's dozens of hankies around somewhere. Look, I'll give you some of mine, if you like.' Irene reached across to the locker at the side of her bed and rummaged inside. Failing to find the small pile of handkerchiefs she knew to be there, she got up to make a more thorough search. 'That's funny, I know I have some somewhere.' She began flinging the contents of her locker onto the bed, only stopping when it was emptied. 'Well, I'm sorry, Dolores, but I can't seem to find them. Wait, there's a clean one in my pocket. You take that and I'll have another search.'

Dolores took the printed cotton square and rolled it between her palms. 'Thanks,' she said.

Irene was now meticulously combing through her possessions.

Dolores gave her a sidelong glance before pressing the rolled handkerchief to her nose. She snuffled loudly.

Irene's head came round in slow disbelief. She stared at Dolores amazed. Comprehension broke over her like a warm tide, and luckily she had sufficient presence of mind to suppress the exclamation that rose to her lips. Turning away she pretended to be engrossed with returning her things to her locker.

Again Dolores repeated her little act with the handkerchief, and this time Irene was ready to offer advice. 'Blow, Dorrie. Open the hanky out, cover your nose, and blow.' She avoided looking to see if her advice was followed, sensing that if she embarrassed the girl over this, their friendship would be damaged forever.

Dolores tried again. This time she spread the handkerchief, and blew loudly through her open mouth reminding Irene of the nursery children when they were first acquainted with this exercise.

'That's better,' said Irene encouragingly. 'But not quite right. Now, if only I could find another hanky I could show you.'

'Use this,' Dolores said promptly.

Irene eyed the cotton square dubiously, then steeled herself to accept it. 'OK, here's what you do. Down your nose, see? Not through your mouth.'

She handed the handkerchief back. Dolores tried again, and again, and finally succeeded. Looking very pleased with herself she offered the handkerchief back to Irene. 'Nobody ever showed me before,' she explained. 'Well, p'raps somebody did, a long time ago, only I forgot.'

This time Irene declined the return of her property. 'No, thanks. You keep that one. I'll ask Mrs Garland if she's moved my others.'

That night, for the first time since they had shared a room, Dolores was the one to creep across the varnished floorboards, and once she and Irene were cosily entwined she poured out the story of a childhood spent without any true home, moving first to one set of foster parents then another.

'At first,' she said, 'at the first place I was sent, they didn't like me. I could tell. So I used to be naughty, crying and kicking, and getting out of bed. I used to rip things, you know . . . and, and smash things,' she hurried on, suddenly remembering the shredded handkerchiefs she had hidden under her mattress. 'Well then I got to a lovely place, my true mum and dad, they were. I was very happy with them. And they loved me. They told me every day, even when I was naughty. They wanted to adopt me, proper, like. I would have loved that, only . . . well, then me real mam, me Irish mam, came and said I had to go back with her. An' I said I wouldn't an' the police came, an' everybody, 'cos I said I wouldn't go, not even if they killed me. And they all said I had to go, an' me Irish mam hit me other mam, an' I cried and screamed, an' then everybody was screaming.'

Irene thought privately that this might be another of her friend's gross exaggerations, but she made no comment, afraid to interrupt, hoping that Dolores would continue.

Dolores did. 'After that I went back to Ireland like me mam wanted. But she didn't really want me. She only wanted to stop me other mam and dad having me, and after a bit she changed her mind and took me back to them.'

The silence following this statement went on for so long Irene wriggled impatiently. 'Then what happened?' she asked, holding her breath in case Dolores should decide against saying any more.

'Then I got stuck with some other people, and then the nuns took me, an' then I went somewhere else. And after that somewhere else again.'

104

'Yes, but what about the lovely people? Your other mam and dad? I thought you said they wanted to adopt you.'

Again the silence stretched tantalisingly before Dolores said harshly, 'They took her away. My other mam. In a hospital, they said. She couldn't stand having me taken away. I think she went to a place where they take mad people. Anyway, they wouldn't let me see her, and I couldn't stay, so like I said I got shoved with anybody who would have me. That's when I started to pinch things. And I went on pinching things 'til nobody wanted to take me any more.'

'Pinch things? You didn't really?' Irene was shocked.

'Yes, I did. An' I'll do it again if they send me out of here.'

'But – but don't you want to go to a nice foster home? Maybe if you tried you could find some people like . . . like those others?'

'No! No, I won't. I won't *ever* have another mam and dad like them. I don't want any more people looking at me and saying how soon they'll get to know me, how soon I'll get used to them. And how much they are sure I am going to like livin' in their grotty homes,' Dolores said savagely. 'They get paid to have me, you know. That's the only reason they do it.'

'Oh, Dolores, I'm sure they don't.' Irene attempted to argue, but the younger girl turned on her in fury, leaping from the bed to plant herself, straddle-legged on the polished boards, her small fists clenched on her hips as she gave vent to the rage and misery built over years of constant upheaval.

'Don't you tell me why they do it. I *know*.' Her small thumb stabbed her chest. 'They tell me they want to make me just like their own kids, just like one of the family, they say. But I know the real reason they take me in, an' that's because they want the money. They don't really care about me. Just so long as I keep quiet an' cause them no bother.'

'Well I care about you, Dolores. So come back to bed before you catch cold.' Irene held the bedclothes open invitingly.

Dolores made no move to get back into bed. 'No you don't,' she accused. 'You only care about your mam and your sister. How lovely they are, an' how much they love you.'

Irene stared at her, gathering courage. 'No . . . No, they don't, not really, Dorrie. They hate me, I think . . . I . . . I only said they loved me 'cos . . . 'cos I felt so ashamed.'

Dolores stared. For a full minute she gazed searchingly into Irene's face, reading in her wide, grey eyes more than words could say. Without another word she clambered back into bed.

Just before she dropped off to sleep Dolores stirred and said drowsily, 'At the last place, the man said he'd give me ten pence if I'd let him put his hand on my thingy. So I kicked him, then I pinched his wallet and hid it. And that's why I got sent here.'

Irene did not hear this final revelation; she was already fast asleep.

Neither girl ever referred to that night of exchanged confidences, and though their relationship remained cordial, it progressed no further. It was as if they had both expurgated themselves and were now free to seek deeper friendships elsewhere. And if Irene experienced some small victory over the younger girl's noticeably less frequent compulsion to lie and steal, that was but a pale shadow of Terry Garland's twofold jubilation.

'You know, I've only just realised that you brought Dolores and me together deliberately,' Irene told Terry on a note of surprise.

He shrugged, bringing his shoulders round his ears before attempting an answer. 'I thought, and I believe I was right, that you two had a need of each other.'

'Her mother must have been a right bitch,' said Irene with feeling. 'To go off and leave her like that . . . and then to come back only to desert her all over again.'

'You feel that was wrong, do you?' Janet asked, watching Irene with interest.

'Of course it was wrong. It was a cruel, wicked thing to do. I could never walk out on my children that way.'

'Yet you punish them – or at least, you punish Lawrence most severely. Wouldn't it be better if you were to leave him? Have him fostered, or adopted, say?'

Irene stared at her in horror. 'No!' she cried. 'No, it wouldn't. Haven't you been listening to anything I've said? I love him. He's my baby. I won't ever let anyone take him away.'

'But you hurt him, Irene. You have hurt him on a number of occasions – hurt him quite badly.' Janet was quietly insistent.

'No I haven't! I didn't. Never! Never, I tell you. It was an accident. An accident! Tell her, Terry. Please.' Irene turned in sudden appeal, and Terry looked away, a sound that might have been a groan leaving his lips.

'*Terry*!' Irene screamed his name. 'What have they done with him? Where have they taken my baby?'

'There was an accident, Mrs Rawding. You said so yourself. An accident. They have taken Lawrence to the hospital.' Janet Fouracres attempted to reason.

'Then I must go to him. Why are you keeping me here when you know he will be needing me?'

'You didn't go to him the last time,' Terry reminded her grimly.

Irene looked at him thoughtfully. 'No,' she said at last. 'No, but I should go now. I can help him.'

'No. No, you can do nothing at the moment, Irene. Only the doctors can help him now. Come, sit down. We must wait to hear from them.'

Irene allowed herself to be led back to her seat, where she slumped forlornly. 'How soon? How soon will they let us know?' she asked quietly, in a departure from her former near hysterics.

'Not long now, I shouldn't think. Look, why don't you continue with what you were saying? We'd got as far as Dolores, remember? And you were telling us how friendly she had been.'

'Yes, well she was – even if he *did* organise everything.' Irene scowled in Terry's direction.

'And?' Janet prompted.

'And I was growing up. They couldn't keep me in the kids' home for ever. I'd done nothing wrong. It was only my mother had me sent there in the first place. I was getting too old to stay there any longer.'

EIGHT

By the time her sixteenth birthday was reached, it had been decided by all concerned that Irene's best interests might be served if she was to move outside the home. Provision was made for the children to remain until they reached eighteen if they continued in full-time education, but Irene was eager to get away from school; she was not academically gifted, and she wanted to find herself a job. Some sort of work caring for children was her objective. And she wanted, more than anything, a place of her own. If she managed to trace her son, and she was ever in hope, she would need a home to which she could bring him.

'You wanted me to take a room at the YWCA,' she reminded Terry Garland. 'But I wanted something better than that. I wanted to find something of my own, a nice little flat.'

'I remember. I also seem to recall that things didn't work out exactly as you had planned,' Terry replied, and filled in the next part of her story. 'I watched you for weeks, chasing after jobs for which you lacked the most basic qualifications. Finally, you were obliged to admit you were making no progress, and came to me for help. I went to Matron who did all she could to get you fixed up with a job.'

'Yes, in a day nursery. She got it through one of her friends. It wasn't quite what I was looking for, it was domestic work mostly, picking up after the children, and some light cleaning duties. But I didn't care. I didn't mind what I did so long as I was working with children. And anyway, I thought it would be a start,' said Irene positively.

The cheap little bedsit she finally secured in lieu of the desired flat had nothing to commend it but immediate availability and a moderate rent. She moved in with the good wishes of Terry and Erica Garland ringing in her ears, and the gift of a home-made dish-cloth from Dolores. For a time the novelty of independence kept her from noticing the comfortless nature of her lodging. Her job drained her strength, and she would collapse into bed with no thought for anything but eight hours' blessed sleep.

As she grew more accustomed to cleaning and picking up after forty under-fives, her youthful vitality returned, and she found time to look around her place of work, and to ask questions.

The state-owned day nursery, known simply as Cherry Street, occupied purpose-built premises and the staff, from the organiser to the menials such as Irene herself, were all the employees of the Social Services Children's Department. The underlying principle was to provide a place of refuge for children considered to be at risk. Only those working there, or those availing themselves of its services were aware of the significance of that provision.

'Why "at risk"? What exactly does that mean?' Irene quizzed the housekeeper who was currently her superior.

The housekeeper pursed her lips, considering her reply judiciously before speaking. 'It means,' she said, watching Irene's alert expression, 'that all the children coming here do so because there are . . . problems at home.'

'Problems?'

'We won't go into that,' the housekeeper said shortly.

Suddenly reminded of little Michelle's appalling injuries, Irene fell silent. It was some time before she could bring herself to ask further questions.

'You don't suppose . . . I mean, would any of the children coming here be adopted children?' She ventured timidly.

The housekeeper eyed her sharply. She was fully acquainted with Irene's story. 'Don't go letting your imagination run away with you,' she warned.

'I'm not. I won't. Only . . . only, if anybody was adopted, it would be because they were really wanted, wouldn't it? A baby, I mean. Nobody would go adopting a child if they didn't really want it, would they?'

There was such pleading in Irene's face the housekeeper

forebore to tell her of the cases she'd seen where a natural child born after despairing parents had resorted to adoption often caused them to reject the baby they had once so desperately wanted. Cruelty frequently found an outlet in these sorry cases, either mental or physical, or sometimes both, depending on the strength of confused emotions. And it was no unusual thing for an adopted child to be admitted to the day nursery for sanctuary.

'No, dear,' the housekeeper said comfortably. 'I'm sure nobody would adopt a child they didn't want.'

'It didn't work out though, Irene, did it? Your job at the nursery. I seem to remember there was some sort of, er, some incident?' Terry spoke the last word as though it were framed by inverted commas. He was reluctant to break Irene's train of thought, but was sufficiently aware of her direction to fear another outburst should she be allowed to continue. He met Janet Fouracre's grimace of annoyance with something approaching defiance. 'You left Cherry Street, didn't you? To work elsewhere?' he prompted.

Irene, however, refused to be sidetracked, and ignored his question. Her eyes narrowed, and her face took on a set expression as the 'incident' Terry had heard of ran through her head like a film on a screen.

There had been one little boy, one little boy in particular, to whom she had felt especially drawn. She had gleaned something of his background from nursery gossip, and knew that his father had been wont to torment him over a puppy which was the centre of the child's life, threatening to have the animal put to sleep, and sometimes hiding it for days on the pretext that this had been accomplished until the lad had become completely neurotic. Irene had been making some progress with the child who formerly shunned all eye contact, and spent most of his days twisting his fingers and hands together as if in constant anguish. He had learned to look into Irene's face, and though he remained without speech, there existed a growing rapport between them. On this particular day he had seemed even more greatly disturbed than usual, cowering in a corner, starting violently when the other children approached. Had she not been given direct orders to the contrary, Irene would have devoted her time to offering him reassurance. But she was after all merely a domestic, and as such was forbidden to interfere. All she felt able to do in her present circumstances was to mention her concern to the child's supervisor, and linger a little longer than was necessary in the boy's vicinity as she went about the performance of her duties.

The storm broke at lunchtime. The children all took their meals in the large dining hall. It was the one time in their day when they were allowed to come together as one group, and every member of staff was required on hand to supervise.

Irene noticed the absence of little Guy as she went up and down the rows, wiping faces, spooning greens. She looked towards the members of staff responsible for his group, risking their censorship by asking after his whereabouts.

'He has been left behind,' the senior group leader said shortly. 'He's growing more and more introverted, thanks to all the attention he's been getting of late.' She swept an accusing eye across Irene's face before adding, 'He has to be encouraged to make his own decisions. Maybe if he gets hungry enough he will think to join us.'

Irene dared make no reply, she had no wish to lose her job by speaking the words on the tip of her tongue.

Lunchtime dragged on, and to Irene, watching the clock, it seemed that the children were deliberately slow with their meal. She could not help but think of the little boy left alone to suffer the torment of his nervous fantasies.

When the tables were cleared at last, and the children were being led away to their group activities, she scooped a handful of biscuits from the table and thrusting them into her apron pocket trod purposefully towards the room where she expected to find Guy still occupying the darkest corner.

Though she had been as quick as she could, and though she flung herself forward in a futile attempt to prevent the little ones seeing, she was too late to do anything about the carnage that leapt out at her the minute she opened the door.

As the children began to scream, Irene felt herself gag.

A small bundle of fur, unrecognisable now as the chirpy hamster that the children kept as a pet, hung limply from the boy's twisting hands; around his feet lay the squashed, flattened splashes of colour that had once swum back and forth in the overturned fish-tank, but more horrific by far than either of these were the bright blue feathers lodged in the blood around the boy's mouth, and the headless body of the budgerigar in the slowly swinging cage. . . .

'He was in torment, the poor little soul,' Irene said with a shudder.

'Who?' Janet asked, watching with a puzzled frown. Was this the breakthrough she was trying for?

Irene disappointed her. 'Guy, the little boy at Cherry Street. I felt so sorry for him, but they refused to let me help. I *could* have helped him, you know.' Her wide, grey eyes fastened earnestly on Janet's face. 'All he needed was love.'

'Isn't that what all children need? What you yourself needed as a child?' Gently the Care Officer tried to draw Irene out.

'Well, I found someone to love that very day,' Irene told her in a sudden change of mood. 'They tried to make out that I was somehow to blame for Guy's breakdown – said I'd given him too much attention. I told them where they could stuff their lousy job, and as I left – in a tearing hurry, let me tell you – I fell over the postman. Leastways, I thought he was a postman, seeing as how he was delivering the mail.' Her eyes grew merry at this recollection, and Janet allowed her to indulge in this little digression from the direction she knew was inevitable.

'You seem to have come in for more than one person's share of misery in so short a time,' she said sympathetically. 'How very undeserved.'

Terry Garland, believing he detected a note of criticism in her words, coloured above his fiery beard, but managed to refrain from pointing out that he had done the best he knew how for the girl in his care.

Ignoring them both, her face alight with tenderness, Irene embarked on a detailed account of the passage she still regarded as the most wonderful time of her life. . . .

She was enjoying herself enormously. She glanced around the crowded coffee-bar, drinking in the atmosphere of animated youth, and released a gusty sigh of pure pleasure before turning to smile at her companion.

Peter returned her smile with interest. His eyes had been fixed on her lively little face since they had entered this steamy, noisy place to take adjoining stools at the high counter.

'Do you like it here?' he asked, not really needing an answer, but eager to bring her attention back to himself.

'Oh, I do, I do,' Irene assured him earnestly. 'I've never been in a café before.'

'Coffee-bar, please. Don't call it a café or you'll offend the regulars.' He ducked as a group of young men passed behind him, feigning punches to his head as they called a greeting.

'Do you come here all the time?' Irene asked, observing that everyone seemed to know him.

'Not all the time, no. But pretty regularly. I meet my friends here – least, I did before I started at college.'

'You're at college?' Irene asked in surprise, and some confusion. 'But . . . but I thought . . .'

'You thought I was your own personal crash-barrier. And so you might, plowing into me like that. But I have to disillusion you, woman; Peter Rawding, second-year student and postman extraordinary, at your service.'

Irene was at a loss for words. Her accidental collision with this young man as she had charged from the Cherry Street premises had given him the opportunity to introduce himself, and ask her out, but he had told her nothing more than his name, and she had assumed, since he was in the act of delivering the mail, that he was employed full time as a postman. She began to feel something of a fool. She had accepted his invitation for this evening partly because she had no real friends and nowhere to go except back to her dismal bedsit, and partly because he had refused to release her arm until she had agreed to the meeting. Had she known he was a college student she would never have allowed herself to be persuaded.

'What's the matter? Is something wrong? You seemed to be enjoying yourself. What did I say?' Peter's broad, homely face registered concern.

'I thought . . .'. Well, I didn't do very well at school. I didn't know you were a student.'

113

'What has that to do with anything?' He was genuinely puzzled. 'I don't see the connection.'

'It's just that, well, you must be very clever, and I'm not. Besides, students are . . . students are stuck up.'

His roar of laughter was lost in the general hubbub, but Irene heard, and her face flooded with quick colour.

'Hey, I'm sorry. I'm not laughing at you, honestly. Please, Irene.' He caught her arm as she would have slid from her stool. 'Don't get mad. I'm no different than anyone else 'cept I'm probably a bit poorer. Students don't get much of a grant, and that's why I'm working the summer vacation as an auxiliary with the Post Office. Don't let the fact that I'm a student put you off. I'm not a bit stuck up, really.'

Despite her initial qualms Irene continued dating Peter, discovering a warm, sensitive nature beneath his robust zest for life. He was not exactly handsome, she decided on their second date. His face had more of a 'lived-in' look about it than any of the pop stars currently in vogue. He was very tall, his six feet and one inch making her five-feet-three tiny in comparison, and his thick black hair had a tendency to become unruly. A sprinkling of freckles across the bridge of his nose denied any pretence to maturity, and his eyes were decidedly green. He was the first real friend Irene had made of her own volition, and all the warmth of her starved, unhappy youth went out to meet him.

Untutored in the art of money-management and careless of material possessions, her lack of employment troubled Irene only in so far as she missed the children of Cherry Street. It was not until the end of the month when the agent called to collect the rent on her bedsit that her situation caused her any concern. She was unable to pay him. She had no money, and, worse, was no longer provided with her meals and had no idea how to shop or budget for food. The money she'd had in her purse when she left Cherry Street was frittered away on high-priced 'convenience' meals that she invariably wasted or managed to spoil on the greasy, two-ringed burner that did duty as a cooker.

For several days she contrived to keep Peter in ignorance of her plight, but weakness induced by hunger brought her close to fainting, and she was obliged to explain her circumstances.

114

'I can't believe this, Irene.' Peter stared at her aghast. 'You are starving, and virtually homeless – and this in the twentieth century.'

'I don't know what the date has to do with it,' Irene said with a rueful grimace. 'All I know is that I have to get my hands on some money.'

'So claim from the dole, or the Social Security. That's what it's for.'

'Oh, no. I couldn't do that.' Irene shrank away from him. She wanted no contact with people like that. They might take her penniless state as an admission of an inability to cope and seek to imprison her in yet another institution.

'Why ever not?' Peter was asking with a touch of asperity. 'You are being ridiculous.'

'Please, Peter. Don't be mad at me. I can't, that's all. I just can't.' Though she had made no conscious decision to deceive Peter about the events in her past Irene found a full admission of the facts impossible to contemplate. How then could she tell him why she was so reluctant to approach the authorities? Her distress became increasingly evident, the shadows under her eyes and the deepening hollows below her cheekbones serving only to emphasise her very real fear of making any formal application for help.

Peter softened in his attitude, feeling the exasperation of moments before melt away as he studied the delicate planes of her face, the long sweep of her lashes against the curve of her cheek, and the silken fall of her silver-blonde hair. 'Oh, Irene. What am I to do with you?' he asked softly, a light kindling in the depths of his eyes that rendered an answer unnecessary.

Helped and encouraged by Peter, Irene managed to stave off eviction and starvation. She found a new job as a nursery assistant in a small, privately owned place that took twenty-six children on a daily basis. The wage was even less than she had been getting from Cherry Street, but at least she was doing something that gave her satisfaction – and her meals were included. From the meagre surplus after she had paid the rent she repaid the money she had borrowed from Peter.

'I don't really need this, Irene. Keep it, buy yourself something nice. Some new curtains, or something to cheer up this place.' Peter sent a quick glance around the small, dismal room, and repressed a shudder. Cracked brown linoleum, scarred and broken furniture, and a threadbare bed-settee were not his idea of home. 'Why do you stay here, anyway? Couldn't you share a place with somebody? Somewhere a bit better? Or maybe you should think about going back home?'

'I'm fine right where I am,' Irene said firmly. 'And I don't want to go home. I . . . I don't get on very well with my mother.'

'But I worry about you alone in this place. It doesn't seem right, and I'm sure you can't be comfortable.'

'Well, I'm not here all that much,' Irene said, looking around as if seeing the place for the first time. 'Only evenings and weekends, and not all the time then, thanks to you.'

'I'll be off back to college soon, Irene,' he reminded her gently. 'I'll come home as often as I can, but I can't make any promises. I'm kept pretty busy with my studies and so on.'

Irene turned away to hide her sinking dismay. 'Yes, I suppose you are,' she said in strangled tones. 'But you don't have to worry about coming back here. I'll be OK. After all, I managed well enough before I met you.'

'Hey, what's all this, then? Am I getting the brush-off?' Peter placed his arms about her, steeling himself for her familiar tense withdrawal. To his surprise he felt Irene relax against him.

'Oh, Peter. I'm going to miss you so much,' she whispered, her face buried against his chest.

She cares! She really cares! The words sang dizzily round and round in his head, and he hugged her exuberantly. 'I'll be back, Irene. As often as I'm able. And I'll think about you all the time. Promise you'll wait for me – promise?' He felt her head move in a small nod of confirmation, and hurried on excitedly. 'I'll write to you. Every week. And you must write to me. Then – then I'll be home for the Christmas holiday, and maybe you could spend Christmas at my house. Mum and Dad would love to have you, I'm certain.'

Once Peter returned to college Irene devoted herself more and more to the children attending the day nursery. These were of a different nature than those disadvantaged unfortunates attending Cherry Street. They were a hotchpotch of happy, outward-going youngsters enrolled at the nursery under no special criteria other than their need of responsible supervision during the time their parents were out at work. They were admitted regardless of age, race, sex or colour, and seemed to find no difficulty fitting into the relaxed, informal programme that governed their day.

Irene found herself much more closely involved with the children here than had previously been the case, and her letters to Peter were full of 'Johnny did's', and 'Cathy said's'.

At this time only one small grub attacked her rosy apple, causing a persistent, disturbing unease, and this in the small defenceless person of the nursery's most recent intake. Little Charles was a Down's syndrome baby; his Mongolism, stamped clearly on his features, rendered him helpless, and created his own special needs.

Irene had been present when Charles's mother first brought the child to the nursery. She caught herself staring in awed fascination.

'Irene, I want you to meet Charles and his mother.' Margery, the senior qualified nurse, had not been blind to Irene's empathy with the children in her care, and was confident of enlisting her aid.

Irene approached the trio with some hesitation, uncertain what attitude to take. Did she pretend to find nothing unusual about little Charles, or did she openly acknowledge his disability?

She was spared further speculation as Margery briskly stated the details concerning the child's affliction, pausing now and again to confirm certain facts with his mother.

'So I would like you to make Charles your protege, if you will.' Margery held Irene's gaze, willing her co-operation as she concluded her recital. 'He must be made to feel secure and cared for before we can attempt potty-training or any constructive education.'

'Education?' Charles's mother was a plump little woman, smartly dressed in a navy-blue suit. She looked to be about thirty years old from the cut of her hair and her figure, but care had traced premature lines on her brow, and pinched up the generous mouth. The mouth now fell slack as she gazed from

117

Margery to Irene as if she feared them insane.

'Charles can never be educated,' she said, clutching the child defensively to her breast. 'You don't seem to understand.'

'Mrs Reynolds, we understand perfectly,' Margery was swift to assure her. 'I worked with handicapped children during my training, some of them far more severely disabled than your little boy. Leave him to us, I'm sure he is capable of learning a great many things which will enable him to reach some level of independence.'

'Oh, if only I could believe that.' Her longing to accept Margery's word was a palpable thing, her face suffused with maternal yearning.

'Trust me, Mrs Reynolds. Trust me.' Margery took the child into her arms and motioned for his mother to leave.

Charles appeared not to notice her going; his flat little face with its drooling mouth and slitted eyes betrayed no emotion.

During the course of the day Irene was given to understand that Charles had been entrusted to their care because of some personal friendship between the nursery owner and his parents. In the ordinary way, he would have been sent to a special school, or long-term hospital if he had not been allowed to remain at home, a constant charge on his mother's energies. His father, she was told, wanted the child out of the way. His mother did not. When the issue began to look like destroying their marriage a compromise was reached, and Charles was enrolled at the nursery leaving his mother free to spend more time with his older brother and sister, and make what effort she could towards patching up her relationship with her husband.

From her initial hesitation Irene developed a real affection for the little lad who sat so helpless yet so stoical in his chair while the other three-year-olds played so busily and actively about him. Following Margery's lead, she did what she could to stimulate the child. Using whatever time she could spare from her regular duties she played with him, talked to him and tried to teach him to walk. Slowly, painfully so it seemed, he began to respond. By the merest flicker he betrayed an interest in her presence, seeming to know how she longed for some indication that she was winning through. The company of the other children appeared to delight him, and he smiled continually as

118

they attempted to involve him in their games, throwing his limbs about in enthusiastic imitation of their co-ordinated activities.

It was only later when she felt they had established some rapport that Irene began to notice the change that took place in Charles each weekend. He was collected by his mother on Friday evenings, a happy little boy, and was returned by her on Monday mornings, an inanimate vegetable.

Irene worried about this transformation, and was finally driven to seek Margery's professional advice.

'It's nothing, Irene. Just that he lacks the attention we all give him when he's away over the weekends. That's why permanent hospital care is often better for children like Charles who are unable to cope with breaks of continuity.'

'But he has his mum and dad, and his brother and sister. Surely they spend some time with him.'

'Possibly. But you have to remember, in the average household there are things going on, chores to be done, jobs that need completion – calls on everyone's time that Charles is unable to understand.'

Irene accepted the logic of this explanation, but she studied Charles's little face, and continued to worry.

The approach of Christmas brought Irene to such a pitch of excitement that all else became secondary. Peter was coming home. For ten whole days they would be together. He had written to say that his parents wished her to stay with them over the holiday, and she was to spend Christmas as their guest. This invitation caused Irene such concern when it arrived, she was at a loss to know what to reply. The thought of staying in their home and living side by side with Peter sent butterflies soaring in her stomach; but the thought of meeting his parents, perhaps having to lie to them about her background, made her write to turn down their offer.

Peter ignored her lame explanation of a promise to attend a get-together with the other tenants in the house where she had the bedsit, refused to consider her excuse of having nothing to wear, and brushed aside her painfully embarrassed admission of being unable to afford Christmas presents as a return for their hospitality.

119

'They are not looking for presents, Irene. Or some fancy-dressed mannequin. They want to meet you, and have you join us for Christmas, and I shall take it as an insult if you refuse to come.'

So, with her one change of clothes in a carrier-bag, a bunch of flowers that had cost her a week's spending money, and a heart beating like an erratic steam-hammer, Irene presented herself for their inspection.

'Don't be nervous, Irene. They'll love you, and you them. I'm certain you will all get along marvellously together.' Peter squeezed her hand as he hurried her lagging footsteps along the short drive to the front of the house.

After her initial shyness had worn away, they had indeed all found each other agreeable.

If Peter's mother had reservations about her only son taking up with a girl who could do nothing to help further his career, she was wise enough to keep them to herself. It was early days yet in their relationship; Peter was very young, time enough to start worrying if this attachment held through his years at university.

Of this Peter and Irene were in no doubt. Their affection for each other deepened over the holiday, and before the New Year dawned, they were making promises to become engaged to be married.

Nineteen-seventy-two augured well for Irene. She was young, she was loved and in love, and the ache to find the child she had lost was at last receding. As the girl in the children's home had pointed out, she would have other children. Peter's children, Irene thought with a rush of warm anticipation. A little boy to help fill the empty space in her heart, and perhaps a little girl to keep him company. In the meantime she was happy to wait, to savour the joy of her first romance, and devote her time to the care of the children who attended the day nursery.

Little Charles started back after the holiday along with the other children, his affliction more severely marked by his total lack of interest in the bright, shiny new toys Santa appeared to have distributed so liberally among his playmates.

'What's the matter, Charlie, my love? Did Santa Claus forget you?' Irene asked as she lifted the child into her lap.

'Not on your life.' The laughing group of children swarming about one of Irene's colleagues parted to reveal a tousle-haired girl on her hands and knees. It was she who addressed Irene.

'Most of this stuff belongs to him.' She indicated a large wooden truck filled with multi-coloured bricks, a gaily painted Noah's Ark, and many other bits and pieces being prodded, pulled, poked or hugged by the nursery inmates. 'I warned his mum not to bring so much stuff – the other kids are bound to break them – but she said they were meant to be played with.'

'Well, I suppose they were, only it would be rather nice if Charles got to play with some of them too.' Irene pointed out.

The girl rose from her knees, smoothed down her skirt, and came to speak out of hearing of their charges. 'He isn't interested, Irene. I tried to get him to join us, he was getting quite knowing before the Christmas break, but I think he's forgotten us all.' She studied the little boy sitting so still on Irene's lap before glancing away to the unflagging bustle of activity created by his contemporaries. 'He's growing worse if you ask me.'

'And ever likely to if you allow the others to take away his toys without including him in their play,' Irene said tartly. 'Charles needs to be stimulated, not ignored.'

'So get on with it, then. If you're so clever, stimulate him. Let's see what sort of genius he turns out to be.' The girl flounced away leaving Irene protectively hugging the unrespon-sive lump that was Charles.

Her colleague's words, so reminiscent of those of the housekeeper at Cherry Street, stirred an unwilling chord in Irene's memory. Was she attempting too much, she wondered? Was she wrong to believe she could help this poor unfortunate? Dreadful recollections of jewel-bright feathers clinging about a child's mouth caused her to look again into Charles's face. Moisture oozed from his pendulous lower lip. His flat, blank eyes gave back no expression.

Very gently Irene lifted the boy from her lap, and placed him on the floor. Better if she allowed him to find his own way, she decided, moving from his painful stillness towards the nucleus of chattering children, like a shivering animal seeking a fire.

For all her brave determination not to become too closely involved, Irene was unable to ignore Charles's special need of loving attention, and found herself drifting back to her former routine. He was the child to whom she devoted any spare moment in her day, and his was the face she most delighted to see creased into a smile. After many weeks of patient application she managed, under Margery's tutelage, to teach him to form a few words, and his unintelligible burblings slowly began to take on meaning. He could now convey some of his most basic feelings, and his training went forward with new impetus.

Charles's mother was a woman transformed. There was hope now in her eyes as she gazed at her son, and pride in her voice when she spoke of his achievements. Irene felt her time and patience amply rewarded.

NINE

Easter came and went, bringing a sheaf of spring flowers and an expensive-looking box of chocolates from Peter. He was working hard for some exams, and did not get home for the holiday. Irene lived for his weekly letters, reading each one at least twice a day, carrying it in her handbag until she received the next. She wrote long enthusiastic screeds in return, sending her love and repeating her promise to wait for him. They fixed the date of their engagement to coincide with Irene's eighteenth birthday on August the third. She counted the days.

The day nursery had closed only briefly over Easter, and it opened its doors as usual at seven o'clock on Wednesday morning.

Charles and his mother almost fell over the step, a full hour ahead of their customary time.

'My word, you're very early.' Margery greeted them with a show of surprise. 'Couldn't you wait to get back to us, Charles? Been missing all of us, have you?'

The child, sitting stolidly in his pushchair, made no response, but his mother answered for him. 'Yes, yes I'm sure he has. Look, I'll leave him with you. I have to get back.' She appeared unusually flustered, and was turning away even as she spoke.

Irene watched Margery take Charles indoors and lift him from the pushchair. She set him firmly on his feet while keeping a grip on his hand, fully expecting him to demonstrate his newly acquired ability to walk. Charles sat down with a bump which appeared to startle him out of his habitual stoical acceptance of all such minor mishaps, for he immediately set up a loud wail.

'Oh dear, are we feeling touchy today? That's what holidays do for you. Come on, let's give it one more try.' She lifted Charles to his feet trying to coax him to the point of balance.

His cries grew more distressed and he sagged at the knees, dragging on Margery's hands as she took his weight. 'OK, lazy-bones, have it your way. No wonder your mum was so anxious to get away.' She lowered him to his hands and knees, prepared to wait while he performed his usual crab-like method of locomotion. Once again the child confounded her expectations by dropping to his tummy, making no effort to move. Margery scooped him out of the way of the door, and thrust him at Irene. 'Take him to the playroom, Irene. I expect the holiday has unsettled him again. It's all those Easter goodies, Charles, isn't it?' she said easily as she handed him over.

Charles grizzled and cried, unusual for him, throughout most of the time it took the staff to greet the other children and get them settled. Once this was done, and her own particular charges were occupied, Irene gave her full attention to soothing the boy. For once Charles failed to respond to her efforts, refusing to be comforted, and sending up fresh wails to her every attempt. He seemed to find difficulty sitting in his chair, yet he refused to walk even when Irene held his hands. It took some time for the light to dawn.

'Oh, Charles. How stupid. Of course I know your trouble,' Irene told him, the frown of perplexity clearing from her brow. 'Why didn't you tell me? Come with me, love. I'll soon have you nice and comfy.' Chiding herself and him for their mutual stupidity Irene bore him away to the toilets.

Since their best attempts at potty-training had been met with unreliable results, Charles was still wearing nappies. Irene placed him on the changing-table and quickly stripped off his pants. 'Now then, my lad. Let's get you out of this,' she said, unfastening the nappy pins. 'Why, that's odd. You're as dry as—' Her words were stopped in her throat as she lifted Charles's legs to pull the folded towelling from under his bottom. His howls began again, deep, guttural expressions of pain that fell on deaf ears as she gazed at the fiery marks on his buttocks. 'Oh, Charles.' Unshed tears clogged her throat as she gazed. 'Oh, Charles. You poor, hurt little lamb.'

Irene did not know what to do. She gathered Charles up into her arms, and tried to stifle his screams. 'Shh, shh. There, there.' She paced the tiled washrooms with him held against her shoulder, the moisture from his eyes and nose and throat making a hot, wet patch against her skin, soaking into the fabric of her dress. 'Oh, Charles, don't cry. Please don't cry,' she begged, then fell to chewing her bottom lip in an agony of indecision. Wanting nothing so much as to rush out of this echoing tomb, and confront the professional staff with the evidence of those shameful blemishes, she did nothing. As the child quietened, she risked another, more searching, examination of his body, releasing her breath on a quivering sigh of grudging relief once she had assured herself the injuries were confined to his buttocks.

All that long, worrying day while little Charles grizzled and fretted, Irene shared his torment. But hers was a torment of the mind. She knew the path she should be treading, and was afraid. If she was wrong in her assumption that Charles had been deliberately maltreated, and she caused an outcry, she would be adding more hurt and pain to the burden already carried by his mother. If she was right . . . if she was right, and she continued to ignore the evidence of her own eyes – she closed them as an involuntary shudder shook her body – that would make her every bit as callous as the deviate who had inflicted those wounds.

But if she told anyone of her suspicions, might she not lose this job as she had the one at Cherry Street? . . . And if she didn't, if she kept her fears hidden, how could she then live with herself?

Finally, Irene went to seek out Margery, and after a great deal of hesitation was persuaded to confess that she had done so because she was worried about 'a rash she had discovered on Charlie's bum,' she improvised, losing courage at the last moment.

Margery fixed her with a commanding stare. 'Now, come on, Irene. You know enough to recognise nappy-rash when you see it. And pressure sores too, by now.'

'Well, it isn't either of those,' Irene assured her. 'Perhaps you'd best look for yourself.'

Wearing an expression of resigned scepticism Margery followed Irene to the playroom where Charles was lying stretched out on his stomach on one of the rugs used for the

125

children's rest periods.

'I, er, do you think we should take him to the lavatories? You could use the changing-table,' Irene suggested.

'No, I'm sure we can manage right here, can't we, Charles?' Margery rolled the child on to his side, and lifted the towelling nappy away from his skin. She became suddenly still. For several long heartbeats she neither moved nor drew breath. Finally, she turned her head to send an upward slanting gaze at Irene's face. 'You say he has these marks all over his buttocks?' she asked, deliberately keeping her voice without expression.

Irene nodded.

'Who else has seen them? Who else have you told?'

'Why, no one. Nobody. I . . . I didn't think . . . I wanted to know what you thought.' Irene's heart beat a mad tattoo. Had she made some mistake?

'Let's get him into the lavatories, away from this din.' Darting quick, furtive glances at those of her colleagues who were engaged in their various duties about the room, she lifted Charles from the mat. 'Come on, Charles, let Aunty Margy take a look. Now there's a good boy, then. He's a brave little man'. The sing-song baby chant she had employed to soothe the child stopped abruptly the minute she had him out of his clothes.

'Have you ever seen marks like this on him before?' she demanded sharply of Irene, who hovered nervously at her elbow.

'No, never. I . . .' She swallowed the urge to rush into an impassioned declaration of her own opinion, and struggled to meet Margery's gaze.

'But you do know this – this rash, as you choose to call it, is not the result of natural causes?'

Irene hung her head. Here, now, was the moment she had been agonising over the whole of this terrible day.

'Answer me, Irene. You do know?' Margery pressed.

Lifting her head, Irene braced herself, and gambled every-thing on her reply. 'Yes, I know,' she said softly. 'I've seen the terrible things some people do to their children.'

'So what do we do?'

Irene started. She had believed that Margery, in her

professional capacity, would find no difficulty in deciding their next move. 'The police?' she ventured.

'What? And Charles's parents thick as thieves with the owner of this place? I should think not!'

'But . . . but we have to do something. We can't allow it to go on.' Shock and outrage lent an edge to her voice as she stared belligerently at her colleague.

'No, of course we can't. It's just . . . look, supposing we talk about this? There has to be some other way.' Silence stretched between them, taut and vibrating as a violin string.

'He's been burnt, you know. With a cigarette end, probably,' Margery said suddenly as little Charles gave vent to a hoarse, guttural outpouring that was his attempt at speech. 'Over, and over, and over again, somebody has applied a burning cigarette to his skin.' Hysteria was building in her, threatening to spill. 'Can you imagine what that must be like?'

'Stop it!' Irene covered her ears, her cry abruptly snapping Margery to her senses.

'I'm sorry. I didn't mean to go on like that. Let's get Charles dressed.' She checked her wrist-watch. 'His mother will be here to collect him very soon. We have to reach some decision before she arrives.'

'Should we . . . do you think it would help if we told the nursery owner? After all, if they are friendly with Charles's parents, they might be able to do something,' Irene suggested.

'Like what? They can hardly ask for a written promise or anything. Besides, I'm not certain they would do very much at all. Charles's mother pays twice the going rate for him to come here. If that was to stop . . .'

'Oh, but surely money wouldn't enter into it,' Irene protested hotly.

'Maybe. Maybe not. This nursery is a business venture, don't forget. Why else do you think they employ unqualified staff? And that's no reflection on you, but we seldom see the people who own the place. How can we be sure they'd welcome our interference?'

In the end, after arguing the matter back and forth, it was decided they would ask Charles's mother to spare them a few minutes in private. They were both of the opinion that the child's injuries had been inflicted by his father, since he was the parent opposed to keeping the boy at home, and they hoped that the knowledge of their support would give Mrs Reynolds the courage to take steps to prevent such a thing happening again.

The ensuing interview was begun in painful embarrassment for all concerned. Charles's mother first flatly denied all knowledge of her son's injuries, then broke down and confessed, amid floods of tears, that she had been present when they were inflicted, but unable to do anything to prevent it.

'Would you like me to speak with your husband, Mrs Reynolds?' Margery offered with genuine sympathy for the woman's plight.

Mrs Reynolds's response was a frantic, gabbling plea to the contrary. 'No, oh, no. Please, please don't approach him. He'd kill me, and Charles too if he thought you'd found out. Promise me, I beg you, that you'll do nothing, say nothing to him.' She grabbed Margery by the arm, her fingernails biting deeply into the soft flesh as she strove to wring a promise from her.

'All right. Don't get so upset. It was just a suggestion.' Margery tore herself free of the punishing grip and endeavoured to soothe Charles's mother.

The woman was utterly distraught. 'I couldn't help it, you know. I couldn't do anything to stop it,' she repeated over and over while Irene and Margery sat helplessly on the miniature chairs in the pleasant little room that was set aside for small groups of the children to use for special activities. After a while she fell silent, and when it seemed she had regained some control Margery made a further attempt to offer assistance.

'We could speak with someone from the NSPCC, if it would help. I'm sure you would find them very discreet and understanding,' she said, and was completely unprepared for the shriek of rage that issued from Mrs Reynolds's wide, gaping mouth.

'Don't you dare! Don't you ever dare! Haven't I told you I couldn't help it? Do you want to see me scorned even more than I am already? Made to look some sort of freak for having ill-treated my child?' Her anger abated as suddenly as it had begun, and Mrs Reynolds began to whine. 'He has to be kept in check, doesn't he? He has to be punished when he does wrong. Surely even you can see that? How else am I ever going to keep him under control?'

Margery and Irene exchanged startled glances. What on earth was this woman saying?

'It's bad enough that he looks like he does, isn't it, without having him behave like a monster into the bargain?' Shrillness returned to pitch her voice on the edge of a shriek.

Margery cut sharply across this seemingly endless cant. Deliberately injecting her voice with cold authority she snapped out her orders: 'Sit down, Mrs Reynolds. And be quiet.'

To her surprise the woman meekly obeyed, and Margery was left, panting with barely suppressed fury. Swallowing a burning desire to slap the woman senseless she took a deep breath to steady herself, and began applying low-voiced, pertinent questions.

Charles's mother answered woodenly, only her questioner's punishing gaze wringing the answers from her. There was little trace in the stiff, barely controlled woman, of the doting parent who daily delivered her son to their care.

A picture emerged that was not so very unusual for all its pathos, of an average, loving family driven apart by the birth of an abnormal child. Unable to cope with the strain, and her inner feelings of guilt, Charles's mother had used many small cruelties to wreak retribution on her unfortunate son. Each time she hurt him she was punishing herself, torturing her soul for having brought forth this sub-human child. Totally unsuspecting of his wife's mental conflict, concerned only with the physical stress to which they, as a family, were subject, Charles's father had urged that the boy be placed in a hospital for the mentally handicapped. His wife had been adamant in her refusal. She needed the child around. Wore his disability like her albatross, feeling the world should be made aware of her penance. The more demands her imperfect son made on her health and strength, the easier she coped with the shame of his birth.

Margery and Irene listened in silence as she poured it all out; the weeks and months of misery, and breast beating that had followed diagnosis of his Mongolism. Her inability to accept

Charles as he was. The progress they had made with him at the nursery, his infinitesimal advancement, served only to exacerbate her self-blame. Other women had babies who were sound of mind and body. What had she done that hers should be neither?

Resisting the urge to sympathise, fighting her instinctive desire to offer consolation to the inconsolable, Margery summoned the cold face of professionalism. 'Mrs Reynolds . . .' She hugged her arms across her chest and took a slow pace about the room, carefully avoiding Irene's horrified gaze. 'Mrs Reynolds,' she began again, 'if you wish to avoid a scandal of the worst kind, I suggest that you go home, and tell your husband that you have suffered a change of heart. Urge him to take every step possible to have Charles admitted to a long-term hospital without delay.' She held up a restraining hand forestalling argument as Mrs Reynolds began to protest, and went on in the same commanding tone. 'In the meantime I want you to go to your doctor and ask him for help.'

Mrs Reynolds collapsed completely. 'I can't. I can't,' she moaned. And now Margery's pity flooded to meet her. 'It's not Charles's fault. I know that. He can't help his illness. But I don't dare tell our doctor what I've done. I'm so ashamed. So dreadfully ashamed, and so sorry. Can you understand? No, no, of course not.' She answered her own appeal, giving them no time to offer a reply. 'How could you? How could anyone? I used to read about women doing this sort of thing. In the newspapers . . . I . . . I always thought what wickedness. Wickedness,' she repeated, beating her clenched hands on her knee. 'If only there had been someone to talk to. Someone who knows what it's like . . .'

'There are societies for the support of parents with handicapped children, Mrs Reynolds,' Margery reminded her quietly. 'You might have approached one of those.'

'No, no, I couldn't. It's not Charles's handicap I need help with. Can't you see that? It's my own. My own.'

'Mrs Reynolds.' Irene spoke for the first time since they had entered the room. 'I think I might know someone who could help you.'

Both Margery and Mrs Reynolds turned to her in surprise.

130

Irene swallowed her sudden nervousness and continued resolutely: 'There is a group – no, a children's home, not far from here. The house-father is a man named Terry Garland. He's a social worker, and a Child Care Officer, and he knows all about . . . about this sort of thing. I'm sure you could talk to him. He's very understanding. And I know he will help you, if you will let him.'

'I . . . I don't know. It's not that easy.' Mrs Reynolds was openly swayed.

Before she could reject the offer, Margery urged Irene to use the office phone to call up this paragon. 'Ask him to come here right away.'

'I just don't understand you, Irene. None of this makes any sense,' Terry Garland burst out angrily. Leaping to his feet, he strode about the room, his flinty gaze occasionally sweeping both women who gazed back at him in a mixture of surprise and dismay. 'You knew enough to call for help when you recognised young Charles was being maltreated – Why the hell did you neglect your own child's needs?' He leaned over her in a threatening attitude.

Irene shrank back in her chair. 'I . . . I don't . . . I *did* call you. I *did*!' She began to weep softly.

Janet Fouracres chose not to intervene. Maybe now she would learn the full story.

'Ah, yes. I was forgetting. You *did*,' Terry said with heavy sarcasm. 'When it suited you – you . . . ahh!' He turned away with an angry exclamation.

Irene continued to weep. 'Nobody wanted to know,' she said finally between gulping sobs. 'I tried . . . I really tried . . . nobody would listen. Nobody.'

Terry could not bring himself to meet his colleague's eye; though she remained unaware, Irene had just made a sad indictment of his professional behaviour. He turned to the window, hiding behind the pretence of looking out, though it grieved him most bitterly to admit the fact that he had failed Irene, just as she said.

Janet allowed Irene time to recover before asking, 'Did you see your doctor? Did you think of that?'

'Yes, I saw my doctor,' Irene blazed. 'And a fat lot of good that did. He wanted to put me on a course of tranquillisers. I tried them, they didn't work, and anyway I don't want to talk about it.' A mutinous expression settled over her face, and she folded her arms across her chest as she brought her gaze to the other woman's face.

Recognising the signal, Janet allowed her to have her way. Deliberately changing her line of questioning she brought Irene to discuss her relationship with Peter, and their subsequent engagement.

'Peter's folks were not pleased. They didn't openly say as much in my hearing, of course, but I could tell.' Irene was calmer now, and more tractable.

'But you went ahead with your plans anyway?' Janet asked.

Sensing a longish session Terry abandoned his pretence of looking out of the window to return to his seat, where he lounged, one leg crossed over the other, the fingers of his right hand playing with the wiry curls of his beard.

'Yes. Yes, we went ahead.' Irene began to show signs of agitation, bringing a lift to Janet's eyebrows. She made no comment, however, merely flicked a swift, interrogatory glance in Terry's direction then looked away as he lifted his shoulders a fraction in a gesture that underlined that he was as puzzled by this shift in Irene's manner as she.

'And you got engaged?' Janet prompted cautiously.

'We got engaged,' Irene concurred. 'With all the usual ceremony,' she added drily. 'We even went so far as to have a notice inserted in the press – that bloody, bloody notice!' Her fist pounded the arm of her chair, and she caught her underlip between her teeth as her voice slithered and slid like water-washed gravel.

It was that dignified insertion in the local newspaper that brought an end to Irene's year of hope. Dorothy Cooper read it through with unbridled anger before crushing the paper to pulp between her fingers.

'I'll kill her! I swear it! I'll swing for the little sod!' Hurling the crumpled newspaper toward the firegrate, she rummaged through her handbag for lipstick and comb. So enraged that she could scarcely control her trembling hands, she made a conscious effort to soften the puckered line of her mouth into a receptive curve for the crimson lip-colour.

Years of heavy drinking had caught up with Dorothy, showing in the puffy bags beneath her eyes, and the loose, unhealthy flesh blurring the line of her jaw. She had been on the way to obesity before a final humiliating and painful showdown with John Forster had caused him to pack his bags leaving Dorothy alone and distraught, unable to eat, drinking herself to skeletal emaciation, a shadow of her former self. Folds of skin, slack and wrinkled, hung like badly washed garments from her shrunken frame, all claim to beauty lost to the contents of too many bottles.

'Bitch!' she said with chilling venom, flinging her lipstick back into her bag before kicking her feet free of her broken-down slippers to squeeze them into painfully high stiletto-heeled shoes. 'Engaged, is she? To Master Peter Rawding. Well, we shall see about that. Yes, we shall certainly see.'

Charging blindly from the house, mouthing a constant harangue beneath her breath, she cannoned into Sandra about to cross the front step, sweeping her aside without apology or breaking her step.

'Hey! Where are you off to in such a tearing hurry?' Recovering her breath, Sandra called after her mother's fast-retreating figure.

Dorothy did not trouble to look round.

A look of utter disgust twisting her pretty face, Sandra watched her until she was out of sight before turning into the house. A mature sixteen-year-old, Sandra had all the poise of a woman twice that age, and she did not suffer her mother's addiction to the bottle with anything approaching understanding or good grace. Spoiled and indulged as her sister had never been, she expected her own wants and desires to take priority, and was constantly ashamed, embarrassed and angered when Dorothy's over-indulgence spoiled her schemes. Closing the door behind her, she entered the untidy sitting room where but for a burning curiosity in respect of her mother's haste she would have ignored the ball of paper lying in the hearth.

Tugging at the tightly wadded newsprint, tearing it again and again, despite the care she exercised, she flattened it as best she could, and was taken aback to discover nothing more earth-shattering than the Births, Marriages, and Deaths columns. A swift scan of the almost illegible print proved unrewarding, and she was about to consign the paper to the firegrate when her sister's name, seeming to leap from the smudged print, arrested her attention.

'Ha, so dear Irene is about to get married,' she said musingly. Sitting back on her heels she considered this piece of information. What was so startling about the fact of her sister's engagement to send her mother racing from the house? Giving up the guessing game, she folded the tattered paper carefully about that particular piece, and propped it behind the clock on the mantel, intending to take the matter up on Dorothy's return.

Had Irene, her fiancé and his parents not lingered overlong at the start of their evening of celebration, Dorothy might even yet have been cheated of her cruel revenge on her oldest daughter.

The evening had begun well enough; Peter's mother and father, having set aside their misgivings, had invited friends to join them and the newly engaged couple for drinks and dinner. The plan was to take apéritifs in the Rawdings' small but delightful garden before moving on to the restaurant where a table had been booked. For once the weather was in kind co-operation, and Irene radiated happiness as she moved across the sunlit lawn handing out drinks and canapés. Every now and again she would catch Peter's eye and smile, and it was as if they were alone in a corner of Eden.

As the sun slid down the sky, and the languid scent of roses thickened on the warm air, Peter's mother belatedly signalled that the time had come for their departure.

Before glasses could be raised to drain the last sip of champagne, a raucous bellow tore through the romantically staged setting, whipping all heads round in amazement, and fastening an icy grip on Irene's heart.

'Where is she? Where's my daughter? And don't tell me to

shush, you whey-faced bitch! She's here somewhere, I know. And I intend to find her.'

Her face blanched a sickly white, Irene sent swift, darting glances about the enclosed garden, searching desperately for somewhere to hide.

'There!' The accusing finger was pointed straight at her, and Irene cringed as Dorothy burst from the restraining grasp Peter's father had taken on her, to hurtle across the lawn.

The guests fell back, forming two separate ranks of festive colour through which Dorothy advanced on her daughter.

Recovering from the stunned surprise that held him immobile, Peter started forwards intending to block her approach. It would have taken an army to halt Dorothy in her present state of dementia. She knocked Peter's husky young bulk aside as if she was dealing with a child, and swept on to confront Irene.

'So this is where you have been hiding yourself,' she accused the cowering girl. 'This is where you came to practise your dirty little games.'

'Now just a minute.' Peter's father joined mother and daughter, determined to silence this woman's tongue.

'Don't you just a minute me, you bastard! I suppose you're like all the rest – taken in by her bloody Miss Injured expression. Well, let me tell you something now, she's not the innocent she's been making out. No, not by a long chalk.'

Peter went to stand by his fiancée who was staring transfixed, her horrified gaze and deathly countenance clearly pronouncing the fear she was in. He tried to draw her into a protective embrace, but Irene was as if turned to stone. Cold and unyielding she stood in the circle of his arms, her eyes never leaving Dorothy's contorted face.

'Oh, got you on a string an' all, has she? Well, never was too particular. Young or old, married or promised, never made no difference to this little tramp.'

A low, gasping moan from the girl at his side drew a forceful response from Peter. 'I think you had better go.' He attempted to manhandle Dorothy towards the house and the street, but she fought him off, and they grappled in front of the shocked and horrified guests like a pair of street urchins.

'Let go of me! Let go of me, blast you. I'm not leaving here 'til I've told that fornicating little bitch there just what she's worth.' She kicked out at Peter's shins.

'Don't you dare say any more.' Panting from his exertions Peter resolutely maintained the grip he'd secured on her flailing hands.

'You wouldn't be so keen to stand up for her if you knew what she did.' Dorothy fixed a look of pitying contempt on her captor. 'Told you she's had a baby, did she? By my bloody fiance? Lovely, isn't it? My own daughter, and the man she'd always thought of as her father.'

A murmur of shock rippled around the assembled guests, and Peter involuntarily loosened his hold on the struggling woman.

'Thought I'd never find out, didn't you? Thought I'd settle for some cock and bull yarn.'

'That's not true! I never said—' Irene bit back her cry of protest as she caught sight of Peter's face.

Her mother was swift to jump into the small pool of silence. 'No, that's right. You never said.' Her expression was frightening. Lips drawn back from her teeth, eyes slitted apertures of hate. 'And no wonder,' she hissed. The sudden shift from shouted rage to sibilant malice caused Irene to draw back. 'You crept about behind my back, you and him. Made a laughing stock out of me with your dirty, incestuous carryings on. Well, let me tell you now. I'll get even with you, slut!' Like lightning her hand flashed, snapping Irene's head to and fro as she slapped it one way then another across her daughter's cheeks.

The crack of flesh meeting flesh jolted Peter and his father from their shocked inaction. Irene's cry of pain lending resolution to their action they pinned Dorothy's arms to her side, and, careless of her drumming heels across their shins, dragged her between them across the lawn.

'You won't get away with this,' Dorothy promised, her screams of rage leaving her spittle-flecked lips in rising crescendo. 'I'll blacken her name in every decent house. There'll be nobody opens their door to her before I'm done.'

Silence floated on the evening perfumes in the wake of Dorothy's passage before crashing like a stone, ripping through the fabric of polite behaviour as the invited guests turned to one another of their fellows with the same scandalised utterings of embarrassment and outrage.

'Oh, Irene, my dear. How dreadful for you,' Janet was moved to utter, most unprofessionally.

Terry Garland took out his handkerchief and blew a loud trumpet in defiance of his emotions, and a long, heavy silence settled over the trio.

'Do you feel able to tell us the rest of the story?' Janet asked, after some time had passed.

Irene stared at her, and blinked to clear her eyes of the mist that caused her vision to waver. 'I . . . he came after me . . . Peter, he came after me.'

'But, Irene, your mother . . . how did she know where to find you?'

'The announcement – in the paper – it had Peter's address.'

'Oh, yes, of course. Of course. I'd overlooked that.' Janet nodded sagely.

'I . . . It was Peter's parents put the thing in the press, maybe they were hoping for something to happen,' Irene said bitterly.

'No, Peter's an only child, isn't he? I'm sure they would do nothing to make him unhappy.'

'Except split him up from me.'

'But they couldn't have known such a . . . a dreadful meeting would follow what was, after all, a proud announcement of their only son's engagement.'

'No, but they knew I didn't get on with my mother. Perhaps they were hoping she'd put a stop to our plans.'

'Now you are becoming paranoid. I'm certain they could have imagined no such thing. In any event they were unlucky, weren't they? Didn't you say that Peter came after you?'

'Oh, yes. Yes, he came after me,' Irene said with feeling.

In the cheerless room she had come to regard as home, Irene sat stony-faced and dry-eyed. Too distraught even for tears, she twisted her handkerchief into rags, shredding the pieces between her hands.

Peter's knock jangled her every nerve, and she felt the swift rush of bile to her throat. She couldn't face him, she couldn't.

He knocked again, and she stuffed her knuckles into her mouth biting down on them, finding relief in the pain as her teeth pierced the flesh.

'Irene! Irene, open the door.'

She sat rigid, a slow trickle of blood snaking across the back of her hand.

'Irene! Please. Please, darling. We have to talk.'

She made no move. Her eyes, wide and staring, were fixed on the door.

'Irene, please let me in. I'll stay here all night if I have to.' Peter stared at the brown varnished panels sensing the presence in the room beyond. He knew Irene was there, though not a sound did she make. 'I'm waiting, Irene. You can't lock me out for ever. If you don't let me in soon I'll break down the door.' He pushed his shoulder against it experimentally, but the old house was soundly constructed, and his weight met with solid resistance. 'Irene, darling. Don't make me beg. Open the door, won't you, please?'

Slowly, as though in a trance, Irene stood up. Moving like a sleepwalker she approached the door, and in slow-motion reached to turn the key.

Peter heard the lock snap back and, leaning his forehead against the dark panel, uttered a silent prayer of relief. He opened the door gently, and closed it quietly behind him, his eyes never leaving Irene's face. 'Irene, don't. Don't look at me like that.' He reached to take her in his arms but she stepped away. 'Irene, you mustn't. You are tormenting yourself over nothing. I didn't believe a word that crazy woman said.'

'Well you should have done then!' Irene screamed at him in a harsh, grating voice so unlike her own. 'You should have done, because every word of it was true!'

Peter stopped as if meeting a brick wall, his arms fell to his sides, his mouth opened soundlessly.

Speech had released the floodgates of Irene's distress, and her eyes filled. She cried silently, making no effort to cover her face as the tears coursed down her cheeks to drip from her chin.

Watching this terrible, melting agony, Peter broke through the barriers she had erected against him, sweeping her into his arms, telling her again and again that he loved her, and that nothing else mattered outside of that.

Allowing herself one brief moment in his arms Irene gathered the courage to do what she had known she must since her mother's voice had shattered the fragile bubble of her happiness.

Drawing the small solitaire diamond from her finger she pressed it into Peter's hand. 'Take it, Peter, please. You must see that I can't marry you now.'

'Why not allow me to be the judge of that?'

Irene had lived too long under the fear of tonight's disclosures, and knew an almost physical need to purge herself. She was unable to prevent the monologue that poured from her lips. With telling lack of expression she quoted chapter and verse of those terrible months when she had been slave to John Forster's whims. Only once did she falter in her narrative, and that was when she came to speak of her brothers' ready acceptance of the lie Forster had told them.

Irene faltered yet again at this point, the remembered pain of that betrayal still keen enough to cause her renewed distress.

'Did you . . . have you seen either of your brothers since that time?' Janet asked quietly, bridging the aching gaps between Irene's smothered sobs.

Irene shook her head, her hands groping blindly for a handkerchief. Terry supplied her with his, his face shuttered and carefully bereft of all emotion.

'And Peter? What was his reaction to all this?' Janet wanted to know.

'He . . . he refused to believe it could make any difference. He loved me, you see. Really loved me.' Irene's voice sank to a whisper. 'Oh, but if only I had been a little more clever. . . .'

TEN

When Irene became certain she was pregnant, the bottom dropped out of her world. 'I can't be. I mustn't be. Oh, please, God, don't let it happen,' she whimpered through teeth clenched against the nausea that had been her first intimation.

'I wanted to kill myself,' she told Janet Fouracres, and there was something in her voice that convinced the social worker this was no hysterical outburst.

'I believe I can understand something of your feelings,' Janet said in all sincerity. 'And how did Peter take the news?'

'I didn't tell him – not at first. He had gone back to college to complete his final year. I couldn't bring myself to interfere with that.' Tears hung heavy on Irene's lashes.

'But he had to know. You can't have hoped to keep it from him indefinitely.'

'No, of course not. And once he came home there was no way I could disguise what had happened. He knew the minute he set eyes on me.'

'So how did he take it? Was he angry – upset? What was his attitude?'

'He . . . he was marvellous about it. I was nearly out of my head with worry, and he just . . . just took care of everything.'

'In what way, took care of everything?' Janet asked guardedly.

'Well, he fixed up for us to get married right away,' Irene said with a touch of impatience.

'I see. And was that what you wanted?'

'Of course it was – well, it was once I was sure it wouldn't prevent him going back to finish his year. I wanted him to get his degree.' Irene's eyes darkened. 'You see, his mum and dad hadn't asked to see me since . . . since the engagement

140

party. . . . . They were hoping he'd drop me, I suppose . . . and anyway, I knew if he didn't go back to finish his course they would always blame me, and . . . and . . .'

'So you arranged the wedding – and then what?' Janet steered towards safer ground.

'Then we got married,' said Irene simply. 'Peter went back to college, I kept on the bedsit, and we planned that I'd carry on working, taking the baby along to the nursery with me, until Peter graduated and could find a job to support us.'

'And is that in fact how things worked out?'

'Do pigs fly?' Irene said harshly.

'So what went wrong?'

'Everything! The baby was a girl, for a start, when I'd been longing and planning for a boy. . . . . It was a difficult forceps delivery. I was very, very ill.'

'So you deeply resented your daughter?'

'No,' Irene said slowly. 'Not once I'd got used to the idea. Only . . . well, Peter had to give up college. I wasn't well enough to think about going back to work, so he had to find a job. He got taken on as a labourer – a labourer,' Irene said with lingering indignation. 'And him so clever and all. It didn't seem right.'

'Then did *he* resent your daughter?'

'Oh, no. No, not Peter. He loved her from the start. He was a bit surprised that I wanted to name her Lauren, he thought it an odd sort of name, but I never let on that it was as close as I could get to Lawrence, which was the name I'd secretly chosen for the little boy *he* made me give up.' Irene jerked her head savagely in Terry's direction.

'That's most unfair, Irene. I didn't make you give the child up. We agreed it was the only sensible thing.'

'Oh, yes, we agreed,' said Irene bitterly. 'Me, a fourteen-year-old kid, and you, my so-clever adviser.'

Terry clamped his jaw against the words he longed to throw at Irene; it would help nobody now to get embroiled in a heated exchange, particularly since his conscience was so dreadfully unclear.

'Then you were reasonably happy, you and Peter, and your little daughter?' Janet felt it expedient to ignore the undercurrents bubbling so threateningly between her colleague and her client.

'Yes, we were . . . for a time.'

'For a time?' Again that interrogative lift of Janet's eyebrows. 'Was Lauren a difficult baby, then?'

Irene gave a deep sigh of weary resignation before plunging back into her story.

When baby Lauren was four months old and beginning to demand her mother's attention, Irene met with resistance to her steady improvement in health. For several days she was listless and out of sorts, the sense of well-being that had been building within her absent when she needed it most. Her returning appetite failed and she lost the gentle bloom which had lately lighted her face.

Wrapped in his own troubles, Peter was slow to notice his wife's problems, and Irene had slipped some way down the ladder before her illness impressed itself on his notice. 'Get along to the doctor and ask him to prescribe you a tonic,' he advised. 'You've been doing too much these last few days, what with the baby and all.'

'I'll be all right, and it's such a drag getting into town. I just can't face lugging Lauren and the pushchair on and off buses. Just give it a few days, then if I'm no better I'll think about it.'

'Damn that, Irene. Leave Lauren with me and go over one evening. They *do* have evening surgery, I believe.' Peter lost patience and resorted to sarcasm.

Irene made no further argument, but the following day dressed herself and the baby, and made the journey into town in sullen defiance of Peter's offer.

In the tiny consulting room she waited with Lauren in her arms, while the doctor doodled on his note pad before delivering his verdict.

'You are pregnant, Mrs Rawding,' he said at last, adding another curlicue to the elaborate pattern shaping under his pen.

Irene stopped breathing. Her eyes widened in shock. Another baby, and Lauren only a few weeks old. She thrust the baby at the doctor, wanting to scream, wanting to run, to yell that it couldn't be true. Air rushed back into her lungs with an audible gasp.

Discarding his pen and taking the child onto his knee, the doctor looked steadily at Irene. 'Sit down, Mrs Rawding. I realise this must come as something of a shock.'

'H-how long?' asked Irene, struggling to find her voice.

'About eight weeks, I should say.'

'Then Lauren will be less than a year . . .' Her voice trailed away as other considerations crowded in on her, pushing her calculations aside. Whatever was Peter going to say? Her pallor deepened visibly.

'Are you feeling faint?' The doctor held Lauren in the crook of his arm while he reached into his desk drawer to produce a small bottle which he uncapped and waved under Irene's nose.

Irene gasped, took another shallow breath; a touch of colour returned to her cheeks. 'Thank you. I'm . . . I'm fine now. I . . . I was just . . .' She reached blindly for the baby and took her back into her arms.

'Go home, Mrs Rawding. Put your feet up, take it easy. Other women have managed.'

Irene stumbled from the doctor's surgery with Lauren in the pushchair, failing to book the appointment he had urged for the following month.

Careless of her direction she tramped through the streets seeing nothing of her surroundings, her whole being concentrated on how she might acquaint Peter with this shattering news. She was under no illusion that he might be pleased; they had agreed they would have no more children until after he had obtained his degree. How was she now to tell him this would no longer be possible?'

Her pace increased as though by hurrying she might outstrip the problem. Stepping out along the pavements, the wheels of the pushchair humming a broken rhythm over the cracks, she arrived flushed and breathless in the busy main centre of town. Obliged by the thickening crowds to slow her steps, she fell to aimless window-gazing. Almost of their own volition her feet slowed to a halt before a display of mother and baby clothes. Stylish maternity wear, appealing layettes, soft, cuddly toys danced before her eyes, and for the first time since she had learned she was to have another child, Irene felt a surge of happy anticipation. Perhaps this time she would have a boy, a male child to fill the never-healed place in her heart. A baby brother for Lauren, a son for Peter.

A smile lifted the corners of her mouth as her glance fell on the blue baby-grow rompers, the fierce little teddy-bears, and the adorable sailor-suits. She could just see her little boy dressed in one of those, his big sister proudly holding him on her chubby knees. . . . On a sudden impulse she entered the shop, and without stopping to consider the senseless extravagance, emptied her purse to purchase the smallest of the sailor-suits.

Peter was rendered speechless. He stared from his wife's pleading face to the blue and white babywear spread across the table. His mouth opened and closed as he gazed, but his voice had momentarily deserted him.

The tremulous smile Irene had conjured wavered and died. 'Are you . . . are you a bit stunned?'

'A *bit*?' Peter spread his hands, palms up in an empty gesture before bringing them into clenched fists. 'Christ almighty, Irene! What the hell are we going to do?'

Irene avoided his eye, made a grimace of helpless acceptance. 'Please don't be angry, Peter. It won't seem so bad once you get used to it. And, after all, there is not much we *can* do, is there?'

'Oh, yes there is! You can get it seen to! We don't have to have kids one after the other like – like oversexed rabbits!'

Irene felt the breath leave her lungs. Peter's angry face swam before her as she reeled under this callous attack.

'Oh, God. I'm sorry, Irene. I'm sorry. I didn't mean that. Please, please don't look at me that way. I'm shocked, that's all. I didn't mean it, believe me, darling, I didn't mean it.'

Irene avoided his outstretched arms, his ill-considered remark ringing like a death knell in her ears.

Peter gripped the sides of the table, his knuckles showing white as he struggled for control. 'Look, Irene, we have to think about this.'

'What is there to think about? I'm pregnant, Peter. No amount of thinking is going to change things.'

'But you don't have to stay pregnant, do you? I mean . . . with it being so soon after Lauren, and everything. There has to be some way . . . something . . .'

Irene dragged a chair back from the table and lowered herself into the seat. 'Just what are you hinting at?' she asked through lips turned to stone.

'Darling, please. You're not so naïve, you must know what I mean.' He looked at her in appeal, but Irene would have none of it and he was obliged to state his mind boldly without prevarication. 'I'm talking about getting rid of it. There are ways and means. Somebody mentioned someone when . . . when we first knew about Lauren.'

'Oh, I see. And you waited all this time to tell me,' she said, hurt beyond endurance that he should have discussed such a thing with anyone else. Then a spurt of anger made her hit back.

'Well let me tell you now, Peter Rawding, there's going to be no gin and hot baths over this baby, chance what your precious friends have to say.' Having delivered herself of this emphatic speech Irene burst into tears.

Peter allowed her sobs to continue, clinging stubbornly to his resentment until her distress pricked his conscience, and his sense of fair play drove him to take her into his arms. 'Don't cry, darling. I'm sorry. Of course there'll be no gin and hot baths. Not that I'd imagined anything quite so crude. Sh, sh, don't cry, we'll manage somehow, I expect. Don't upset yourself.'

Aware that he must now abandon all thoughts of returning to college, Peter faced his new responsibilities with as much grace as he could muster. Irene was not a good housekeeper, she'd had no one to teach her the basic rules, and money ran through her fingers like water. Not that they ever had a great deal, but Peter put in all the overtime he could while the weather was fair, and the days long enough to allow the men to work extended hours on the building sites. This time there was no question of Irene working to help swell their capital, no hopes that she would eventually get another job, not with two small babies to nurse. The cramped, inadequate accommodation afforded by the bedsit grated on their nerves, made them edgy with each other, sparked sharp, bitter rows that did nothing to ease the mounting tensions. This pregnancy, greeted with tears

145

and despair, continued along the same miserable vein. Irene was continually sick, and made wretched by low stomach pains that prevented sleep, her legs and ankles grew puffy and out of shape, and her fingers swelled making the most simple of tasks awkward and time consuming. Their lack of funds meant she must go without even one loose cotton dress that might have made her increasing bulk halfway bearable. The pinafore and wrap-around skirt she had worn when she was carrying Lauren was pressed into second service, their want of inches bridged by safety pins. Irene was uncomfortably larger in this, her third pregnancy.

'The doctor wants me to have a scan. He thinks we might have twins,' she told Peter on her return from her third visit to the ante-natal clinic.

Peter drew a deep breath, holding it as a buffer before it escaped him in a long drawn sigh of resignation. 'How soon will we know?' he asked weakly.

'Couple of weeks.' Resentful that he had made no pretence of enthusiasm, Irene was deliberately sharp. She had not expected him to be pleased, but she felt he might have attempted a few words of encouragement. 'I suppose you're hoping I'll miscarry,' she flung at him bitterly.

'Irene, please.' He tried to disguise the jolt her words had caused him, unwilling to admit, even to himself, that she might have come close to the truth.

'Oh, don't Irene please me. I know you never wanted this baby.' She knew also she was being unfair, but she had need of some outlet for her own nagging distress, and as always of late, she made him her whipping boy, pouring out her resentment of the trap they were in, seeking to allay her feelings of guilt.

'Knock it off, Irene.' He gave her curt warning before turning away.

'And if I don't?' Fear of even greater poverty than they currently endured goaded her into provoking him further.

'Then have your bloody kids in some home or other – and get them all adopted as you did your first!'

Before this cruel hurt had wiped the rage from his wife's face Peter had slammed his way out of the room.

Irene heard the door bang behind him, followed by the

clatter of his feet on the uncarpeted stairs dropping down to the street. Like a slowly deflating balloon she crumpled into a shapeless huddle of misery, and, locking her arms about her swollen stomach, she rocked backwards and forwards in a scalding paroxysm of grief.

Slow tears trickled down her cheeks as Irene recalled this incident, and she scrubbed them away with her borrowed handkerchief.

'You must have resented Peter very much at this point,' Janet Fouracres said with telling certainty.

'Yes, I bloody well did! Him and the baby – both!' Irene's eyes flashed back at her.

'Which baby, Irene?' The words dropped like pebbles into a still pool.

'Both of them – all three of them, Goddamn you!' Irene yelled. 'All of them. And especially the two I was lumbered with. There I was like . . . like a bloody inflated frog, one kid bawling away at the side of me, the other kicking away at my guts!'

Terry Garland's face took on a dark mask of disapproval at Irene's choice of words, and he leaned away from her as if to dissociate himself with this new face of the girl he had believed he knew so well.

To confound him, his colleague's approach grew warmer, and even more sympathetic. 'And was this the first time you ever . . . struck your baby?'

Irene glowered at her. 'I didn't strike her,' she said in some disdain. 'She . . . I couldn't get her to settle . . . I was feeling like death. I wanted to die. I thought it would be the best solution for us all if I just turned on the gas taps, and ended it there and then.'

'But you didn't? Turn on the gas taps, I mean?'

'What was the use? I have enough sense to know that natural gas wouldn't poison me,' Irene said dully.

'So you . . . smacked your baby . . . to get her to quieten?'

'No, I tell you. I didn't smack her.'

'So what did you do?'

'I got into bed and took her in with me . . . then . . . then I

147

covered her face with my pillow.'

The silence holding the trio took on the quality found in the vaults of a deserted church. It stretched achingly until Irene, releasing her breath with a ragged sigh, said with composure, 'Once she had quietened, I put her back in her cot.'

'Didn't you realise you might have killed her?'

'No, I wouldn't. I wouldn't. I made sure she was breathing. It was just to make her stop crying.'

'Did you tell Peter about this?'

'No, why should I? There was nothing to tell.'

Terry and Janet exchanged a long, meaningful glance before the latter returned to her steady questioning. 'How often did you . . . employ this method of putting your baby to sleep?'

Irene shrugged. 'Not often . . . only when . . . only when her crying started to get on my nerves.'

'She cried a lot, then?'

'Not really. Like I told you, she was a pretty good baby – and besides, once we moved out here, and we weren't all on top of each other, I felt a lot better about things . . . . They told me it was a false alarm about me having twins, that helped, and then getting this flat . . . it was like we were getting engaged all over again.

'Was the new baby born after you moved in here?'

'Yes, just a couple of weeks.'

'And that was an easier birth?'

'Yes.'

'Was she a good baby, Irene?'

'Yes.'

'Then you didn't need to . . . to use a pillow to get her to sleep?'

'No.'

'Were you upset because this was another girl?'

'Well, no. Not really. She was company for Lauren . . . and Peter . . . Peter got himself a much better job. A proper job, in an office. We had more money . . . I thought . . . I thought – hoped – I might find out where Lawrence, my little boy had been taken. I thought I might get him back.'

'But you must have known that was impossible,' Janet began to remonstrate gently only to find herself facing a virago.

'No I *didn't*! It *isn't*! I could get him back! He isn't dead, is he? He's out there somewhere.' Irene's hand flapped vigorously towards the window, her cheeks flooded with colour, her lips drawn back from her teeth.

'But you have a new little boy now. He's Lawrence, too; doesn't he deserve some of your love?' Janet continued quietly, refusing to be intimidated by Irene's outburst.

'He isn't the same. Don't you see, you stupid bitch!'

'Is that why you hurt him – because he isn't the son you gave up?'

'I didn't hurt him. Don't I keep telling you it was an accident? Why won't you believe me?'

'Then tell me exactly what happened. You say you were not responsible, that you didn't hurt him, so tell me how he came to be in need of help.'

'He . . . he . . . I don't really know. . . . I wasn't in the room.' Irene pouted, refusing to meet Jane Fouracre's gaze.

'But there have been occasions when you have hurt him, Irene. Tell me about those.'

'I don't know what you are trying to get me to say. I . . . ask him,' she said in a sudden show of temper, nodding to Terry. 'He's the one you should be asking all these questions. He's the one, not me. I didn't hurt Lawrence, it was an accident. And anyway, I nearly did find my own little boy,' Irene said irrationally. 'It was on the day our Lauren started school.'

Lauren's first day at school was a milestone for the whole family. For Lauren herself it was an adventure; for her sister, deprived of her constant companion, it was a crying shame; for Peter it marked the beginning of real opportunity, since this was the day he was first asked to travel abroad as a representative of his company. And for Irene it brought the start of a terrible new chapter.

Waiting with Debbie at the gate of the school playground for Lauren to come out of the classroom, Irene scanned the tide of bright, eager-eyed infants spilling from the school buildings and found her gaze riveted to a boy whose height distinguished him as one of the second-year children. Her breath caught in her throat. She started forward, her eyes devouring every line of his

149

face. It was . . . it had to be . . . the likeness was unmistakable. This was surely Lawrence.

Without stopping to think she started towards him, releasing her daughter's hand, her arms outstretched.

'Lawrence! Oh, Lawrence. My own little love.'

The child stared at her no less amazed than Debbie or Lauren who had joined her sister in an open-mouthed gape at their mother.

For the space of a heartbeat the tableau held, then the boy turned to race away from Irene's reaching arms, calling to his companions to follow as he sped down the street.

Irene remained in a stooping posture, her arms embracing the space where he had been, an expression on her face of anguished bereavement.

'Mummy! Mummy!' Her daughters' fingers plucking her sleeve, their cries of bewilderment pierced the vacuum she had entered, and she shook herself before meeting their gaze.

'I'm sorry, darlings. I . . . Mummy must have been dreaming.'

'But you called that boy your own little love,' Lauren said accusingly.

'Did I? Oh, dear. Well, well, that just shows how much I have missed having my big girl around today.' She bent to kiss her daughter's cheek. 'Debbie and I have been so lonely, you wouldn't believe. So come on, tell us all about school. We want to hear every little thing.'

Having succeeded in diverting her daughters' attention, Irene gazed over the bobbing heads hoping for a further glimpse of the boy she was convinced was her son. But in this she was to be disappointed; the child was gone without trace.

Irene was so keyed up by this encounter she scarcely listened as Peter explained about the chance he'd been offered to visit South America to work on a project for his company.

'It's a marvellous opportunity, Irene. If I do well at this, there'll be no stopping me,' he enthused. 'Just think of it, today South America, tomorrow the world.'

When Irene failed to respond to this extravagant boast, he looked at her sharply. 'What's the matter, Irene? Something wrong?'

'I, er, no, darling. I'm sorry, what were you saying?' She turned to him in polite enquiry.

'For heaven's sake, Irene. I'm just telling you I've been asked to fly out to South America for three weeks. Can't you think of anything but the kids?' Peter had listened patiently to his wife's account of their daughter's first day at school, waiting until he felt she had talked the subject to death before making his own exciting announcement. Now he felt let down and cheated by her obvious lack of interest.

Irene decided against telling him of the discovery that was occupying first place in her mind, and made every effort to pay attention as he outlined the details of his trip. It might be they would need to move abroad at some time in the future if her plans to have her son restored to her came to fruition, she thought dreamily.

The next day, and all the remainder of that week, Irene hung around the infant school playground, watching for her son. She saw him enter the school every morning, watched him at play during the morning recess, and was there by the gate when he left every night. He was a fine looking boy, well built, tall for his age, with her own wide, full-lashed grey eyes, and just the suggestion of a dimple in his chin. She loved him on sight, as she had always known that she would, and longed to place her arms about him, to smother him with the kisses they had been denied.

As the children emerged from the playground on Friday afternoon, and she was faced with the thought of a weekend without sight of Lawrence, Irene grew desperate. She had to do something about this situation. She could not go on week after week, living for these few barren moments outside the school gates.

Luck was on her side in the form of a teacher who came hurrying along in the wake of the dispersing children. Irene planted herself firmly in the woman's path.

'Excuse me, would you mind . . . Can you tell me, please, what is the name of that boy?' She pointed at Lawrence.

'Oh, that's Michael Greenway. Why? Is he up to mischief again?' The teacher glanced at the two little girls clinging to Irene's hands.

'What? Oh, no. Nothing like that.' Irene had been astounded to hear her son referred to as Michael.

The teacher, after giving her a curious glance, made as if to pass.

'Um, do you happen to know where he lives?' Irene asked.

'Not offhand. I could find out for you if it was important.'

'Would you? Would you, please?'

'Well, I would need to know why you are asking,' the teacher hedged.

'I . . . I must speak with his mother.'

'I knew it. He has been up to some mischief. His mother will go mad. What with him and his brother, she hardly knows a minute's peace.'

'His brother? Does he have a brother?'

'Two. But Danny, the oldest, is no trouble at all, while that young rip and the next one up, well.'

'How . . .' Irene found it impossible to go on.

'Pardon?'

Gathering herself for the question, Irene held the woman's gaze. 'How old is Michael?' she asked in a voice scarcely above a whisper.

'He's coming up seven. Lord help us all when he gets a bit older.'

'Are you sure?' The sky fell in on Irene as the woman confirmed Michael's age. Not even her obsessive folly would allow her to believe a child could grow younger. Lawrence would now be nine years old, going on ten. Why had she never thought of that?

Out of bitter disappointment grew an idea so filled with longing Irene dared not speak of it aloud. Only to herself did she whisper her plans. 'Peter is sure to be eager after three weeks from home,' she breathed to her reflection in the bathroom mirror. Wide grey eyes returned her stare, sparkling in excited anticipation. 'And what he doesn't know is not going to kill him,' she added as she flipped the tiny round pills from their foil strip. 'We'll have another baby, this time a son, and he'll be so thrilled.' Only for a moment did she pause to consider before dropping the pills into the lavatory basin. 'Maybe I'll just put the idea into his head; then, when it happens, when I'm pregnant for sure . . . Oh, he's going to love baby Lawrence.'

'No way, Irene. Don't even think of it,' was Peter's response. 'We're just beginning to get on our feet. All the work I've put in with my company is coming good. I'll get all the plum jobs from now on, then we'll have enough money to get out of this place, and buy that house with the garden we always promised ourselves.' Peter spoke without heat, lying relaxed and utterly content after their hungry, tempestuous love-making.

Irene had chosen this moment with care, certain that Peter could refuse her nothing. She nibbled his ear before planting butterfly kisses along the firm line of his jaw, then tried again. 'I don't really mind not having a place of our own. I'm happy enough as we are. This place is comfortable, we've made friends, the girls are settled. It would be a pity to move.'

'Ah, but if we had any more kids, we might have to move. There wouldn't be enough room, 'specially if we should have a boy.'

Angry with herself for not having foreseen the trap she'd walked into, Irene abandoned all attempt at logical argument, and sought to get her way on the strength of feminine wiles.

'We could afford another baby, Peter. Just one,' she pleaded in a little girl voice, her fingers gently teasing the sensitive flesh of his inner thigh.

'No, my love. Not even one. We have all the family we need with Debbie and Lauren.' He kissed her soundly, hoping to soften his refusal, and was glad to feel her respond. 'I know you are feeling a bit lost now the girls are starting school, but why don't you get a little job? Go back to nursery work, eh? It would give you a bit of pocket money.'

Irene's teasing nibbles were having effect, and Peter was done with words. Three weeks of bachelor living had sharpened his appetites.

Another twelve months flew past, and as Peter predicted he was now being offered more lucrative jobs with further assignments abroad. Debbie followed her sister's lead in starting school, and still Irene schemed and planned, longing for a son. Her failure to conceive became a bitter irony she strove to keep hidden

153

while losing no opportunity to remedy the situation. Finally, when her hunger became a constant ache, when she was so desperate she wept at the sight of pregnant women, her calendar gave her to hope. Her period was late – by only a day, then two, then four, then six until at last she was certain. Her joy knew no bounds. This child would be the son she had so long been seeking. She took on an inner glow which reflected in her face like a beacon. Soon she would break the news to Peter, but not yet. For the moment she was content to keep her secret, waiting for just the right, magical moment, hugging the wonder of this precious new life to herself.

Peter waited until Lauren and Debbie were in bed before attempting to tell Irene his news. He was not sure how she would take it – and he needed her co-operation. He watched her as she moved about the room, picking up after the children. She had seemed so happy lately, so content, was he being purely selfish in wanting more than he had already?

Irene became aware of his gaze and looked up with a smile. Maybe now, tonight, would be the right time to tell him her news.

'Come and sit down,' Peter invited, patting the cushion next to his.

'I have something to tell you,' they said in perfect unison, one of those strange flukes that sometimes occur between people who share a close relationship.

They laughed at themselves and kissed as Irene joined Peter on the settee, snuggling into the circle of his arms. 'You first,' she said, knowing what she had to tell him would needs be followed by some discussion.

'I've had the offer of a job,' said Peter, slowly. 'It's doing pretty much as I do now, only it's with an American company at nearly three times the pay.'

Irene was startled into sitting bolt upright, her face expressing pleasure and disbelief in equal mixture. Surely this must be a sign, she thought, almost delirious with happy relief. If Peter was going to be earning that much more money he couldn't help but be pleased when she told him about the baby.

'Well, say something. Speak to me,' Peter teased. 'Only before you do, I think I'd better warn you – that was the good news.' He allowed a silence to develop in order to underline what he had to say. 'The bad news is that I have to go out to the States.'

'The States?' Irene gazed at him, unable to comprehend.

'They want me over there for two years – well, not two years exactly. I'd get a break of twelve weeks in the middle, so it would be like two stints of just over ten months apiece.' He rushed at the explanation, anxious to present as favourable a picture as was possible.

'The States, the United States, you mean? For two years? Oh, Peter, you can't.'

'But, darling, listen. Listen, it's not really for two years. It's ten months, then another ten months. No time at all, really.'

Irene studied his anxious, pleading expression, and felt her objections melt away. Peter had always been so good to her, so loyal. He'd given up his home and a promising career for her sake; how could she ask him now to do that over again?

'You really want this, Peter, don't you?' she asked, holding his gaze.

'More than anything. No, no, that's not quite true.' He corrected himself hastily. 'Most of all I want you and the kids, but if you're willing to give me this chance . . . Oh, Irene, if only you could manage. I know it wouldn't be easy, but the girls are both at school now, you're not so tied. What do you think?' He waited tensely for her reply.

'When? When would you have to go?' Irene was doing sums in her head.

Peter gave a bark of rueful laughter. 'Next month. They want me over there as soon as possible.'

'Then you'd be back in August.' By her reckoning the baby was due in early June.

'In good time for your birthday,' Peter promised.

'Oh, but you would miss Christmas,' she wailed.

'I'll send you presents from America, you and the girls.'

Irene knew she had only to tell him she was pregnant for him to turn down the job. He would be understandably dis-appointed, and angry, but he would never leave her to cope alone. And in time he would come round. . . .

'We are going to miss you,' she said.

ELEVEN

Never once in all the long letters she wrote to him did Irene give Peter a hint of their forthcoming child. Not when things began to go wrong and she had to spend days at a time in the hospital, and not even when her friend who was to have cared for the girls when the baby was born went back on her promise, with the result that Lauren and Debbie had to be taken into care.

'That was the worst thing of all,' Irene said, sweeping both Terry Garland and his superior officer with an accusing glance. 'They were like . . . like strangers to me when I got them back.'

'But they had to be cared for, Irene. Surely you can understand that?' Terry felt moved to defend an action that had been outside his jurisdiction.

'Yes, I know that, but why did nobody bring them to see me? Why weren't they told what was happening to them? They thought they were being punished – that I'd deserted them.'

Though feeling obliged to defend the authority for which they both worked, neither officer was able to present a convincing explanation for this want of understanding.

'Lauren told me she hated me. Little Debbie . . . she wouldn't even speak when I got her home. . . . Can you imagine that?' Irene demanded. 'My own children, my babies, not wanting me to touch them, or go near them, and when I did . . . when I tried to take them in my arms, they fought and kicked. I almost went crazy. I cried so much over the next few weeks I could hardly get my eyes open.'

'You should have contacted your husband. It was his place to take charge of things while you were not well,' Terry said firmly.

'How could I? What could I tell him?'

'I should have thought the truth would be sufficient.' Terry maintained his stand.

'Oh, yes, you would, wouldn't you! Come home, Peter. Give up the only half-decent job you'll ever have because the woman who cheated you out of your degree has done it again. She's tricked you into getting her pregnant, and what is more, she's turned your two little girls into swearing, spitting little wildcats you wouldn't even recognise, let alone love.'

'You exaggerate,' Terry said flatly.

'Do I? Oh, do I? Well let me tell you, it didn't take Peter long to decide whether I did or not once he got back.'

Janet leaned forward in her chair, her face a study of consternation. 'You don't mean to tell us you allowed him to continue in ignorance of the situation?' she asked faintly.

'It . . . it seemed the best way, at the time.'

'But, Irene . . .'

'I know. Don't go on about it. Perhaps if I'd . . . Well, just don't go on.'

'I'm sorry. I didn't mean to preach.' Janet paused to consider what she knew in the light of this information. 'Did you . . . were you aware of this?' she could not help but ask of Terry.

He shook his head wearily. 'Not at the time, no.'

'And later?'

'Later, I discovered a great many things I found hard to believe.'

Irene pounced on his words. 'There you are, you see? You don't believe anything I've been telling you,' she cried.

'But, Irene, you've made so many difficulties for yourself!' Janet exclaimed.

Irene stared at her, as if daring her to make further comment. Janet shook her head over her own stupidity. 'I'm sorry. You must have done what you thought was best. But Peter, how did he cope with this new development?'

Irene proceeded to tell her.

Peter came home all unsuspecting to find his family greatly changed. The close, loving bond that had latterly united his wife and their daughters was obviously lacking. Though Irene was as demonstrative in her affections towards them as ever, neither

157

Lauren nor Debbie responded to her hugs and kisses with the enthusiasm he remembered.

'What's with you guys?' he asked, displaying his transatlantic connections. 'You're all so edgy with each other. And what about me? Don't I get a "welcome home, Daddy" from my two favourite girls?' He stooped and held his arms out to them, and they looked to each other for confirmation before entering his embrace. Peter straightened, a child on each arm, their faces close to his own. 'So tell me about it,' he invited, expecting to be acquainted of some childish squabble, and was disturbed by his daughters' refusal to look into his face. He looked to Irene for an explanation, but she was staring down at her fingers, twisting and untwisting, as though they had independent life of their own.

'OK, you guys. Scoot. Go play with your dolls.' He set his daughters back on their feet, and gave them a push towards the hall and the door of their bedroom.

Irene started forward, a warning to them to play quietly, not to wake Lawrence, choked back at the last minute. Slowly she turned to face her husband; apart from his first bruising embrace and his exuberant dispensing of lavishly wrapped packages, they had not greeted each other after his ten-month-long absence. Her heart pounding so heavily she could feel it shaking her whole body, Irene was brought to face the moment she had been rehearsing over and over. Her mouth was suddenly too dry for speech and she struggled to free her tongue.

'Hey, what is this? Some welcome I got from the three of you.' Though he spoke jestingly Peter glanced at her suspiciously. Something of her distress communicated itself to him, sweeping away the joy of his homecoming.

'Come.' Unable to say more Irene held out her hand and took hold of Peter's to lead him across the hall to their own bedroom.

Once inside the door she halted, and, still without speaking, jerked her chin in the direction of the cot drawn up to the side of the double bed.

Peter's face was a study of bewildered incredulity as he looked from his wife to the sleeping baby.

'Whose?' he croaked, after a pause that held everything of blank amazement, speculation, and hardening suspicion.

Irene's lips moved as she worked the gummy saliva in her mouth trying to articulate just the one word. 'Ours,' she managed finally, and waited for him to say something.

'You . . . you mean you've adopted it?'

She shook her head.

'Well, what, then?'

'He's ours, Peter. Our son.' Her face remained carefully blank of all expression.

'Oh, no. No, you don't pull that one on me.' He stepped away from the cot. 'Yours, he might be. Mine, he is not!'

'Oh, stop talking like a blasted American film actor.' Irene had endured too much over the past few weeks; stress made her belligerent. 'He is ours, I tell you. Yours as much as mine. I was pregnant with him when you left for America.'

'I don't believe you.' Peter dropped like a stringless puppet to perch on the edge of the bed. 'I just don't believe you,' he repeated.

'And what does that make me?' Irene had played this scene over and over, night after night, since Peter had left. She had planned it, stage-managed it, scripted the dialogue, but strangely, she realised now, she had never imagined Peter would take this attitude. Anger, she was prepared for. Shock, surprise, even rage, but never in her wildest imaginings had she allowed for the hard condemnation she saw so plainly in her husband's face.

'You . . . tell . . . me.' Peter dropped the words one by one, like tiny bombshells into the waiting silence.

'Why, you . . .' Irene launched herself at him, fingers hooked, raking for his face. 'He's ours, I tell you. Yours and mine.' She panted and writhed in the punishing grip he had taken on her hands, unable to free herself as he dragged her down across the bed to bring his face within inches of her own.

'No, Irene. Not mine! Never that! You are not saddling me with somebody's bastard!'

Peter left without troubling to unpack. He simply picked up his cases and went. Irene had no idea where to contact him; he sent no forwarding address. Approaches to his company were useless as they refused to disclose if he remained on their payroll. For weeks Irene pretended to herself that he would return, that his going had been merely a fit of pique. But she knew in her heart, as she had known from the moment the door closed behind him, that he would not be back.

The baby lay in his cot and screamed; screamed until his puckered face began to turn blue, and his flailing arms and legs were drawn up to his stomach to lend strength to the sounds pouring from his throat. Irene, lying sleepless in the wide double bed, paid him no attention. He was always crying. He had cried almost continuously since the day he was born, and the fact that he cried now offered her grim satisfaction. Let him yell. He'd soon learn that he couldn't have everything he wanted just by kicking up a din.

She made no effort to stem his screams or to discover the cause of his discomfort. Swamped by her own misery, and the depression that had followed his birth, she endured the ear-shattering wails without moving.

Soon an enraged thumping on the ceiling warned that his noise had awakened the tenants of the flat above, and shortly after that her bedroom door opened to reveal her two daughters clad in their nightgowns, their faces streaked with tears.

'Please, Mummy. Stop him crying,' Lauren begged for them both. 'The people upstairs are knocking and me an' Debbie can't go to sleep.'

'All right. Go back to bed, sweethearts. I'm sorry he disturbed you. I'll take care of it now.' Irene waited until the girls left the bedroom before reaching over to drive her clenched fist into the baby's chest.

His screams ended abruptly as the air was forced out of his lungs. When, after what seemed an age, he drew breath with a desperate, painful whooping, Irene picked up the empty pillow next to her own and dropped it over his head.

His screams were quietened now, only a muffled cry escaped the stifling feather pillow, and soon that too petered away into silence. Irene lay flat on her back staring sightlessly up at the ceiling, the unbelievable silence settling over her like a mantle. She had not known such peace since the baby was born.

Suddenly, she sat bolt upright, her head turning from side to side as if she had awakened in a strange room and had no knowledge of her surroundings.

The baby! Where was the baby? Why was he so quiet? Flinging aside the bedclothes she ran round the bed to the light switch, looking back over her shoulder like a child as she switched it on. 'Lawrence. Lawrence, my lovely. What have I done?'

Her fingers pressed to her mouth, she moved with tiny reluctant steps toward the cot. Slowly, she reached over the side rails, and lifted the pillow. 'Baby, baby, baby. Oh, my sweet, sweet love.' Tears pouring from her eyes blinded her as she caught up the tiny bundle that miraculously breathed in the light, shallow rhythm of a sleeping infant. 'Lawrence. Oh, Lawrence, my precious, my own precious son.'

The child awakened and began to cry. Irene dashed away her own tears, and clutched him tenderly to her breast, staring down at him as if seeing him for the first time. His pathetically naked skull and tiny, aimlessly waving hands clutched at her heart. She had not been able to feed this baby as she had Lauren and Debbie as she had been too ill immediately after his birth. And then, when she was stronger and her milk came, he had grown accustomed to the bottle and refused to suckle. Somehow there had seemed no good reason for her to cuddle this child, he took his feed just as easily whoever held the bottle, and her contact with him had become almost perfunctory.

'Oh, Lawrence, my poor little lamb. What has Mummy done to you?' She carried him from the bedroom to the kitchen where she put his bottle to heat before stripping him of his sodden nightclothes. A dull red patch on his rib-cage felt hot under her fingers, and his cries increased in volume as she touched the angry flesh.

'Shh, shh, don't cry, little man. It won't happen again. You and I are going to get along just fine, wait and see.'

Irene's voice faltered to a stop. She had been so engrossed with this terrible chapter as to forget her audience. She scowled at them defensively. 'You tricked me. You planned this between you.' She began to grow angry. 'You came here, both of you, to try and make me say it was me that hurt Lawrence.'

'Irene . . . it *was* you who hurt Lawrence. Admit it . . . tell us. We are here to help you, not . . . not to apportion blame,' Terry said earnestly.

'Ah, no.' A sly look crossed Irene's face. 'No, you don't catch me like that. You *know* it was an accident. You can't make me say it wasn't.'

'But you already did.' He spoke gently now, pleading with her to accept the truth. 'You just said,' Terry reminded Irene, 'that you punched him . . . and tried to smother him.'

'No!' Irene sprang to her feet. 'No, I never said that. I said . . . I said I was a bit . . . a bit rough with him . . . but I never said I'd . . .'

'So what did you mean by that? What did you mean when you said you were a bit rough?' Terry remained seated hoping to defuse the heat of Irene's stubborn anger. His ploy had some effect for she looked about her uncertainly before slowly sinking back into her chair.

'I didn't mean anything. I've told you, I won't be tricked.'

Terry eyed her dispassionately. 'And you never laid a finger on him, I suppose?'

'No. I . . . well . . . I . . . Once, once I shook him a bit – but that was his own fault. I . . . you have to understand.'

'I'm listening, Irene.'

Irene gave him a long, speculative glance before returning to her story.

In spite of the very real effort she made, Irene was unable to find a place in her heart for this long-awaited son. Unlike her little girls, his coming brought no instant rapport, no warm glow of tenderness, no motherly love. He resented her, she could feel it, and she scowled at him fiercely.

The baby scowled in response, his round, characterless little face lost its identity with all infants of a similar age, and took on a closed expression that seemed to shut Irene out completely. She soon gave up all attempts to become close to her child, often neglecting to change him or feed him until he cried himself into exhaustion. Following her lead, the girls grew accustomed to ignoring their baby brother, and the three of

162

them, mother and girls, bent their energies towards forgetting his very existence.

Though she had never seen him since the day he'd stormed from the flat, Peter now corresponded with Irene through his solicitors. He settled a generous allowance on each of the girls, and wrote from America to say he would be seeking a divorce. Terrified this would mean he'd fight for custody of Debbie and Lauren, Irene wrote back begging him to reconsider. His reply was short, sharp, and to the point – and posted in the UK.

He told her a reconciliation was out of the question. He wanted to spend some time with his daughters, however, and warned her he would be along to collect them for the day that Sunday week.

Irene watched from the balcony as he walked away clutching Debbie and Lauren by the hand, her fear of heights completely forgotten, driven out of her mind by the even greater dread that he might choose not to return them to her.

'Seven o'clock,' he had said. 'I'll have them back by seven at the latest.' His face had been without the hint of a smile for Irene, though he had managed to laugh at the exuberant reception he'd received from the two little girls.

It was now twenty minutes past seven, and Irene braved the balcony yet again to search the distant horizons for some sight of them. By eight o'clock she had worked herself into a frenzy of mindless anxiety. Thoughts of her babies on some transatlantic jet leaving her and England for good, a car crash, an accident, both of them dead, and Peter . . . She clutched at her chest trying to stifle the agony that thought had caused her. She loved him still in spite of the cruel things he had said.

The baby was crying in the other room, his wails beating at her, bringing her grief to unbearable crescendo, sending her running in to him to snatch him from his cot to shake and shake his tiny, helpless, warm little body until his breath caught in his throat and he went limp and quiet in her grasp. Pushing him back into the cot, she dragged the bedcovers across him before running back to keep vigil on the balcony.

Once, she saw a distant but familiar figure turn into the road leading up to the flats, and she leaned over the waist-high rail with a glad shout that was dashed as soon as she recognised the man was alone and wearing a railwayman's uniform. He was the man who had the flat below hers, coming home from his shift. She and Peter had seen him many times when they'd moved in, and wondered about the hours his wife must spend alone. Now it was to be her turn – she was the one to be left endlessly waiting.

It was nearing midnight by the time Peter brought the girls home. Irene did not hear the taxi pull up eight floors below. She was unaware of the rumbling progress of the lift as it climbed from the ground floor, and heard Peter's fist pound on the door as if in a dream.

Not until they called out to her, Lauren's shrill young voice echoing her father's, did she rouse herself with a cry from the stupor of despair that held her sightless, deaf, and immobile.

'Where have you been? What happened? How could you – *Debbie*!' The questions and reproaches pouring from her lips were silenced as Peter carried Debbie, white-faced and strangely huddled, across the threshold.

'She's had an accident. She's all right. Broke her collarbone.' Peter held Debbie protectively against his shoulder, avoiding Irene's grasping hands. 'Don't try to lift her. She's heavy, and still under the effects of the stuff they gave her. Which is their bedroom?'

Irene opened the door, stepping aside to allow him to carry Debbie across to her bed.

'Don't try to undress her tonight. Just make her comfortable, and leave her to sleep it off. They've strapped her up. She's going to be perfectly OK.'

'We went to the hospital, Mummy. Debbie cried a lot,' Lauren informed her solemnly.

'Why didn't you come for me – let me know? Why wasn't I told?' Irene blazed, raising her fists to strike Peter in her anguish.

He caught her wrists, and held her easily. 'There wasn't time. And anyway, I couldn't leave her. You aren't on the phone, there was no way.'

'But I should have been there. I'm her mother. I should have been told,' Irene protested, close to tears.

'What good would it have done, except to ease your mind –

and I'm sorry about that, but like I said, you're not on the phone. Besides, you could hardly have turned up with a baby in your arms. There were enough children in casualty, heaven knows, without another,' he said in bitter reference to the child he still refused to acknowledge as his own.

Peter stayed long enough to explain how they had been on their way home and were in fact just getting of the bus. He had turned from lifting Lauren to the pavement too late to prevent her sister leaping from the high step. Debbie had landed awkwardly on the pavement edge and had fallen, knocking her shoulder against the metal bus-shelter. 'I'm sorry we were so late, you must have been very worried,' he finished on a note of contrition.

Relief was making Irene shaky and tearful; she turned away. 'Don't mention it,' she said tartly. 'And don't come expecting to take them out ever again.'

Peter let himself out of the flat without further argument.

The following morning Irene was too taken up with her daughter's discomfort to ponder the cause of her son's unnatural silence. Not one murmur or cry did he make throughout the day, not one scream of hunger, not one whimper of protest at the soaking bedclothes in which he lay, white and still, just as Irene had left him the night before.

Halfway through the evening Irene thought to check on him, and was assailed by the choking stench of dirty nappies when she turned back the cot covers. Holding her breath she bundled everything, covers, pillows, nappy and baby into the bath. Lawrence made no outcry as the water washed over him, and did not open his eyes as his mother cleaned the excrement from his skin.

For a further twenty-four hours he lay comatose in this fashion until Irene won the argument with her conscience, and called for the doctor.

'I want you to look at my little girl's arm,' she told him when he arrived. 'She broke her collar-bone at the weekend, and I think it should be checked.' Drawing Debbie forward she gazed expectantly at the doctor.

The doctor supressed his anger. He'd had a busy night and silly, hysterical women who didn't know when to bring their children to surgery took up valuable time.

'This has been professionally treated,' he said after a cursory glance at Debbie's shoulder. 'There is nothing for me to do here. When does she return to the hospital?'

'I'm to take her back in about three weeks.'

'Then I suggest you do that, Mrs Rawding. And in the future, please don't ask for house-calls unless it is absolutely necessary.' He turned and would have been gone, but Irene caught at his sleeve.

'I'd like you to take a look at the baby. He . . . he's not been very well,' she said timidly.

The doctor sighed. 'Where is he?'

Irene led the way to the bedroom where the doctor, after one glance at the baby's complexion, turned his penetrating gaze on her face. 'How long has he been like this?' he demanded.

'Like this?' The question was both stupid and unnecessary. Neither of them was in any doubt that the child was in need of medical attention.

'Unconscious, woman! How long?'

'About . . . about a couple of days. I, I didn't want to bother you,' Irene babbled feverishly. 'I'm sure it can't be anything much.'

She was talking to herself; the doctor was intent with his examination of the baby. 'Are you on the telephone?' he snapped suddenly, abruptly cutting off Irene's inane babble.

'I . . . there's a pay-phone on the ground floor,' she said.

He was halfway across the room before she had finished speaking, and she heard the outer door bang before turning to stare down into the cot.

'They won't take him away from me, will they? They won't?' Clutching her daughters to her sides, Irene gazed earnestly at the nurse. 'I mean, it's not as if . . . I only gave him a little shake, he was crying and crying. I thought he would choke. They won't take him away?' Tears ran unchecked down her face.

'I have no idea, Mrs Rawding. Lawrence will have to stay here for some time.' She examined Irene in a cool, professional manner. 'Perhaps after that . . .' She allowed a small shrug to complete her sentence.

'But you don't understand. He's my only son. I want him at home. He can't be so very ill.'

'There could be some brain damage. You *were* told, Mrs Rawding. We won't know until the results of our tests come through.'

'No. No, there isn't. There can't be. And I want my baby back. You can't, you mustn't take him away.'

The phrase became a litany as Irene was sent from doctor to doctor, clinic to clinic. She grew as thin and as gaunt as she had while suffering the torments heaped on her in childhood, and she haunted the corridors of the paediatric ward begging that she be allowed to take her baby home.

Her pleas were finally rewarded, and as she sat facing the consultant paediatrician with Lawrence fast asleep in her arms, she could find no words to express her gratitude.

The doctor glanced from Irene's glowing face to that of the student earnestly taking notes, and waited until the busily scratching pen came to a halt before continuing with his instructions.

'You must bring the baby back for further tests on the first of next month,' he explained patiently, as if talking to a backward child. 'He's done very well over the past couple of weeks, but we want to be perfectly sure. Do you understand?'

'Yes. Oh, yes, Doctor. I'll bring him, never fear,' Irene was swift to assure him.

'And you do understand you must not shake him? Not even a little, no matter how much he cries or tries your patience? If he gives trouble taking his food leave it for a while; he takes a little longer to feed than some babies, that's all.'

'Oh, yes, Doctor. I know, and I *will* be careful.' Irene's expression was so sincerely contrite, the whole of her slender figure so imploring that she wrung pity from even the most stony of hearts.

'Off you go then, Mrs Rawding. I'll see you and this young man again on the first of next month.'

Irene scrambled from her chair, and babbled her thanks. The young student doctor crossed to open the door, subjecting her to a frowning scrutiny as she passed through the doorway with

Lawrence clutched lovingly to her chest.

'Do you think we've done the right thing, there, Mr Gibson?' the student asked, keeping his voice deliberately neutral.

His superior was in no doubt of his meaning. 'Oh, yes. Young woman like that, harassed by the cares of running a home, two other children, trouble with the marriage, a perfectly under-standable impatience with a fractious baby, I should say. No doubt at all that she has learned her lesson, gave her quite a scare, and if we're lucky no lasting effects on the infant.'

'Her younger daughter had a broken collar-bone when they brought the baby in.' The student was not making polite conversation, there was a watchfulness about his expression as he waited for Gibson to make some reply.

'I am aware of that, Maskray. It's all on our records. I took the trouble to look at the girl's notes. She was taken into casualty by her father – there were witnesses to the accident. For God's sake!' He suddenly lost patience. 'Are we to question every parent who brings a child to the hospital? We are not the Gestapo!'

Echoes of a case that had rocked the whole country and shattered those connected, however loosely, with the welfare of children, rang in his consulting rooms. Little Maria Colwell had been dead since 1973, but her passing in that most dreadful, horrific fashion was the tragedy responsible for the young student's scepticism. Doctors and the welfare workers through-out the country were now advised to consider potentially threatened children, and any suspicion of non-accidental injury invited closer scrutiny.

Jason Maskray looked an apology to his superior before adding an appendage to his notes. 'Are you ready for the next patient?' he asked placatingly.

Aware of increased public sensitivity in the matter of mal-treated children, Irene watched over her family like a neurotic mother hen. Her fear that one or the other might be taken from her took its toll of her health, and she grew nervous and jumpy and deeply suspicious of people in authority. Peter had insisted on visiting his daughters every day following Debbie's accident, but he never asked to see the baby, or commented on the absence of all the little things that normally betray the presence of a child. Irene chose not to tell him that their son had been admitted to the hospital, and swore the girls to silence. She would give him no opportunity to brand her unfit as a mother.

She need not have feared; her devotion to her daughters was so obvious that even Peter, who had thought to fight her for their custody, was satisfied their best chance of happiness lay with her. He would continue to send maintenance, he told her, and he would keep in touch with Lauren and Debbie by mail, but he wouldn't be coming around to upset them with wranglings for their affections. He was returning to the United States where he now intended to set up a permanent home.

Irene watched him leave from the window, her tears blurring her last sight of the man she knew she would always love. Peter did not look back, not even to wave farewell to his daughters who stared down at him from the balcony; to Lauren and Debbie there was nothing final in this parting, their daddy was going in a plane back to America, where he worked. They had yet to be told he was never coming back.

For some weeks following his discharge from the hospital, Irene handled the baby as if he were made of glass. He didn't cry quite so much now, or seem so robustly active as he had before he'd had what Irene referred to as his 'little accident'. Left alone in his cot he would lie for hours making no attempt to climb out, blue eyes wide and blank stared at nothing, and his few words of speech seemingly forgotten. The reports from the hospital were guarded; it was possible he had suffered some brain damage, but how much, and how badly he would be affected, it was impossible to determine at this stage.

The more helpless and feeble her baby son, the more Irene worried over the health of her daughters. It became a ritual for her to take them along to the family practitioner, sometimes as often as once every week, to seek his advice on some minor ailment either real or imaginary. It was useless for him to assure her that the girls were perfectly healthy as she refused to believe him. She worried that Debbie's shoulder had not properly healed, that she might grow deformed. It took a visit to the X-ray department of the hospital to lay this fear to rest. She fretted over an attack of nettle-rash that followed a trip into the country, and was fastidious in the care she took over applying creams and unctions to reduce the itch. The girls suffered all this with good grace since it was tempered with an abundance of warm affection, and they were constantly told that their mother's concern sprang only from her love of them both.

Lawrence was nearly two years old before he started to toddle. The regular hospital checks, having produced no evidence of permanent brain damage, were now spaced out to six monthly intervals, with Irene taking care to ignore him as much as possible between each visit. His increasing mobility brought him constantly to her attention and made greater demands on her time. Try as she would, she could not love him as she did her girls. There were times when she took him up in her arms, and held his warm body snuggled against her, his face tucked into her neck, seeking an answer to this mystery. And times when he would look at her with such appeal she came very close to surmounting the barriers she had erected between them. Only when she considered the possibility of his being taken from her did her basic maternal instincts override all else, and she vowed she would fight tooth and nail before she would give him up. At moments like these he was her own precious son, a substitute for the child she had given up, and as such infinitely precious.

She found him less delightful when he continued to resist all attempts to potty-train him, and was free with her slaps as she changed his clothes again and again. 'I'll leave you in them, that's what I'll do,' she threatened, her patience at an end as she struck out at him with the flat of her hand.

Lawrence stared at her solemn-faced, his lack of expression exacerbating her anger. 'Well, don't just gawp at me, damn you. Get from under my feet.' Sweeping him aside she returned to the mountain of ironing she had been engaged with before breaking off to see to his needs, and soon forgot his presence as she struggled to smooth the over-dry linen and restore some crispness to the tricky, intricate pleating on her daughters' dresses. Not until she turned with the last little blouse swinging from its hanger did she rediscover her son – and the game that had kept him so quietly occupied while she worked. Faithfully imitating his mother, Lawrence had taken the carefully pressed clothes from the chair where she had hung them, spread them out over the floor, and there he crouched on top of the dresses using one of Irene's discarded shoes as a flat iron, pounding away in happy oblivion of the dirt-streaked creases he was making.

The blouse fell from Irene's fingers. Without making a sound she picked up the hot iron she had been using and pressed it down on her little boy's hand.

Screams beat at the walls all about her, screams of agonising, unbearable pain.

'Stop it! Stop it! Stop it!' Hands clasped tight to the sides of her head in a vain attempt to shut out the sounds, Irene stared in horror at her baby's charred flesh. Suddenly she spun about and was running, running for the door, running away from the accusation of those terrible screams that followed piercingly in her wake as she sped out of the flat.

Without waiting to summon the lift she ran for the stairs, miraculously keeping her footing down three flights of concrete steps. Reaching the lower landing she tore along the corridor to a door at the end where she hammered double-fisted until it sprang open.

'Irene! What the hell is going on?'

'Carol. Oh, Carol, you've got to help me. It's Lawrence.' Panting, sobbing for breath, she tugged at her friend's arm. 'I've burnt him, Carol. With the electric iron.'

Carol resisted Irene's clutching hands. 'For God's sake! Is that all? I thought the flats were on fire at the very least.'

'You have to help me. Carol, you have to.' Irene was fast becoming incoherent.

'Hold on, hold on. I've got things cooking inside. I can't just go tearing off. Wait while I switch off the oven.'

'Oh, hurry. Please, please, hurry.' Irene begged.

Carol took her time attending to her domestic duties. In her opinion Irene fussed far too much over her kids. Look at the row there had been when she had gone into hospital before Lawrence was born, you'd have thought it was the end of the world just because she'd put her foot down and refused to be saddled with those precious daughters of hers. They'd been well looked after, anyway, in some home or other, but to hear Irene go on . . . She checked the heat under the saucepans, and paused to remove her pinafore. And all the rubbish Irene spouted about somebody taking them away – she should be so lucky! Personally, she'd be over the moon if somebody would offer to take her kids off her hands.

'Right, I'm ready. Oh, wait, I need my key.' Some demon made her delay further while she went back into the flat for her door key. 'OK, I've got it, now let's go and see what it is you are getting so het up about.'

The two women climbed the stairs with Irene leading the way, and Carol refusing to be rushed. Halfway to the eighth floor the sound of a child sobbing in pain carried down the stair-well to speed her dragging feet.

'It wasn't my fault, Terry. You do see that, don't you?' Irene reached out to clutch at his sleeve. 'I wanted to tell somebody . . . the doctors . . . anybody . . . I wanted to tell, but they didn't ask, and I knew . . . I knew that I needed help.'

Terry began to look distinctly uneasy, a fine sheen of sweat beaded his face, and he swallowed convulsively. 'When you burnt him, when you burnt Lawrence's hand, did no one question then?' he asked hoarsely.

'Well, I didn't take him to the regular place . . . to the local hospital. I knew . . . I knew they would have records.'

'But you have just said you wanted someone to know. You can't have it both ways.' Guilt lashed at Terry exacerbating his temper, and his tone was both harsh and condemning.

'Did you tell anyone of the things you were doing to Lawrence?' Janet spoke quietly, drawing the heat from the situation they could all feel building.

Irene shook her head miserably. 'I tried, really I did. The doctor who dressed his hand was very kind. I . . . I told him I'd been angry with Lawrence. He . . . he asked me if I got that way very often.' She fell silent, remembering.

'And did you tell him?' Janet pressed. 'Did you tell him anything of what you've told us?'

'Y-yes . . . I said I got this . . . this feeling.'

'And?'

'And he said could I explain. So I told him . . . well, I told him that sometimes, sometimes I smacked Lawrence – on his legs – when, when he wet his pants.' She ducked her head, hiding her face, and Terry also looked away, staring at the dark square of the window, feeling the burden of error bearing down on him.

'So you told the doctor you smacked your little boy, Irene. Did you tell him anything else?' Only Janet remained outwardly imperturbed at the climax she felt approaching.

'I was afraid. . . . I thought . . . I thought if I told him about . . . about shutting Lawrence outside on the balcony . . . and other things . . . I thought he'd . . .'

They waited, the three of them, for the strength to go on. Finally Irene voiced the words that Terry had been so dreading to hear. 'Then I remembered Terry,' she said, as a bankrupt might say of his savings account. 'And I knew I could go to him. I was so sure he would put everything right.'

TWELVE

Irene was up and dressed in the grey light of early dawn. She watched the sky grow light from the open door of the balcony, and knew if she'd had the courage to step out to the railings she would have seen the street lights in the distant town go out one by one. Though she had never lost her own fear of this high perch, she considered it deliberate provocation that her little son screamed his terror every minute of the hours she forced him to spend locked out here. She stood in the open doorway, her hands grasping the frame for additional security, and wondered how soon she might start out to find Terry Garland. Big, solid, dependable, Terry Garland, her one hope in all this dreadful, terrible mess.

The children's home where Terry worked was some distance from the flats, and she would need to take Lawrence in his stroller. Better if she went early, then she could be sure of getting back in time for the girls coming home from school. She never intended to allow them to arrive back at an empty house ever again – not after their misery when she'd had no choice but to leave them. She agonised over that unhappy time as she made her way across town.

'I'm sorry, Mrs Rawding. Mr Garland left here some time ago. You see, this is not a children's home any longer. The building has been taken over by another department.'

Irene stared at the speaker in mounting dismay. Having so far convinced herself that only Terry Garland could deal with her problems she was both blind and deaf to all other avenues she might have been expected to try. 'Do you know where Mr Garland has gone?' she asked.

'Why, he's still with the Children's department. His wife died, you know, but he continued with his work in the Social Services.'

'Where can I find him? It's very important.'

'Wait a minute, I'll just check my records.' Lugging an untidy reference file from an overflowing cupboard, the woman placed it on her desk and began to leaf through the torn pages. 'Now, let me see. . . . Ah, here we are, Garland T. Child Care Officer. He's with the East Side Social Services Department. You are in luck, my dear, that's just around the corner from here. Go out of the front door, turn right, cross the first road you come to, then turn right again. You can't miss it. Ask for Mr Garland at the reception.'

Irene was already on her way. She had started out of the once familiar room with its dusty aromas that reminded her so poignantly of the years she had spent within these walls, and tugged open the door before the woman had finished speaking.

Terry Garland was just as she had remembered him. A little older, perhaps, a little less hair, but basically the same, bluff, friendly giant who had steered her through the time she had spent in the care of the local authorities.

'You hadn't changed a bit,' Irene said to him now. 'You were exactly as I remembered you.'

Talk to her, Terry. Janet willed silently. Pick up the lead she is giving you, and use it to help her along.

As though receiving her telepathic message, Terry forced a smile to his lips, and nodded. 'Yet it must have been all of ten years,' he said encouragingly.

'Not quite. Eight, probably. Eight and a bit,' she said, basing her assessment on the age of her oldest daughter. 'But you know all that, because . . . because . . .' Her voice died away.

'Because we have already talked about the last time we met, haven't we?' Terry had picked up the lead now and was preparing to run with it. 'It was when I came out to the nursery to see the little Mongol boy and his mother.'

Irene licked her lips nervously, waiting for him to continue.

'She was needing help too, Irene, wasn't she? Needing someone to show her what to do. I believe you remembered that, and that was why you came looking for me, right?'

Irene nodded, her eyes never leaving Terry's face.

'And we arranged for the little boy to attend a special school,'

175

he said, as if speaking to a backward child. 'A school where he would be well looked after, and be safe.'

'But you won't send Lawrence away, Terry, will you? You wouldn't do that. There's nothing wrong with him, is there? I mean, he's not a Mongol, or anything.'

'No, he's not a Mongol, Irene,' he said placatingly, a spasm of anguish momentarily twisting his features before he regained control, and slid the mask of kindly understanding over the torment of his guilt. 'But you did come to me for help.'

Terry knew, as did most case-workers in child care, that the perpetrators of cruelty were often disturbed, isolated, and in need of help – sometimes to an even greater degree than their hapless victims. He accepted that this was the case with Irene. Irene, he told himself, deliberately ignoring the expostulation that echoed from his wife's grave, was special. Accordingly, he had turned up at her flat that same evening unprofessionally bearing the gift of a bottle of wine as an entry.

'Hi. Brought some plonk. Thought we might have a drink and take up where we left off this afternoon. Do you have a corkscrew?' Giving Irene no time to offer any excuse, he entered the flat waving the bottle of wine under her nose.

'Oh, but I . . . Yes. I'll get it. Um, you'd better go through.' She indicated the half-open door, and Terry let himself into the sitting room where Lauren and Debbie turned from watching some television programme to stare in surprise.

'Hello, ladies. I don't believe we've met. I'm Terry Garland, some people call me Judy, but probably she was before your time.'

Irene's daughters clapped their hands to their faces and giggled through their fingers at this strange man with the beard like untidy flames licking his chin.

'Aren't you going to introduce yourselves?' he asked seriously.

'I'm Lauren, an' this is Debbie. She's my sister,' Lauren said before ducking her head to send him quick, darting glances through her lashes.

'That's nice. I'm a friend of your mother's.' Terry's keen eye noted the comfortable disarray of the sitting room, the books and children's toys littering the floor, and the predictable, naturally childish behaviour of the two little girls. He experienced a certain relief to find all this supportive of his guess that any ill treatment was currently confined to the boy.

'I've only got these sort of glasses. Will they do?' Irene entered the room carrying two glass tumblers, and a tin opener which did double duty as a corkscrew.

'They'll be fine.'

Irene hesitated, unsure of herself in the unaccustomed role of hostess, and puzzled by Terry's relaxed attitude. She couldn't imagine why he had come. In spite of the urgency that had driven her to seek him out, she had said nothing of any particular significance this afternoon, and she had since regretted her haste. She took a cigarette from a packet on the table and lit it before remembering her manners.

'Oh, sorry. Do you smoke? Funny, but I can't seem to remember.'

'No, thank you. I never did use them – and neither did you when I had the care of you.' He smiled in a teasing, conspiratorial manner designed to put Irene at her ease.

Irene's mouth quirked in a rueful expression before she drew on the cigarette. 'I only started quite recently . . . after . . .' She shot a glance towards her daughters, excluding them from the facts hidden behind the words she was using. 'After Peter went to work away.' Her eyes begged Terry's co-operation.

He grasped the situation instantly and hastened to reassure her. 'Helps pass the time, I suppose. Until he gets home. So come, drink your wine, let's enjoy ourselves a little.'

'My daddy is in America.' Despite the play-acting by the adults Debbie had sensed the undercurrent, and abandoned the television programme to come and stand close by her mother.

'Yes, so I've been told,' Terry said.

'He *is* coming back.'

'Of course he is, darling. And soon. You have got to be a good girl, and be patient.' Irene smoothed the child's straight, mousey-coloured fringe from her eyes as she spoke.

So that's the way it is. But why on earth doesn't she tell them, Terry wondered. She was merely postponing the agony, and making things ultimately more difficult for herself by pretending the separation was only temporary.

After the girls had gone to bed – half an hour later than usual, Irene pointed out with mock severity – Terry began to point the conversation towards the reason behind his visit. At first, Irene resisted all his attempts to persuade her to talk about the breakdown of her marriage, but his display of genuine concern, coupled with the tongue-loosening effects of the wine, eventually wore down the barriers.

'You could have some tests done, Irene. Blood tests, and so on. They might serve to convince your husband that Lawrence is his natural son.' Terry sipped at his drink, giving her time to consider this suggestion.

'No, I thought about it, but the real issue behind our break-up wasn't the fact of the baby's parentage. . . . It was the things Peter allowed himself to believe about me. The poison he was so willing to accept. . . . There could be no going back.'

'That being so,' said Terry gently, his eyes intent on her face, 'it is hardly surprising that you resent the boy so much.'

For a second he was afraid Irene would deny everything. She bridled like a startled colt, her eyes snapping fire. Then just as suddenly she subsided, became a woman tortured by guilt. She gulped at the wine in her glass, waiting for its warming release before attempting a scrappy, disjointed, unintelligible outpouring of her reasons for her rejection of her baby son.

'He isn't Lawrence, you know. He's just a . . . a replacement. He doesn't need me, and I don't need him. We don't belong together. I'm no more a mother to him than . . . than he is a brother to Debbie and Lauren. He doesn't care about us. Not really he doesn't.'

'No, Irene. You have it all wrong. He is just a baby. An infant. He has to be taught about love before he can respond. You are mixing him up in your emotions, getting him confused with your husband. It isn't Lawrence who has deserted you, my dear. He has never been given a chance to show whether he cares for you or not. Come on, now, you know that's the truth.'

Keeping her eyes fixed on the glass she held with both hands, Irene mumbled a few words Terry was unable to catch.

'Sorry, what was that?'

'I said . . . I do smack him sometimes.'

* * *

178

At this point Terry's brave determination to have everything brought into the open suffered a minor setback, and he faltered, hearing again Irene's low-voiced admission, accepting his own incompetence. He had been blinded by his own conceit, had failed to hear the warning bells – and even when their clamour became too persistent to be ignored had acted without due regard to essentials. He found himself unable to meet Irene's accusing gaze, and made a pretence of needing to stand and stretch his legs an excuse not to do so.

Janet guessed something of the pain he was feeling and remained quietly unmoving, waiting patiently to learn the full extent of his involvement with Irene at that time.

Terry coughed unnecessarily and cleared his throat, pacing the short distance between his chair and the window, before attempting any further speech. He recalled the sense of shock and outrage he'd experienced when his questions had led Irene to confess to having deliberately burnt her baby's hand; all his professional training had failed to prepare him for the jolt he had felt. And then, even then, armed with this knowledge, he had failed to take appropriate action, he reminded himself miserably. He rubbed his hand wearily across the back of his neck before bringing his attention back to Irene. He had allowed her desperate plea for the custody of her son to influence his decision.

'They won't take Lawrence away from me, will they? You wouldn't let them do that? You'll help me, won't you? Won't you, Terry, please? You'll show me how to make it up to him,' she had begged. And he, like the great, gullible, egotist that he was, had given in to her.

Colour flooded his face as he recalled his pompous admonition to Irene. 'I'll help you,' he had promised, 'only if you will make shift to help yourself. If you are prepared to face up to the fact that you are in need of professional assistance.'

Terry groaned aloud for his own pathetic vanity, and again his eyes leapt away from Irene.

'You sent me to see my doctor,' Irene said woodenly, her gaze fixed at some point in the centre of the leaf-patterned carpet. 'But he was just like all the others. He didn't really want to know . . . didn't want to take me seriously.'

Irene's doctor listened to her incoherent, rambling attempt to appraise him of the many cruelties to which she had subjected her infant son, and dismissed most of it as hysterical twaddle. Too much publicity, in his opinion, had been given to the few, isolated instances of real child abuse. Only the pathologically insane would deliberately set out to wound or maim their own child. In his experience ordinary people, like this overwrought young woman, were just not capable of such acts. They simply got carried away by the media and imagined all sorts of ridiculous things.

'I'll give you some tablets,' he said, reaching for his pad of prescription forms. 'I want you to take one of these three times a day. Come back in a couple of weeks if you are feeling no better.'

Irene gaped. Was that it? Didn't he understand what she had been at such pains to tell him? 'You mean . . . you mean I can go? You won't be reporting me, or anything?' It had been her secret belief that Terry Garland had sent her along to tell her story in the hope that the doctor would relieve him of the responsibility for her punishment. If that was not so, then what was she doing here?

'Reporting you, Mrs Rawding?' The doctor was puzzled.

'To . . . to the police . . . or the . . . the NSPCC?'

'Good heavens, is that what you were thinking? I don't make a habit of reporting my mothers to the police, or anyone else, for that matter. Now, you get that prescription filled out, young woman. I'm sure you'll find those tablets will help.'

'But . . . but you have seen my baby before. You were the one had him admitted to the hospital,' Irene persisted.

'That's right, I did. Some time ago now. I have the details here in his notes. An unfortunate accident, Mrs Rawding. Most unfortunate, but you mustn't allow it to play on your mind. The child made an excellent recovery.'

Irene crumpled the prescription in her fist before thrusting it into her pocket. She felt, as she had so often felt before, embarrassed for being such an obvious nuisance, apologetic for giving everyone trouble, and, most of all, frightened that the situation in which she felt herself trapped was becoming a nightmare way of life. If all she could hope for in the way of help was a packet of tablets . . . if there was no other way out of the morass . . . She sobbed helplessly as she turned for home. She didn't want to keep on hurting her baby. She didn't, she didn't!

Terry Garland was extremely pleased with his protege's willing co-operation, and confident of his ability to see her through her troubles. He visited Irene and her family as frequently as he was able to make the time, treating Irene as a friend in need rather than one of his clients. He made no official report of his visits, kept no case-papers that might be discussed with his colleagues. He told himself he knew enough about Irene and her background to deal with the situation out of hand, and felt no need to recourse to office files.

Irene swallowed the tablets as she had been directed; they made her drowsy, gave her a feeling of couldn't-care-less. She went through her days like an automaton, and slept through the nights as though practising for death. She didn't report back to her doctor when her supply ran out; she hated the thick, fumbling clumsiness of their effect, and they had done nothing at all to counter her feelings of resentment towards Lawrence. He was such an easy target for punishment, so stoical now in his acceptance of her punches and slaps. Sometimes, the very way in which he looked at her as she inflicted the blows was enough to drive her to frenzy.

She made no mention of this to Terry.

'How do you feel about things now you have been able to tell someone what you were doing?' he asked on one occasion.

'Well, sort of relieved, I suppose.'

'Good. That's great. And what are your feelings for Lawrence?'

'I . . . I want to make it up to him, make him feel better.' Brow wrinkled in concentration, Irene did her utmost to offer an honest answer. 'I feel sort of . . . well, sort of unreal. As if the person doing those terrible things can't really be me.'

'*Was* doing, Irene. *Was*. You are getting better now. You won't do them again.'

Irene stared at him blankly. Didn't he know? Couldn't he guess?'

'Go on,' Terry prompted in his role of helpmeet and adviser.

'I . . . I never thought I would do things like that – not after the way things were between me and my mother. I always promised myself . . .'

'Now, now. No need to distress yourself. The worst is behind you. Just keep telling yourself that.' Terry beamed through his curly red whiskers, his expression that of a jovial Santa Claus. 'I'll keep a close eye on things for a time, and if you ever feel that you can't cope or . . . or anything, then you have only to say.' He watched her face carefully, searching for some indication that she understood. 'You should get out a bit more, Irene. Get a little job, or join a social club. And try to encourage the girls to take more of an interest in Lawrence. I'm sure they'd love to babysit while you went out for an hour or so.'

Irene considered this suggestion thoughtfully. 'Yes, yes, perhaps I will. Maybe I'll go to night-school like Carol downstairs.'

'Good girl.' Terry was quietly jubilant. His efforts were beginning to bear fruit.

He continued to make regular visits to the flat, making every opportunity to watch Lawrence without giving the appearance of excessive supervision. The child seemed sound enough, no unexplained marks or bruises, no indication that he might be in any distress. The burns on his hand had been a long time healing, but were now clearing up nicely, though he would carry the scars to his grave. He was not a boisterous child, Terry noted, given more to playing quietly by himself in the bedroom he continued to share with Irene than romping around the sitting room in company with his sisters.

It took several months and many visits before Terry began to suspect all was not as it seemed. He had not seen Lawrence for a week or two, had not caught so much as a glimpse of the boy, and always the explanation was the same – he was said to be playing downstairs with Carol's son; and always the door to the bedroom remained firmly fastened.

'Irene, I would like to see him. Am I to go down to your friend's place, or will you go yourself and get him?' Terry was not in a mood to be fobbed off with further excuses. His instincts told him something was wrong; his initial, premature feelings of triumph and well-being suffered a severe check.

'Go and get him, Irene. He's in there, isn't he?' He jerked his head at the bedroom door.

Irene backed slowly away from the deliberately expressionless mask Terry had assumed. Her heel struck the door timbers, and her hand crept slowly across the painted woodwork to close on the handle.

'Get him, Irene. Go in there, and bring that boy out.'

Terry waited through the eternity it took for Irene to return with her son, schooling himself to neutrality, drumming up all his reserves of professionalism to deal with this situation.

Even so, even after telling himself he had seen all there was to see of the heinous brutality inflicted on children, even half knowing what he might expect, he was unprepared for the sight that met his sickened gaze.

Never display anger or revulsion when confronting a client, the textbooks all said. Never allow yourself to forget that parents who batter their children are in need of your help. Terry fought hard to keep all this in mind as he stared at the pulp which had once been a baby's face.

It was Terry who took Lawrence to the hospital, he who waited while the child was examined and admitted, and he who shouldered full and awful blame for those terrible injuries.

'They have strapped his ribs and set his arm. It was broken in two places.' His carefully unbiased expression slipped a little as he confronted Irene. 'They can do very little about his face . . . only time . . . but they are of the opinion that his sight is not impaired.'

Silence, thick with guilt and recrimination stretched between them. Finally Terry managed to expel the word that had been riding on his tongue ever since he'd returned from the hospital. 'Why?' he asked, the one word expressing his total inability to understand.

'I . . . The cupboard fell on him,' Irene said slowly.

Terry gaped.

'It *did*. It really did. He . . . he wouldn't wait for me to open it for him. He started tugging and pulling, and . . . and, well, it just fell on him.'

Terry ran one hand over his face, the dry sound of it echoing the disbelief he took no pains to hide. 'Try again, Irene,' he invited quietly. 'Which cupboard? Where? And if that is true, why didn't you get him straight to the hospital?'

'The kitchen cupboard. That big heavy one. He climbed up and . . . and it toppled over.' Despite her stubborn, childish perseverance in this obvious lie, Irene was unable to meet Terry's eye. She looked away, her head turning first one way then another as she sought refuge from his penetrating gaze.

'And the hospital, Irene? You knew he was badly hurt; why didn't you call an ambulance?'

'Because I *knew* nobody would believe me. See? Even *you* don't believe me.'

The sudden flash of righteous anger startled Terry, gave him to pause and consider afresh the nature of the child's injuries. But before he could say any more the spark had died leaving Irene to stare at him in mounting dismay and accusation.

'Why, Terry?' she cried. 'Why in God's name did you let me do it?'

Her question hit Terry full in the stomach, driving the breath from his lungs as surely as any physical blow. He buried his fingers in his beard, gripping his jaw in an excess of self-condemnation. His late wife had always said he would one day grow too big for his boots, now he had felt those boots pinch more painfully than he could have imagined.

Terry and Irene turned their heads like a matched pair of clockwork toys, their eyes groping for each other across the space dividing them. It was as if they had each reached an identical place in their recollections. Neither remembered the presence of Janet Fouracres.

'I . . .' Terry's voice was merely a croak. He cleared his throat and tried again. 'I failed you, Irene . . . when you needed me most.'

'No.' Janet had to strain to catch Irene's all but inaudible denial. 'Not me, Terry. Lawrence.'

'Christ!' The harsh rasping sound of a man crying was all that broke the poignant silence.

* * *

184

Only this morning, in that strangely remote other life, Irene had gone along with Terry to bring Lawrence home from the hospital. She could not find the courage to enter the doors, but the minute Terry appeared on the hospital steps, her son in his arms, she was out of the car and running across the pavement towards them.

'Lawrence! Oh, Lawrence. My own precious boy. Let me look at you.'

The child drew away from her, hiding his face against Terry's collar, drawing his legs up, making himself as small as possible.

Irene stopped, arms outstretched, and stared uncertainly at Terry.

'I tried to warn you, Irene, you are a stranger to him now. You should have visited as I advised. Take it slowly, let Lawrence make the advances in his own time.'

Feeling her child's rejection as a slap in the face, Irene stepped aside.

'Now don't take it personally,' Terry warned, reading her expression. 'Remember, he's been through a traumatic experience; snatched from his home, thrust into a strange environment peopled by strangers, and then, just as he grows accustomed to that, he finds himself moved on again.'

'He doesn't like me, Terry,' said Irene tearfully.

'Of course he does. Give him time, show him a lot of affection – not too gushing, mind, take it gently and he'll soon respond.' He made as if to hand Lawrence into her arms while he opened the car door, then thought better of it, setting him down on the pavement, a small, lost little figure who gazed after him anxiously until he turned to lift him into the rear seat. With a few, quiet words of encouragement he persuaded the child to release him from the strangle-hold he had taken about his neck.

'Get in the back next to him, Irene. Don't try to touch him. Just pretend not to notice he's there. His curiosity will draw him out.'

They arrived at the flats without any noticeable change in Lawrence's attitude. He huddled in the corner of the car seat, his eyes apparently unfocused, staring straight ahead.

'You're not going to leave me alone with him, Terry? I mean . . .' Irene gestured helplessly.

'I'll see you indoors and get him settled, then I really think it would be best for me to leave you two to get re-acquainted. You'll manage far better at this stage without a third party on the scene.'

Terry was as good as his word, refusing to stay longer than a couple of minutes once they reached the flat. 'I'll look in on you later this afternoon,' he said with a glance at the clock. 'The girls will be home in a couple of hours, you'll manage very nicely until then.' He paused on his way to the door. 'You are taking your pills?' he asked, then continued on his way, reassured by Irene's what-do-you-think? grimace.

It was strangely quiet once he had gone. Lawrence sat in the armchair where he had been placed, staring at nothing. Irene eyed him apprehensively. What should she do now? She wanted to go to him, to say she was sorry, to show him how glad she was to have him home, but she didn't dare. Terry had said she must wait.

She tried to busy herself about the flat, re-arranging the ornaments, tweaking the cushions, tidying the books the girls had left lying about. Lawrence sat as though carved from stone, completely ignoring her activities, taking no interest in the toy fire-engine or the giant stuffed panda she had bought to welcome him home.

Irene glanced at the clock. It was only twenty minutes or so since Terry had gone; suddenly that seemed like eternity.

'Are you hungry? Would you like some lunch? How about a biscuit, Lawrence? Some milk?'

The child gave no indication that he had heard her questions.

'I bet I know what you would like.' Irene tried to make her voice sound encouraging as she struggled to think of something with which to entice him. 'How about some ice cream? Now you'd like some of that, wouldn't you, Lawrence? Lovely ice cream with chocolate sauce? Shall Mummy get you some?'

Lawrence met her coaxing smile with the same blank expression he had worn since leaving the hospital.

Once again Irene counselled herself to patience. She lit a cigarette and picked up a newspaper, pretending to read while she studied the silent, unmoving little boy over the top of the spread sheets. After a few minutes she found her arms ached and she crumpled the paper into her lap making as much noise over the action as she could.

Lawrence did not even glance in her direction.

She drew heavily on the cigarette. 'Lawrence, you have to look at me. You can't shut me out. I'm your mother.' She paced across to his chair and sank to her knees in front of him. 'Lawrence, baby. Please . . . Please don't just sit there staring like that. I bought you a fire-engine, look.' She grabbed the neglected toy from the floor and thrust it towards him. 'Look at it, Lawrence, isn't it a beauty? It has a little ladder on the top, see? And . . . and there's the firemen and the driver inside.'

Lawrence did not even squint as the smoke from her cigarette drifted into his eyes. Irene moved the cigarette away, offering the fire-engine again. No flicker of interest lit the child's face. He made no move to take the toy from her.

'Well the panda, then. Perhaps you'd like that.' Irene stubbed the cigarette and went to fetch the enormous panda occupying the other armchair. 'There, how about this splendid chap, Lawrence? Isn't he a whopper? I'll bet he can eat more honey than you. Would you like to try him and see? If I cut some bread and honey we could feed him together.'

The child remained mute and apparently unseeing for he made no move to reach for the soft, furry creature Irene had found so irresistible.

'Ah, poor panda, Lawrence doesn't like him.' Irene turned from her son pretending to comfort the huge panda, stroking the black and white silky fur, and watching Lawrence out of the corner of her eye.

Still the boy demonstrated no interest.

'All right. If you don't want him, I'll give him to some other little boy. *And* the fire-engine. They can both go.' Irene watched Lawrence closely now, expecting some gesture or cry of protest. When it became obvious that neither was forthcoming she flung the toys from her and returned to a crouching position in front of her son's chair. 'Look at me, Lawrence.' There was a hint of command in the tone she used to address the boy, and for an instant she thought she detected a deliberate concentration in his blank gaze. His eyes had focused very briefly on her face, she was sure of it.

'Lawrence. Lawrence, darling. Mummy's so sorry for the things that she did. She didn't mean to hurt you. I love you, darling. I really and truly do. You are my own sweet, precious little boy.' She took his hands, limp and unresisting, into her own, and drew him slowly towards her. 'Lawrence, you funny little man. Why won't you say hello to me? I'm not going to bite you.'

Their faces were now almost touching, and suddenly Lawrence ducked his head catching Irene sharply across the bridge of her nose. She dropped his hands and fell back, clasping her hands to her face, her eyes watering with the pain.

'You did that on purpose.' Shrill and uncontrolled, her voice rose to an accusing shriek. 'You did it deliberately. Look!' She held the palm of her hand inches in front of his face. 'Look, you've made my nose bleed.' Specks of blood smeared her palm, and she dabbed tenderly at her nose with her handkerchief.

Lawrence had drawn well back in his chair, his steadfastly blank expression lost in the pucker marking his brow. He gazed at Irene through lashes deliberately lowered to mask the fear in his eyes.

Irene stared at him coldly. 'You miserable little sod! I bet you talked to the nurses all right. So why can't you talk to me? I expect you told them everything, didn't you? All about me? All about me smacking you? Well, just you be careful, or I might just do it again.'

With a shock Irene heard herself saying the words, heard her voice making the threat, and she jerked away from her son as if pulled by strings. What was she saying? What was she thinking of? She had better take some tablets and get herself in hand.

Her fingers shook as she extracted the strip of tablets from the box; another strip fell to the floor as she pressed two of the torpedo-shaped tablets from their packaging then squeezed out a couple more. Better take a double dose, just to get started, she told herself, and swallowed them down without water.

'I'm going to make a pot of tea, Lawrence,' she said without so much as a glance in his direction. 'And some sandwiches. We'll both feel a lot better after we've had some lunch.' She went purposefully to the kitchen, keeping her eyes deliberately

188

to the front. She did not want to look at him, to acknowledge his presence; she needed a few minutes alone to gain control of herself.

On her return some ten minutes later, she paused as she entered the room. She sniffed audibly, a frown creasing her face. She sniffed again, then turned her head with infinite slowness to stare directly at her son.

He sat as she had left him, well to the back of the upholstered armchair, his feet stuck out straight in front of him, and an expression of almost fatalistic resignation on his young face. Not a sound did he make as his mother crossed the room walking steadily towards him, not a murmur left his lips as she reached his chair. It was not until she upended the teapot, emptying its contents in a scalding cascade over his head and shoulders, that he was at last able to scream.

EPILOGUE

In the pink and white, sweetly feminine bedroom the two little girls clung to each other. Through the thin walls they could hear the rise and fall of voices from the next room. Some of the words carried quite clearly, others were muffled, sometimes the conversation was lost to them completely, at others it was painfully close.

'Lauren, I'm scared. I don't like that man talking to Mummy that way.'

'It'll be all right, Debs, don't worry. He'll be gone soon.'

'I know, but I want him to go now.' Debbie was on the verge of tears.

Her sister did her best to offer comfort while grappling with her own growing apprehension. In addition to being the oldest, Lauren was of a more robust nature than the younger, overly sensitive girl, and readily assumed the role of guide and counsellor. 'Let's just sit on one of the beds and wait for him to go,' she suggested, leading Debbie towards the twin beds with their matching pink-and-white spreads.

'But he's shouting.' Debbie pulled away. 'I can hear him. Why is he shouting at Mummy, Lauren?'

'Take no notice. I expect he doesn't even know that he's doing it. Here, I think you had better nurse Victoria; I expect she's frightened too, she seems to be crying rather a lot.'

Debbie obediently seated herself on the edge of her bed, and took the baby doll into her arms. 'Don't cry, Victoria,' she crooned in a high, piping voice. 'Mummy's here now, she will look after you.'

The sound of voices from the next room dropped to a murmur, and Lauren plonked down on the bed next to her sister, listening for some indication that the conversation had drawn to a close.

At the sound of the outer door being opened the girls looked to each other in satisfaction. 'He's going,' Debbie said, half-rising to her feet. Her action was arrested by the unmistakable sound of high-heeled shoes tapping along the hallway. They heard Janet Fouracres introduce herself before the closing of the sitting room door cut off her words, muffling the sound of her voice.

'Who's that?' Debbie asked fearfully.

'How should I know? Shh, if you're quiet we might be able to hear something.'

They listened intently, but the steady drone issuing from the next room gave them no clues.

'You don't think they're going to take us away again, do you?' Debbie's fingers pinched into the flesh of her sister's arm.

'Aw, let go!' Lauren rubbed her bruised skin.

'Well, do you? Do you, Lauren?' Debbie was beside herself with anxiety.

'No, no, of course they're not. Mummy promised, didn't she? She said she'd never let anybody take us away, ever again.'

'But why are they here? What do they want? I don't like it.'

'It'll be all right, don't worry. Nothing's going to happen to us.' For all her brave words Lauren's face took on a scared expression and she drew closer to her sister. 'I wish you would quieten that child,' she said in a brave attempt to divert their thoughts. 'Her noise is getting on my nerves.'

'I know, but she's always like this in the evenings. I don't know what's the matter with her.'

A shriek from the next room, a piercing cry from their mother, caused both girls to abandon their places on the bed. Clutching the doll in one arm, Debbie grabbed for Lauren with the other. 'Lauren, I don't like it. Make them stop.'

'Shh, listen.'

Terry's voice carried to them pitched at a low murmur. As Debbie made to speak her sister signalled her to keep silent. They could hear Irene now; she appeared to be pleading, begging for some concession. Her voice trailed away, to be wiped from their straining ears by a steady, droning monotone from the strange woman. The listening children found it strangely reassuring.

'It's all right, Debbie. They're friends again now.' Lauren sighed with relief, and relaxed her strained attitude. Her sister's hand relinquished its grip and the girls resumed their seats on the bed.

'Just listen to this naughty girl,' Debbie piped, the doll lying across her lap. 'She's crying again – and for no good reason. I fed her and changed her before we went out.'

'P'raps she's got wind,' Lauren said seriously, calling on her fertile imagination to bring realism to their game.

Debbie lifted the doll to her shoulder, and firmly patted its back. 'No,' she said after a few seconds. 'It isn't wind. I think she's just playing me up.'

'What she needs is a good smack,' said Lauren with conviction.

'And she's going to get one if she doesn't shut up,' said Debbie with a hint of malice. She held the doll on a level with her face. 'Shut up, you naughty, naughty girl. Be quiet, will you?' She gave it a vigorous shake.

'You are too soft with her, that's your trouble. I'd soon give her something to cry for if she were mine,' Lauren said with disdain. 'You should let her know who's boss.'

Debbie shook the doll again, its plastic, sleeping eyelids rattling loudly in its head. 'Now don't let me hear another sound!' she threatened.

Lauren tutted sharply, her glance indicating that she found this leniency over-indulgent.

'I'm warning you, Victoria. I shan't tell you again.' Debbie took the doll's arm in her fingers and gave it a vicious twist.

'Lock her in the cupboard,' Lauren advised. 'That'll soon quieten her.'

'I'll do better than that!' Debbie stripped off the doll's panties before turning it on its face over her knee, and proceeded to administer some very heavy-handed slaps to its moulded pink buttocks. 'There, maybe that will be a lesson to you.' She was panting from her exertion, and the palm of her hand glowed red. 'Now, don't let me hear another peep, or it will be the worse for you.'

'I should think so too, and not before time,' her sister said with grim satisfaction.